THE EL GRECO PUZZLE

Also by John Murphy

THE GUNRUNNERS
THE LONG RECONNAISSANCE

THE
El Greco Puzzle

JOHN MURPHY

Charles Scribner's Sons   New York

To Mrs. G., with all my love and all my thanks for the light and the laughter.

THE EL GRECO PUZZLE

I'D FINISHED MY CHORIZOS AND SCRAMBLED EGGS and was on my first cup of coffee and first cigarette when Carlos came along the sidewalk toward the terrace.

"Como estais vos!" he called cheerily. "Mbaexapa! 'Ow are you!" He is Argentine and tends to overdo.

"Fine," I said in the last language he'd spoken. I watched him walk up to the table and sit opposite.

Nelida rose from her place beside me. She is a patriotic girl and dislikes Argentines. She went across the narrow terrace and through the kitchen arch, her back rigid.

Carlos shifted to Spanish and stuck to it. He complimented me on the morning and on my healthy appearance, and asked what my plans were for the day.

"You tell me," I said.

He shrugged all over. "The Frenchman wants to see you."

"When?"

"Ten minutes ago. Now. As soon as can be."

I'd been planning on going out on the river for dorado and surubi. Hell. "Okay. I'll be about fifteen minutes behind you. Go tell him."

"Of course, mi General." Carlos could never end any conversation without being sure he was ahead. He parodied a salute, and left the way he'd come.

After he'd disappeared, Nelida returned. "Cure py," she

said. Paraguayans call Argentines "pig skins." Goes back to their big war, and has something to do with the equipment of the Argentine soldier of that time. Hard to explain and understand, but gives satisfaction to the Paraguayans and irritates hell out of the Argentines. "I heard him," she said. "Will you have to travel again so soon?"

"Maybe. Sometimes Du Vigny simply wants to talk or play chess. I'm afraid if we're going to eat fish tonight, it will have to come from the market."

She made a face, looking at her watch. "It's late, all the good fish will be gone." It was actually only seven o'clock, but in accordance with the differences it keeps from the rest of South America, the whole Republic of Paraguay wakes up at four-thirty in the morning. In Asunción the rush hour, if it can be called that, is at six.

Nelida came with me while I changed from my fishing clothes to jacket and tie. She seemed to like me and to miss me when I went away. She was a shade over five feet tall and in a few years would probably be plump, but right now she was firm and ample on a small scale. Her face showed plain the Guarani, yet Spanish blood had rounded the angles and softened the cheekbones. She was pretty, bright, a great companion, and possessed more than the usual Paraguayan female's independence and hardheadedness. I gave her a kiss and a pat and told her I'd let her know as soon as possible what was up.

Outside, I got in the Brazilian-made Jeepster that Du Vigny provided and drove off. Since Nelida's chalet was in Sajonia I had to go across most of Asunción to reach Du Vigny's villa on the Avenida Mariscal Francisco Solano Lopez. It was mid-April so the summer heat was over and the sweet Paraguayan fall underway. The late blooming flowers were starting their display.

2

Paraguayans are not among the world's best drivers but, thank God, they're better than those in Saigon and lack the maniacal spirit of competition one finds in Buenos Aires and Rio. The main Paraguayan failing is a belief that an automobile should have something of the spirit of self-preservation that is found in a smart horse or a dumb burro. Paraguayans are often astounded when an automobile willfully crashes into a tree merely because it is steered at it.

Du Vigny had a sprawling villa surrounded by a ten-foot-high brick wall. It was one of the five completely air-conditioned houses in the city, and whether done on purpose or not was a near but larger replica of the French embassy located about seven blocks down the avenue.

Patricio was on the entrance gate. He gave me a big "Mbaexapa" but it was all right for him to talk Guarani. He's a native and in fact his Spanish isn't the best in the world. He speaks pistol quite fluently, though. Patricio and I have the same name-day so I chatted with him an obligatory three or four minutes and then went up the walk to the house.

The main door opened before I reached it. Patricio would have buzzed from the gate. Andres, the major-domo welcomed me in. He was a skinny, fussy, rather pompous man, but he'd been trained in Buenos Aires and Madrid and was an expert major-domo.

I walked into the hall as Andres bowed. Against the side walls were two of the inlaid chests the country people keep their clothes in. They weren't fine cabinet work and the inlays were slightly out of true, but they'd been lovingly done and the clear, golden grain of the wood glowed. Set in a niche to the front was a painted carving looted from one of the old missions. It was a saint done in lapacho wood and although the paint was chipped in spots the colors were as fresh as the day three hundred years before when some Indian had put them on, a robed Jesuit checking over his shoulder. The wooden vestments looked as if a breeze would blow them about. The face of the saint had higher cheekbones than I expect you find in Castile. I envied Du Vigny that carving.

Andres said, "The patrón is on the terrace," and turned to lead me through the long main salon. Du Vigny liked the Directoire style. I didn't envy him the salon. It was all brain and balance with a bare trace of living heart. The trace of heart came from the pictures. Most of the artists I'd never heard of, but one was an Ingres portrait.

Du Vigny was seated in a chair made of spidery wrought iron at a glass-topped table. "Good morning, Major," he said. He was one of the few I didn't mind calling me by my old rank. Du Vigny knew Spanish well but was reluctant to use it for some reason, and since I had no French, we always spoke English. He, being spare and compact and, although short of sixty, white-haired, resembled nothing more than the older Charlie Chaplin except his intense blue eyes made it plain he'd never amused anyone for a living. He was wearing a short sleeved white shirt and pale blue slacks.

He asked me to sit down. "I'm sorry I had to call you abruptly," he said, "and I'm also sorry that I must send you to Paris again and as soon as possible."

I was sorry too, but that was what he paid me for. "No problem," I said. I visualized airline schedules in my head. "I can catch the three o'clock Caravelle to Buenos Aires and get the night flight out of there. It'll be quicker than going through Rio."

"Fine." He took a cable form from his shirt pocket, opened it and frowned at it. "I got this from Pierre this morning."

That explained why I was going on a sudden trip. Pierre hardly ever communicated directly with his father and then

4

only to send some code phrase that usually resulted in my being dispatched to bring back details.

"Pierre can be a dunce at times," said Du Vigny, still looking at the cable. "This thing says, 'I send you best wishes from your friend in the south.' The best wishes is enough to get him you. The mention of a 'friend in the south' is simply confusing and unnecessary. It could be any one of several men except he doesn't use the word '*midi*,' which would seem to eliminate anyone French. Tell Pierre that all he's done is puzzle me and probably alert the police. They'll seize on that phrase and worry it to death." He sighed. "The trouble is, the poor idiot is probably trying to give some pleasant word to his old father. I can think of one man I'd like very much for this to refer to and Pierre may be trying to tell me that. Don't be brusque with him but make it plain I'm not pleased."

"Yes, sir."

"What were the police like last time?"

"Fairly easy. On arrival they didn't give me a body search, and they even gave back a magazine I'd been carrying to entertain them. On the way out the same, except they kept the magazine."

A line appeared between his brows. "You and Pierre. There is no point in uselessly goading those people. Please do not carry magazines again."

"Yes, sir." Those bastards goaded me pretty good and I'd gotten considerable solace from imagining the grand time they'd have with the magazine.

He eyed me sardonically. "The military refuge—stolid agreement. I wouldn't be surprised if this trip doesn't demonstrate that you made an error and Pierre has unwittingly compounded it for you."

"Yes, sir."

"Merde." He fished another paper from his pocket and

passed it to me. "Since you're going you might as well carry this also."

Written on the paper were five groups of letters and numbers, seven characters in each group. I studied the paper for a few minutes. I don't have a fancy memory but I have a good one, and once, while not having anything better to do when I was on the 8th Division staff at Manheim and thinking to make myself a better Assistant G-3, I'd taken one of those courses that teach you various tricks of mental association so you can astound your friends at parties with feats of memorizing lists of unrelated items or the like.

I passed the paper back, and Du Vigny restored it to his pocket. "I'd suggest some chess, but I suppose you have arrangements to make." He smiled sympathetically. His face warmed when he smiled. "Sometimes I think I don't pay you enough. All that traveling."

"You pay me enough. Of course, you could start sending me first class. I'm a bit large for tourist seats."

He chuckled. "You should know better than suggest to a Frenchman that he send anyone else anywhere first class. But I have a new picture. There's time for you to see that."

I followed him back through the Directoire salon over to the long side gallery. He stopped at the door to turn on the lights. He'd designed the system and was proud of it. Du Vigny could buy anywhere except inside France and he had a wide-ranging collection, most of which I liked except for a few specimens of the young abstract school which I couldn't stand. On the other hand he'd once bought a big Pop art picture for the pleasure of burning it and had kindly invited me to the ceremony.

We stopped in front of the new picture. Du Vigny said, "Hayden's sent it on approval. I've heard of this new school of realism and asked him for a sample." Hayden was Du Vigny's

New York dealer and he apparently made a pretty good thing of it.

At first I thought the picture was a color photograph of a wooden fence, but on examining it closely I could see the minute brush strokes.

"What do you think of it?" Du Vigny asked.

"Not much. Someone's done a hell of a lot of work and hasn't produced anything that looks like a painting."

"You are too conservative. There's no composition, but I like the way he's treated the light on the texture of the wood. I'll give it a week more before I make up my mind."

He saw me to the door. I said that I should be back by Thursday, the day after next. He told me he'd be looking forward to my report.

WHEN I BOARDED THE AEROLINEAS PARIS JET IN Buenos Aires, I knew by sight most of the stewardesses aboard. I said hello and they said hello back but they were never entirely sure what to make of me in view of my usual reception at Orly and what they'd almost certainly heard about me and Du Vigny. Still, I always got good if wary service. There were one or two I'd been tempted to pinch like peaches one wants to check for ripeness, but I never got the chance to stay in Buenos Aires long enough to warrant the action.

Just before landing, I borrowed the on-board electric shaver. I never dared to carry one of my own.

Three men in civilian clothes were standing by the foot of the gangway at Orly. I recognized Raspière in the cold, gray light. It was going to be an unhappy couple of hours. "Good morning," I said neutrally. Raspière infuriated easy. "I have only this attaché case. No other baggage."

Raspière nodded dourly. He was tall and pallid; close-shaved as he was, his black beard still gave his long jaw a bluish tinge. He wheeled and his two minions fell in on my flanks. One of the minions took my attaché case. My fellow passengers made a small buzz as I was led away.

We went across the tremendous, many countered customs hall to one of the side examining rooms. As I walked in, I saw among the waiting men the tall blond medical orderly in his white jacket and trousers. "Oh, Jesus," I groaned. I didn't get him every time and never missed him when I didn't. He grinned broadly and waved a pair of rubber gloves at me.

"Bien," said Raspière. "Strip."

I undressed, handing each article of clothing to one of the customs men. In a corner, I could see a crew busy with my attaché case. After I'd had a good leather case ruined early on, I traveled with only the flimsiest plastic one I could find. Inside it was one shirt, one change of underwear, one pair of socks, and one handkerchief. Two men in the corner had a black light lamp and were giving everything the works.

One of the customs men put the contents of my pockets on a side table. Raspière poked them around. There was Paraguayan, Argentine, and French money, matches and a mostly used pack of cigarettes, a fairly clean handkerchief, and my passport. Ever since the complications when the bastards had taken away my return ticket for further examination, I've always picked up my return at the counter once they turned me loose.

It's bad for your morale to be the only naked man in a cold room with ten other busy dressed men.

"No magazine?" said Raspière.

Du Vigny was right. I shouldn't have goaded them. It had probably cost them hours of work to find that the magazine was innocuous.

"No, no magazine," I said.

He beckoned to the medical orderly who got busy with his gloves and a vaseline jar. I turned, spread my feet, and bent over, supporting myself by leaning on the side table. The orderly did his dirty work and patted me on the ass.

I straightened. "Prostate still okay?" I asked.

The orderly beamed and nodded and passed me some toilet paper. "No change in size. Ver' firm. Ver' helty."

"Thanks a lot."

Then he took me into the neighboring room to the fluoroscope which always bitched me off. If they were going to fluoroscope me, they goddamned well didn't need to do the previous bore sighting job. And I didn't think that getting fluoroscoped once a month or so was good for me. I kept my mouth shut and stood where told and gritted my teeth. I'll say this, he was quick. He took me back into Raspière and reported in rapid French. Raspière nodded. He never had much to say during the examination.

I waited for them to finish. There was one new wrinkle. They not only confiscated my cigarettes and matches which I had expected, they switched my paper money too, giving me new and different bills for what I'd had. Where they got Paraguayan money I didn't know.

I finally got back my rumpled clothes and was permitted to dress. Raspière crooked a finger at me and I followed him out into the big main hall and down to another door which gave into a small room furnished with a green tacky-looking metal table and two scarred wooden chairs. He pointed to one chair and took the other. I sat down.

"I know where you have it," he said. His English was nowhere near as good as Du Vigny's.

I was silent.

"Yes," Raspière nodded. He reached over and tapped my forehead with a hard forefinger. "In Algeria, I would have had it out quicker and easier than we now take your handkerchief out of your pocket."

I sat still. I was going to get the Algeria speech.

"Instead of a finger up your ass, we'd have put an electrode," he told me. "I've seen men break parachute harness webbing guaranteed for five hundred kilo stress when we turned the current into that for them."

He went into further familiar detail as to what he would have done to me in Algeria. This didn't do me any good, and I doubted it really did Raspière any good, but he must have gotten some kind of interior satisfaction, probably akin to that which causes a man to pick at a scab or squeeze a boil or bite on an aching tooth. Or maybe he simply liked to reminisce about the good old days.

Raspière wound up, unattractive drops of spittle in the corners of his mouth. I far preferred his pal, Levasser, who looked like a poor man's Maigret and was the kind man of the pair. Levasser even smoked a pipe and often would let me have one of my own cigarettes, too.

One of the customs men came in and handed Raspière my passport, my plastic attaché case, considerably the worse for wear, and a sheet of paper. "Your belongings," Raspière said. "Sign the paper."

The paper was the customary statement in English and French that although I had been subjected to rigorous search, I had not been mistreated nor had my individual rights been abused. I allowed myself a snotty smile and signed the goddamn paper.

Raspière sat and stared at me for a while. Finally he spoke. "I can't understand why an officer with your service will work for a toad like Du Vigny."

To think that my military record was the only aspect of my life of which Raspière approved was even more depressing than the search.

"Get out," said Raspière. I did as told. The Aerolineas people had my return ticket waiting at their counter. I picked it up and went for a taxi.

I drowsed during the long ride into town. Sleep on an airplane comes hard to me. To anyone with Buenos Aires

11

experience, the Paris traffic is almost soothing. I arrived at the Hotel Sylvie without incident.

I called Pierre du Vigny from my room. "Glad to hear from you, Clancy," he said. "Are you free for lunch?"

"Yes indeed."

"Excellent. Let's meet in the usual place at one. Is that agreeable?" Pierre's English was even better than his father's. Du Vigny had once told me Pierre had gone to Harrow.

"That's fine. Thanks much."

"Au 'voir," he said and rang off.

It was not quite ten o'clock. I left a call at the desk for noon, undressed, and stretched out.

The two hours' sleep did me good. I took a quick shower and changed into my well-fingered linen, throwing away the dirty clothes and the busted attaché case. I told the room that I was going to the Place de la République. I would have to work off that nonsense of the magazine.

During the taxi ride, I was as observant as I could be. No matter how short a time between trips, Du Vigny always had questions about how Paris looked and what people were wearing and doing. Paris was certainly handsome, but it was an overcast day and the people were behaving much like those of any large city in the world—trying to avoid being run over and not having a great time at it.

I was a few minutes early so I hung around the Magenta entrance to the Métro and tried to spot my tail. I couldn't. The Place de la République roared around me.

Pierre came up a few minutes after one. We shook hands. He was younger than I, in his early thirties, and took after his father. He was another compact, taut man, with hair already beginning to gray and tight lines of strain around his eyes.

"You're looking well, Clancy," he told me. "Sorry you had to return so quickly. Let's get it over with."

We went down into the warren of the République métro station. One o'clock is the midday rush hour in Paris. Hordes of people scurried around through the echoing corridors. It was like panic in an anthill. République is the biggest subway junction point in the city; five lines cross. We went along tiled tunnels and through arches until Pierre finally halted against a wall. We each could see over the other's shoulder. The racket of the crowd echoed and reverberated around us so that we had to shout in each other's ear, but nobody could stick his own head into our conversation, nobody could use a directional pickup, nobody could even read lips. It was a wearing but safe process.

"Let me give you my messages first, Pierre," I hollered. "Your father is cross with you. I'm to tell you he doesn't approve of your having said anything about a friend in the south. Sorry about that."

He nodded.

I went on and recited the numbers and letters I'd memorized from the paper Du Vigny had shown me in Asunción. Pierre's eyes glazed as he listened. I'd told him once about my memory course and he'd taken a French equivalent. He rarely asked me to repeat.

When I finished, he was silent a minute or so while he fixed my message in his mind. Most of the messages I carried back and forth were like that—strings of meaningless numbers and letters varied only by an infrequent phrase or two about buying or selling stocks and bonds. I figured I was helping with rotating numbered Swiss accounts and the mechanics by which Du Vigny was cleaning off the money he'd taken and moving much of it back to France in such a condition the authorities couldn't recover it but his son and his grandchildren could.

13

"Now I'll explain why I sent for you," Pierre said. With a break or two to rest his voice, he told me a story.

Pierre was in the habit of taking daily walks along the *quais* for his health and because he didn't have much else to do. He had been in the banking business although not his father's outfit, and had found it better to resign. Two days before, he had been leaning on a rail looking at the Seine, when a man had turned out of the stream of strollers and taken a position a few feet away. Pierre had paid scant attention until the man suddenly asked out of the corner of his mouth if Pierre were under police surveillance. The man spoke French, but with a definite accent.

Pierre sneaked a look at him. He was old but vigorous and well dressed and was acting determinedly nonchalant. Pierre also realized that the man was familiar to him, although he couldn't remember why. Pierre said he certainly was under police surveillance and why did the gentleman want to know? The gentleman had sworn in low-toned Spanish and said they must talk as he had a message for Pierre's father. Pierre was digesting that and wondering if the old man were a trick when there was Pierre's tail at their elbows, waving his police card and demanding the old man's papers.

Anyone who's ever bored and lonesome in Paris has a simple remedy. Hunt out Pierre du Vigny and try to strike up a furtive conversation with him.

Fifteen difficult minutes ensued. The old gentleman was at first haughty, then incensed, and at last flew into a spark-throwing rage. A large audience formed and listened with interest. After repeated requests, the old gentleman disgorged some impressive papers indeed. He was a Spanish historian who was visiting Paris with the scholarly motive of consulting French records and besides his passport he had letters from the secretary of the Spanish Academy to prove it

14

and it was not acceptable for him to be set on by a low thug. His name was Don Jaime Pedro de García Mendoza y Zibaru of Toledo and he ought to have known better than come to a police state. This had irked the cop—not illogically so, considering Don Jaime's point of origin—but had immensely pleased the crowd. The cop had had to return the Spaniard's papers and make abject apologies, and had then taken himself off, biting his tail, to resume surveillance.

Pierre's face had lightened when he'd described Don Jaime's fireworks. It must have been a real treat for him.

When they were alone again, Don Jaime had sworn some more in Spanish, apologized to Pierre for attracting police attention, and said he still had a message. They'd gone openly to a café, and Don Jaime had whispered, "Pass this to your father. The Grand Duke never got them. The last Villenas kept them all and I think I know what happened and where they are now. I found papers in Simancas. I'll wait two weeks."

"That's it," said Pierre. "Father knows Don Jaime, and I remembered him at last. I met him only once several years ago. I know a little of this matter and I don't want to know more. Father will understand. Have you got the message clear?"

I repeated it and he nodded. He laughed shortly. "Don Jaime is not cut out for intrigue and neither am I. I was an ass to have mentioned a friend from the south," he said. "I hate this way of living and can see no end to it." He met my eyes. "Let's go to lunch."

I had many questions but it was plain Pierre was through talking. We fought our way back up to light and air.

We went to Prunier's and had a highly satisfactory meal—Marrennes oysters and sole and Pouilly Fuisse—during which we talked mostly about Paraguay. Pierre was interested in the country. "Perhaps in a few years they will let me have a passport and I'll be able to visit Papa," he said once but with no firm confidence. There was a strong filial feeling between that pair. There had to be for Pierre to keep on.

Back at Orly Raspière gave me the full treatment again—up to and including the fluoroscope. I was going to have to get a film badge like the ones x-ray technicians wear. Even with no baggage, I barely made my plane.

3 ═══════

I LANDED AT ASUNCIÓN AT ELEVEN IN THE MORNING. Nothing would have appealed to me more than to go right to the chalet, drink a couple of martinis, and sack out with Nelida to keep me company, but duty called. The Jeepster was waiting where I'd parked it about forty-eight hours earlier. I got in and tiredly drove to Du Vigny's villa.

He was on the back terrace reading through a stack of French newspapers. He had shipments sent regularly up from Buenos Aires. Du Vigny politely insisted that I be served a drink before beginning my report. I wanted to make my report. This old Spaniard talking about a Grand Duke was a welcome change from the usual.

When I finished the story of Pierre's encounter with Don Jaime Pedro de García Mendoza y Zibaru, Du Vigny was sitting bolt upright, his eyes sparkling. He erupted into rapid French. Then he shook his head at himself.

"I must have been wrong!" he said intensely in English. "Completely wrong! Masséna didn't get them! They never left Spain! If Don Jaime says he knows—" He cut himself short, and sat back in his chair. "I should not burden you with this."

I was staring. It was the first time since I'd known Du Vigny that his hard polish had shown the least crack. I knew the name Masséna from somewhere. It came to me.

17

"I am as bad as Pierre," said Du Vigny. "You are easy to read, Major. What have I told you?"

"Not a lot, but wasn't Masséna one of Napoleon's marshals? And didn't he command in Spain around 1808 or so?"

He sighed. "I am worse than Pierre. Still this does no great harm. How do you know about Napoleon's Marshal Masséna?"

"They give you a lot of History of the Art of War at our Military Academy. While a cadet, I spent months on Napoleon's campaigns."

"As a Frenchman I am flattered. As an individual I am rather distressed. I strongly subscribe to the military principle that no one should be told anything he does not need to know. I have bored you with tales of my experience in the *maquis* but I promise you I've never forgotten the lessons of that time. Please try to put the name of Masséna from your mind."

I nodded. I thought it wasn't so much he'd not forgotten the *maquis*, he'd gone back to it. He'd stolen around thirty million dollars, left France, and gone back to his underground. He'd left poor Pierre and all his family behind, and Pierre had no *maquis*.

Du Vigny sat gazing across his garden. Then, as if he caught some echo of my thoughts, he said, "Well, I am an old, tired thief—but a successful thief. I can indulge myself. I'll have to do some thinking." He turned to me again. "I forgot to ask you. How were the customs and police?"

"Awful. As bad as I've ever seen them both in and out. Body search, the fluoroscope, the whole bit. Raspière was in charge. He's taken a dislike to me."

Du Vigny expressed himself in crackling French for a sentence. "They got Pierre's message, and they'll surely connect it with Pierre's encounter with Don Jaime. I will have to do a lot of thinking, and there will have to be inquiries and arrangements. Thank God communications will not be a major problem. We'll talk again in about a week. I'll send for you. Until then I think you can count on no more travel. My respects to Doña Nelida."

I smiled. Nelida thought he was a wizard—a literal wizard. They have them in Paraguay. Anybody there will tell you. Nelida would be dubious about receiving the respects of a wizard.

I put my plans for a lunch and a siesta with Nelida into effect and unwound the knots of travel. That night I got more than a little drunk. The urge came on me at times.

====== *4*

SHORTLY AFTER I'D ENTERED DU VIGNY'S EMPLOY
and it seemed I'd be staying around Asunción for some time,
I'd joined the Club Nautico and bought a second-hand
outboard runabout. The Club Nautico does not have what
might be called exacting standards for its membership since
they were happy to accept me, but it's a pleasant place. It's on
a cove, south of Asunción's main harbor on the Paraguay
River, and the club owns a couple of piers and provides people
to take care of your boat. The clubhouse is set on a slight rise
and has a spacious veranda overlooking the river. Everything is
a tad rickety, but neat and clean and brightly painted.

A week after I'd returned from Paris bearing an exciting
message, I went out early on the river. By ten, I had three nice
surubi—the local equivalent of catfish—about ten pounds
each, and a good mess of things that looked like bluegills. The
latter were small but from each Nelida would trim a pair of
narrow tasty filets. It hadn't been a bad morning and some
cold beer would go well.

One of the boat boys came to help me tie up. He took the
fish to gut and put on ice in the cooler I had in back of the
Jeepster. I walked over to the clubhouse.

The veranda was sparsely populated at that hour. There
was a family group including several kiddies at one end and a

couple of stocky serious well-known experts gravely discussing something at a table in the middle. They nodded to me and I nodded respectfully back. I didn't rank as an expert and wasn't invited to sit with them. Izzy Meyer was at a table against the rail. He waved at me. I told the *mozo* to bring beer and went to join Izzy.

Izzy resembles a five-foot-four-inch replica of a child's tan plush teddy bear that has lost most of its fur through hard use, but still remains cuddly. You even want to pat him every now and then when you're talking to him. God knows how old he is or what his past has been, though he must be close to sixty and once when I happened to talk about Munich he knew the places I mentioned. He was the resident honest man for the nice smugglers, the ones who wouldn't handle dope.

There are some remarkable statistics about Paraguay. For years, it has imported more US cigarettes than any other country in the world. Its appetite for Scotch whisky and light electrical appliances is also astonishingly high. What happens, of course, is that various groups of importers, airplane owners, pilots, officers, and government types diligently work to send all this stuff over the border into Argentina and Brazil. Since no one absolutely trusts anyone else, they have to have a man like Izzy who holds the money involved in any one operation until it's completed to the satisfaction of all when he makes the payoffs, taking a small fee for himself. At times Izzy must be one of the richest men in the country.

Izzy asked how I'd done and I told him, exaggerating hardly at all. He wasn't much of a fisherman and wasn't often at the Club Nautico but in the nature of his business, Izzy moved in many different circles.

"Hear you been to Paris a couple of times since I saw you last," he said.

There are few secrets in a city the size of Asunción, but it wasn't like Izzy to bring up a man's business first. "That's right," I said and waited.

"Doesn't your boss know he can send a letter for maybe seventy-eighty cents registered?"

"Izzy, you know better than that."

"I do, but there are other ways of sending word. I know a couple–three and as a matter of fact I know your boss knows them too." He looked down at his Fanta soft drink. "But I figure he trusts you pretty good and to him it's worth the extra expense."

"Tell me something, Izzy, did you come out here this morning looking for me?"

"Yes. Yes I did, Clancy." Izzy even told the truth most of the time. "I'm not being nosy, nothing like that, but a couple of friends of mine are curious about something."

Izzy's friends were not people you wanted to have needlessly curious. I said, "You explain what this is about and I'll comment, okay?"

"Sure. There's an Englishman calls himself Arthur Grey came in a couple of days ago. He's staying at the Hotel Guarani. He says he's a tourist and he has a camera and all that, but he speaks good Spanish. Last night in the Guarani bar he got to talking with Glavin. You know Glavin?"

I nodded. Glavin was an ex-USAF type and according to report could do amazing things with an overloaded C-47. One of these nights on some unmarked strip in the Pampas he'd surprise himself.

"Yeah," said Izzy. "The Englishman mostly just listened, which is something any man talking to Glavin does a lot of, but he did ask if Glavin knew anything about your boss."

"Du Vigny?"

"Yes, the Englishman said he'd read about Du Vigny in

the papers when he left France and thought it was an interesting story. Well, Glavin told everything he knew, the way he always does to anybody and that would be about four times what's real. So my friends thought you should hear about this and they're wondering if Du Vigny maybe knows an Englishman called Arthur Grey."

"I've never heard him say so. Grey could be a newspaperman. Those birds have been interested in Du Vigny before."

Izzy sighed. "Well if he's newspaper, my friends will know what to do, and if he's a friend of Du Vigny's they'll know what to do, and if he's neither one, they'll know what to do, too. But there's three different what-to-do's there. Maybe you could talk to Du Vigny?"

"Sure. He'll be glad you told me about Grey. I'll pass on anything he says, but he doesn't tell me much."

"Well, that's all a man could ask, Clancy, that you talk to your boss and tell what he says. Everybody'll appreciate that. In case you want to take a look at the Englishman, the two days he's been here he's had his lunch at the Guarani and drinks in the bar before. He's nearly as tall as you with black hair going real gray, even though he can't hardly be forty. No mustache. Good tan and seems healthy. Quiet like English are supposed to be, but you notice him."

"I'll go by. How about a beer?"

"Well, not a beer, Clancy. It don't set good for me. One of those Fanta lemons though?"

The *mozo* brought me beer and Izzy his concoction. "I don't want to be prying into your affairs, Clancy," Izzy said, "but we're sitting and talking nice and friendly. Did you really kill all those people they say you did?" His light brown eyes met mine. "I've thought about it and you don't really seem that kind of guy. I know that kind of guy."

23

I cleared my throat. "Yeah, I killed a lot of people. Not as many as you've probably heard."

"You put bets on how many you'd kill? You and your general? Was that right?"

"Yeah, sometimes we made bets."

"Clancy, you know I don't think the Germans ever bet on us?"

"From what I hear, the Krauts killed you people like fish in a barrel. What was there to bet about?"

"You shot them from a helicopter, Clancy?"

"Mostly."

He moved his head slowly from side to side. "I like you Clancy, but you got a bad streak. Killing people and betting on them. How much? Couple, three dollars?"

"Izzy, why are you doing this?"

"No more. I took an advantage. Might do you good that I did." He smiled again. "You got a bad streak but I've seen a lot worse men. Not far from where we're sitting, too. I was only wondering what went on in your head."

I drank beer. Most of Izzy's capital would be knowing what went on in peoples' heads. "I didn't know you took such chances, Izzy."

"I don't very often. You mad?"

"I can't tell yet."

He chuckled. "Can I come round your place tonight around seven?"

"Sure. I better get going." I finished my beer and stood. "Take care, Izzy."

"Likewise. And thanks for the Fanta."

THE GUARANI HOTEL IS ON THE PLAZA DE LOS HEROES
in the center of Asunción. The plaza itself is all tremendous
lapacho trees with some palms and lots of hibiscus and it's
mostly ringed by old tile-roofed colonial buildings. By every
cannon of taste and rule of harmony, the Guarani Hotel should
fit into that setting as well as a Warhol giant tomato can would
into Du Vigny's Directoire salon. The Guarani is a fourteen
floor, glass and aluminum, triangular tower thought up by
some advanced Italian architect who was probably an early
experimenter with LSD. And it looks grand. The Paraguayans
love it so dearly they have even put its picture on the hundred
guaraní note. Guarani is a big word in Paraguay.

I went into the spacious, glittering, slightly mad lobby.
Mueller, the portly German manager, was talking to one of the
reception clerks. He smiled and bowed at me. I smiled and
nodded in return. Mueller is an ex-*Wehrmacht* artillery major
and claims that he shelled Moscow once in the winter of 1941.
Could be telling the truth.

The hotel is usually fairly full of Argentine and Brazilian
tourists who come to see quaint, cheap Paraguay. Some
Argentines can make the ugliest American seem attractive.
There are also a fair number of associates of Izzy's friends who
come in and out and a sprinkling of US and European tourists

who have heard about the country and decided to see for themselves.

I went up a weird stairway to the leather upholstered mezzanine bar and ordered a Bloody Mary, something Leodegar, the bartender, does well. There was a party of three Brazilian couples at a side table, making a cheerful racket and having a great time. There was also an Argentine party of four pretending they were having a better time than the Brazilians who couldn't have cared less. Two associates of Izzy's friends were at the bar, drinking whisky and doing some low-voiced arithmetic on an envelope. Standing alone at the far end of the bar was the Englishman. He was drinking the local beer and looking at nothing.

Arthur Grey was as described. Quiet but someone you noticed. I chatted with Leodegar who isn't a member of the Club Nautico—not because of class prejudice but for lack of having the initiation fee—but who still claims to have caught many huge fish and who is willing to explain his system. As I talked I glanced in the bar mirror from time to time. I couldn't figure out what there was about Grey that was striking. He didn't fit in the Guarani bar but nobody did, not even Leodegar. It could have been a feeling he gave of not being very much interested in anything that made you look at him again.

I finished my drink, paid, said so long to Leodegar and left. It was just short of noon and Du Vigny lunched at one.

Du Vigny was in what he termed his *bureau*, putting a sarcastic inflexion into the French word. It was a square room, with a wide window on the side garden. The walls were completely covered with books from the ceiling to the floor except for a small space reserved for an efficient gray four-drawer file cabinet with a triple combination lock. Du Vigny didn't like desks. There was a simple, handsome table of what I thought was mahogany in the center of the red Chinese rug. He was seated at his table writing when Andres ushered me in.

Du Vigny stood to shake my hand. He took me to one of the two armchairs by a smoking stand which were the only other furniture in the room. There was the business of arranging some hospitality. I asked for a martini on the rocks and Du Vigny decided to let himself have a vermouth.

"All right, Major," he said, after his first sip of Campari. "I know something must have brought you. What is it?"

I recounted my morning. Du Vigny listened intently. When I finished he frowned at the rug for a moment. He shrugged. "You can tell Izzy Meyer that I know nothing of this Arthur Grey and have no reason to expect attention from any Englishman at all. Tell him also that I am grateful for his information."

"Yes, sir."

"Grey is probably harmless. I hope Meyer and his friends do nothing out of the way. I understand the general is anxious to encourage tourism." There are more than a few generals in Paraguay, but when one talks of "the general" he means "*the* general." The general would be utterly unamused if an inoffensive Englishman disappeared or worse, were found.

I shook my head. "They won't do anything to get the general down on them."

"Expressly, no; however that lot are not always cool-headed."

That seemed to take care of the matter of Arthur Grey. I went to work on my martini. Du Vigny noticed. "Don't hurry," he said. "I've been making arrangements as a result of Pierre's message and your detailed instructions are about ready." He pointed at his table. "I've been writing them in a convenient form for you to commit to that excellent memory of yours. They'll be finished tomorrow. You can study them in this room. And only in this room."

That had a slightly ominous ring.

"Do you know Spain?" he asked.

"No, sir. I've never been there."

"You're going. You'll like it. It's been said that Spain is a desperado among the nations, but it's a good country for soldiers. I used to know it well.

"Ostensibly and actually you will be going to buy some pictures for me. There is a fine collection of French impressionists in the hands of the Quintinar branch of the Medina family. The Medinas have long been grandees of Spain. One of them commanded the Armada against England, poor fellow. The grandfather of the present Conde de Quintinar spent much time in Paris at the turn of the century. He probably had a stronger interest in models than in art, but he brought back many paintings and tertiary syphilis. Fortunately he'd already provided for the succession of the family. The present Conde is disposed to sell these pictures for some reason or other—to improve his estates or pursue some phantom of his own. Philip Hayden, that man of mine in New York, cabled me a month ago about the matter. He wanted authority to act for me, but I've told him I'm sending you. There's a Monet and a Pissarro I might be interested in, and I'll want you to look at them and make an appropriate offer."

"Well, sir—" I started.

He raised a hand. "You have a good eye and I wouldn't mind trusting your judgment, but you will be accompanied by a specialist. Hayden is providing her. He is undoubtedly disappointed not to be named my representative because he would have extracted more money from this transaction than otherwise, but I'm still paying him a good finder's fee, so he's anxious to stay in my good graces."

"Her?" I said.

"Yes. Her name is Susan Allgood. You shouldn't be dubious. There are many women in the art business and the specific specialist you'll need was not easily found. I told Hayden to get me someone who was not only an expert in European art but also highly skilled in the field of treating, handling, and restoring paintings. Miss Allgood is apparently exceptionally well qualified in both areas. I expect the deft feminine hand is good at the latter work."

"Are these French paintings in poor condition?"

"I have no reason to think so." He smiled. "You may need Miss Allgood's technical expertise more in your other mission." His mouth twisted and the smile went away. "Your other mission borders on the quixotic, appropriately enough considering where you're going."

He fell silent. I waited.

Abruptly he asked, "How much money do you think I stole, Major?"

I pulled at my ear. "I've heard it was around thirty million dollars."

"Tchah! It was a shade over twenty, and that was before the expenses of moving here. But even so you can see I have money to spare."

"Yes, sir." I could see that all right.

"I'm willing to spend a fair amount of it on this project. Your principal mission in Spain will be to see Don Jaime de García Mendoza and act according to your best judgment on the matter he will explain to you. As of this moment, you go on double pay. If you bring Don Jaime's matter to what I would call a successful conclusion, I will pay you a bonus of fifty thousand dollars. If in addition you are able to bring one item to me here, I'll pay an additional hundred thousand dollars over and above the first bonus.

"You'll go to New York to pick up Miss Allgood, then to Madrid. Don Jaime lives in Toledo, which is only seventy kilometers to the south. Your tickets and hotel reservations have been arranged. You will be pleased and I trust stimulated to know I'm sending you first class. I expect you have some questions?"

"I've got a couple of hundred," I said. "What is this item that's worth the extra hundred thousand?"

He smiled. "What do you think it is?"

"With this expert Miss Allgood who's coming along, I'd say it was an old painting."

He approved of me. "Excellent. I'm not going to go into details because if I have misread Don Jaime's message or Pierre has garbled it, I would rather not expose my aging dreams." He gave me a speculative look. "However, I shouldn't be too rigid even though you've already taken me aback several times during our acquaintance by showing knowledge one wouldn't expect an infantry officer to have. Does 'El Espolio' mean anything to you?"

"No, sir, other than it's Spanish for the looting or despoiling."

"Good. Just remember that I'd prefer 'El Espolio' but don't insist on it. Don Jaime will understand."

I didn't. I tried another tack. "Could you tell me anything more about Don Jaime?"

"Ah, yes. I wish I could see Don Jaime again. I have a large envy because you will. He is a scholar, a true scholar, but he fought on both sides in the Civil War and managed to be esteemed by both—a difficult feat in any Civil War, almost impossible to understand in a Spanish Civil War.

"I am qualified to say so. I fought in that war myself in one of the French battalions of the International Brigades. I've told you of my service with the *maquis* because that was experience of my manhood. I haven't told you of my time in the Spanish war because that was my youth, all of it, and it's hard to talk of one's youth. I trust you are not offended."

"No, sir," I said.

"There was little philosophy in my going with the International Brigades. There was a war the other side of the Pyrenees and I wanted to have a war. I met Don Jaime then. He'll tell you about it. Anything else?"

There was one more key question. The extra bonus wasn't being offered merely because he wanted a trustworthy messenger to carry a painting from Spain to Paraguay. "How interested are the police going to be in this?"

"Deeply. I'm not asking you to behave in a dishonorable way, but if you win the bonus, you will certainly be acting beyond the edge of the law. You have an Interpol dossier with green tab and the word of your arrival in Spain will stir a commotion in the Quai des Orfèvres who in turn will harass the Ministerio del Gobierno in Madrid. Thank God there is no love between the Spanish and French police, but the Spanish will have to respond to French proddings, and the Spanish in their own way are able men. Being Spanish they are hard to anticipate. The police will be a peril."

"This Allgood woman may not be willing to cooperate."

"Very possible. There'll be adequate funds. You handle her." He didn't seem disposed to answer more questions.

"I'll look at the written instructions you're preparing and then there may be some other points, sir," I said.

He pinched his temples between the thumb and fingers of a hand. "You conduct yourself well, Major. I don't think there is a good chance of your succeeding, but I want you to very much. Now that the dreary financial manipulation I've been playing at since my theft is close to finished, I need something to want. A man without an interest or an end turns into a husk.

Wanting nothing is only slightly less bad than having all wants satisfied, and I could finish in both conditions if I am not careful. Please come back tomorrow morning. The detailed instructions will be ready—addresses and telephone numbers and the manner of passing money and reports and the like."

"Yes, sir." He was a knotted, contradictory man and one who'd been kind to me when I needed it. "You know, I'm looking forward to this."

"At least you'll see Spain. Everyone should see Spain. It is a country entirely lacking in moderation and proud of the fact."

Driving back to Nelida's house, I decided I really was damn well looking forward to visiting Spain. Not only would it make for a change, but if I could get one hundred and fifty thousand dollars I could do a lot. Eat, drink, and screw myself to death, or buy land in Paraguay and settle down, or maybe even go back to the States. Going back to the States would be hard.

NELIDA WAS DOWNCAST WHEN I TOLD HER THAT I'D be leaving soon on what could be a long trip. I cheered her up by saying that when I came back we might go over to Rio for a few days. She'd never been outside Paraguay and I should have thought of taking her on a jaunt before.

Izzy dropped by as he'd said he would. I passed on what Du Vigny had said about Arthur Grey, adding that I was going to Spain to buy some pictures for Du Vigny and that Izzy's friends shouldn't leap to any conclusions about that. Izzy seemed sincerely grateful.

The next day he was back. Grey had departed the country. He apparently came down in the morning according to Izzy, got himself booked on the Varig plane to São Paulo, and sedately went on his way, leaving a few small nagging doubts behind.

The day after that I left myself, traveling, by God, first class. It was well over a year since I'd been in the States. The trip was dull but the plenteous free drinks helped. It took damn near as long for me to get through customs at Kennedy as it did at Orly, but at least at Kennedy I wasn't being treated any worse than anyone else. Even though I was scheduled to leave the same evening, Du Vigny had ordered a hotel room for me to rest in. He was being very considerate.

It was close to eleven when I checked into the hotel. I

called the number I'd been given for Philip Hayden's gallery. The secretary recognized my name. She said, "Mr. Hayden's been waiting for your call, Mr. Clancy. Just a moment, please."

There was a click or two, and a rich baritone voice came on. "Mr. Clancy," it said, "this is a pleasure. Welcome to New York. I hope your trip was smooth."

"It was fine. I'd like to see you this afternoon."

"Of course. I hate flying and usually have to rest for at least a day after a flight, and here you are leaving again this evening. Couldn't do it myself but I compliment you. Can you lunch with me perhaps?"

"Thanks, but I do want to get my head down for a couple of hours. How about three o'clock at your gallery?" I not only was tired, I didn't want to dodge questions I didn't have very good answers for.

"That will be fine. I'll have Susan Allgood here. You'll be impressed with her. I know of no one who better meets the qualifications Du Vigny specified. We're lucky to get her."

Since I knew that Miss Allgood was getting a thousand dollars a week and expenses, I thought she was fairly lucky, too. I said, "I'm looking forward to meeting Miss Allgood." Very accurate statement.

He paused a second. "There's one thing I believe I should mention. She's rather female-lib. I don't mean aggressively so or anything like that, but she does not like to be called 'Miss.' You know, prefers 'Ms.'" He spelled the last word and repeated it a couple of times, making it rhyme with "fizz."

Jesus. "I'll keep that in mind," I said.

Hayden made sure I knew the address of his gallery and we rang off. From his voice I estimated that he was qualified to sell expensive art. I'd never met an art dealer, but Hayden sounded the way I'd imagined one would.

I wondered how Ms. Allgood would react if it ever turned up that I'd be going over the edge of the law. I could always fire her or something. There was no point in worrying until I knew more.

I had two martinis and an omelet sent up to the room and disposed of them quickly enough to get a solid nap before having to leave for my appointment.

Hayden's place was up in the East Sixties. It had a severe front, only about thirty feet wide, with a narrow door at one side and a display window taking up the rest of the space. The door was brass-bound dark wood, the brass was polished to a gleaming gold. The window was framed in yellow painted metal, probably steel to hold the spread of glass. Three' pictures were on display. One was a three-foot square example of Op Art—an intricate conglomeration of distorted squares and spirals in green and hot orange that made me shift my feet to keep from losing my balance when I looked at it. The other two were something that seemed to take after the Wyeth school of eerie realism and a small medieval triptych. This Hayden didn't specialize.

I went through the narrow door. Before I could look around the softly lit interior, a living version of the Op Art piece in the window popped up before me. I guessed it was male because of a wispy goatee and mustache. He was wearing plush pajamas that also were green and hot orange and he tinkled like a set of wind chimes because of the layer of necklaces he sported. He had streaky blond hair to his shoulders and a narrow face hard to make out through the overgrowth. He squeaked at me.

"I'm Mr. Clancy to see Mr. Hayden," I said.

He squeaked some more and tripped away. I sighed and followed him to a big room at the rear of the building. Two men were occupied at long tables on one side and two girls were seated at desks on the other. The men at the tables were busy with wood and sharp tools, the girls had typewriters hammering away. The place smelled of oil, turpentine, cedar and scented girl.

The thing I was with made noises again. The girl at the first desk said, "Thanks, Jerry. Mr. Clancy, Mr. Hayden is expecting you." Whatever it was went back from whence it came. The girl rose and opened a door, said, "Mr. Clancy is here," and as soon as I'd passed through, closed the door behind me.

I was in a handsomely appointed office. The furniture was old English or damn good reproductions and a Persian rug covered the floor. A man came from behind the desk toward me. A girl in her late twenties was seated at a side armchair.

"Very glad to meet you indeed, Mr. Clancy," said the man, shaking my hand. "I'm Philip Hayden and this is Susan Allgood."

Hayden's voice may have fitted my idea of an art dealer, but the rest of him didn't. He was dressed like a banker in a conservative dark gray business suit and vest which fitted him a way my clothes never do. He was smaller than his voice, too, being no taller than Izzy Meyer and slim. His grip was strong enough. His hair and eyes were dark brown. The eyes were not a warm brown and they didn't seem glad to see me. Hayden's skin was odd. He was all over the way most people are only at the points of their elbows which gave him a faintly fuzzy aspect.

Susan Allgood remained seated and made no offer of a hand so I half-bowed to her and said, "How do you do." I'd have to practice Ms. a few times before I tried it out.

From the length of leg displayed below the miniskirt of her simple lavender dress, she looked to be taller than Hayden.

I guessed that if she'd thrown her bra away she'd never really needed it, though she was not flat-chested by any means. Her glossy black hair was straight and long, reaching nearly to the tips of her breasts. Her face was oval with a firm chin. She didn't seem to be wearing any make-up other than pale lipstick. She also didn't seem ever to pluck her eyebrows which damn near met. Their dark bar put a heavy note on an otherwise delicate face. Her deep blue eyes were regarding me from under the eyebrows much as if I were a six foot roach. She returned my greeting in a firm, impersonal contralto.

Hayden pointed me to an armchair by the other corner of his desk and retook his place. I sat, feeling gloomy. Of course, maybe this female looked at all the boys that way.

"I certainly envy you two this expedition," Hayden said. "Lord, a trip to Spain to visit a count and negotiate for beautiful pictures. I hope you'll spare some sympathy for me back here trying to survive a New York spring. What's your first name, Mr. Clancy?"

Susan said, "Perhaps he'd prefer Major Clancy, Philip."

Ah, that was it. "My first name's Patrick, and I resigned from the army so no 'major.' Appreciate your thinking of it, though."

Her expression never altered, but Hayden's eyes slid to me and away. He said, "Patrick. Certainly most appropriate. Have you been to Spain before, Patrick?"

"No, but I do speak Spanish, which is the principal reason Du Vigny's sending me."

"I understand you'll be handling the actual selection and purchase of the pictures?" said Susan.

"With your advice, and I'll need plenty."

"May I ask what your background in art may be? To give me an idea as to the kind of advice you'll need."

Hayden came in hastily. "I understand it's extensive. Du Vigny was high in his praises. Patrick's been helping him reconstitute his collection."

"Since he had to leave one in Paris, you mean," said Susan.

Better I try to soothe this prickly girl than stir her up. Someday I might be really needing help from her. "You're being a little too kind, Philip. I'm not doing anything like helping Du Vigny put together this new collection. He just tries some of the pictures out on me. I promise you, Susan, I'll welcome any advice any time you care to offer it. Just act as if I were some Hottentot placed in your care and I'll be grateful."

That didn't go over worth a damn. When I said "Hottentot," her noticeable eyebrows went up and she nodded slightly to herself. I may have convicted myself as a racist in addition to other defects.

Hayden was curious about which pictures of the Conde de Quintinar's collection most interested Du Vigny. I had the specifications of several in my head but didn't think Du Vigny would want Hayden to know or he'd have told him himself. I made some general statements.

This conversation was ended by Susan rising. I'd been right. She was a good couple of inches taller than Hayden. "It's been interesting meeting you, Mr. Clancy," she said. "I suggest we meet at Kennedy in the TWA terminal at six, since our plane leaves at seven. Is that all right?"

"Sure." I was also on my feet. "See you then, Susan."

I would have left, too, but Hayden said there were a couple of other matters he wanted to talk to me about, so I waited while he saw Susan out. She apparently didn't refuse normal gentlemanly courtesies.

When Hayden was back at his desk—that chair seemed to

be the only one he was comfortable in—he said in a confidential tone, "Susan sometimes can create a false impression. She's most jealous of her independence and I must tell you rather liberal in her outlook—quite active in the antiwar movement and the like. But I'm sure you'll find her a charming and friendly companion besides being, as I've told you, superbly qualified."

He seemed to be trying to sell me Susan. Could be he was worried about whatever commission or fee he was getting. He shouldn't have been. I did what Du Vigny wanted.

"Susan and I will get along great," I said. I realized that Hayden's chair behind the desk must have been skillfully built up. Hayden sitting appeared taller than Hayden standing.

He continued confidential. "You know there's one point that I don't understand. Du Vigny laid much stress on the qualifications of your adviser. The need for an expert in European art is fairly obvious, but the requirement for an expert on handling and restoring paintings is not so apparent. Some of those French paintings may need cleaning but no more than that. The air of Spain is famous for keeping paintings in good condition." He waited expectantly.

I said, "Du Vigny's main objective is the Quintinar paintings but he also wants me to take a general look around to see if there's anything else interesting. For example, he'd like a couple of samples of the Flemish school to give some historical continuity to his collection. Susan will be very helpful there." I was repeating phrases from Du Vigny's instructions. I wouldn't know a sample of the Flemish school unless it bore a label with four-inch letters.

"Oh, I see. Thanks for answering my question."

That may really have been all he wanted to know but it took another ten minutes to break away. When you came right down to it he was a fancy rug merchant who wouldn't be successful unless he could smell money and there was certainly the smell of money about this trip. A hundred and fifty thousand dollars had been waved under my nose.

Hayden saw me to the door. From the way the thing in the display room cavorted around at the sight of him, I formed a question or two of my own about Hayden.

There was one salient advantage to having Susan as an adviser. She might be difficult but she was infinitely preferable to something like Hayden's little orange-and-green horror.

7 ==================

THERE WAS A BOOK STORE IN THE HOTEL LOBBY. Before leaving for Kennedy I bought a *Guide Michelin* to Spain in English and a *Concise History* of the country. The guide had a fair map and I located Toledo, which as promised lay about seventy kilometers southwest of Madrid. I also discovered a place called Quintinar de la Orden about a hundred and twenty kilometers southeast of Madrid. I wondered if that was where the Conde de Quintinar came from.

In the cab to the airport I considered lines of action with Ms. Susan Allgood. This trip promised to be more entertaining than anything I'd done in a long time. I'd have to establish a workable relationship with her or the trip would have more than a few grim moments, not to mention that I might need at least her acquiescence if I had to go illegal to win Du Vigny's second bonus. Apparently she saw me as a card-carrying war criminal. I'd never felt like one, but she wasn't alone in that opinion. The best bet might be a frank discussion. I didn't think I'd succeed in explaining anything but it wouldn't hurt to clear the air, and if need be I could make it plain that I gave the orders and she was paid to follow them.

She was waiting by the first-class check-in counter, tall and still heavy browed. The trace of disgust I'd seen before returned to her face when she saw me. She was wearing a dark blue pants suit that went well with her figure and long legs.

Slung from one shoulder was a large square kit bag like the cases advanced camera fanatics carry.

Since it was only ten to six, I didn't apologize for being late or keeping her waiting, but merely wished her good evening. She was polite. She'd already checked herself in and reserved seats for the two of us. Neighboring seats they were so she wasn't determined to be extreme.

After I went through the dreary rigmarole of having myself and my bag accepted by the airline, we wended our way out through large, entrail like, concrete tubes to the side concourse from which we would board. I suggested a nip at the bar and Susan agreed. She wasn't liberated enough to suggest we toss for the tab, which was an encouraging sign.

Our flight was called and we boarded. I did like traveling first class. Room for my legs and for me and when I wanted a drink I got a drink, bang, without having to wait for someone to push a cart around. We settled ourselves, Susan by the window. She was careful of her shoulder bag. During dinner I asked her what kind of a camera she had and she told me very civilly that the case held her traveling gear as an art expert, and although it included a small camera for taking pictures of paintings that was the only kind of photography she did.

I had decided to open the frank discussion as soon as the stewardesses cleared away the dinner trays, but Susan anticipated me. We had just been given coffee and I'd lit a cigarette for her when she said, "I can guess at least one of the things Philip talked to you about when I left. He told you that I am completely against the war you were in and that I'm a supporter of the women's liberation movement as well as most other attempts to secure the rights of the individual."

She wasn't asking a question but I said she was right.

"I know the recent past of your employer as well as your own," she went on. "You may be wondering how I can reconcile my beliefs with working for Du Vigny and with you. It's easy. I'm being paid well for whatever use you're going to make of my knowledge and skills. This is an opportunity to practice my profession, which is art."

That was delivered in a cool tone. I scratched my head. The air didn't seem to be clearing the way I'd hoped. I said, "Susan, would you tell me what you do know of my recent past?"

She turned to look at me. "I don't know why you ask but all right. In Vietnam you had a position on the staff of a General Jonas. It seems that when you had nothing better to do the two of you would go out in the general's helicopter and hunt Vietnamese in what I think were called free fire zones where you could kill anyone you wanted to, firing your machine guns from the helicopter. Between you and the general, you killed two or three hundred people, some of them possibly enemy and others not, some of them women and children. You and the general used to place bets on who'd kill the most, or on who would get a certain target—some human being trying to hide from your invulnerable machine in a ditch or a rice paddy. Unfortunately for you, one of the helicopter pilots told the story to a newspaperman who investigated and then published. The army went through the motions of bringing you and General Jonas before a court-martial but it ended in a cover-up. Nothing was done to you. Nothing at all.

"That's what I understand." Her voice had stayed level, scarcely loud enough for me to hear her above the constant low engine sound, but it had become more intense as she spoke.

She paused, then asked, "Are you going to tell me I'm mistaken."

"You're right about the main points, I guess. General Jonas and I did hunt Viets from his helicopter in free fire

43

zones. We kept score and more than a few times we made bets. You're wrong about being able to kill anything in a free fire zone. You had to identify it as enemy in the day time and it had to be out and moving at night. We didn't kill anywhere near two or three hundred and I don't think we killed civilians, but I won't swear that every man we got was VC. We landed to check when we could but often there'd be heavy ground fire and we couldn't. We killed only one woman that I know of. The men she was with were all armed with the Chinese automatic rifles the VC used so we figured she was a VC nurse or good friend or something. We never killed a child as far as I ever knew.

"The army didn't make a cover-up. The army wanted to try anybody who got his name in the papers the way General Jonas and I got ours. They ran their investigation and took all sorts of depositions and there simply wasn't any reason to try us. We might have been over-zealous practicing our profession, but we hadn't busted any Articles of War. When everyone in the My Lai thing but Calley was acquitted, the army gave up on us. That's all."

Her eyes weren't convinced. "But you did kill men and make bets on them."

"Yeah. I was a soldier and I believed then—still do—that a soldier's work is killing the enemy. As for the bets, I don't think I could ever explain that to you. Whenever anybody talks to me about this, the bets are the point that seems to get them most. Betting made sense to me at the time. I think I'd do it again under similar circumstances. Oh, and one thing more. Helicopters aren't exactly invulnerable. We were hit more than a few times by ground fire. The General and I each got one Purple Heart from those expeditions. Anyway, nobody ever made a rule you had to fight an enemy even." I didn't tell her that his Purple Heart was one of the things General Jonas was looking for. He'd missed the Second War and hadn't been wounded in Korea. He'd brooded about that. Happiest man in the world when he took a round through the thigh. Didn't do him any real good, though.

Susan said, "I really don't understand why you thought it necessary to tell me all this and I must say my opinion of you remains the same—you are basically a brute who shouldn't be allowed at large. However, I can work with you."

"Fair enough," I said. At least now she wasn't the high priestess condescending, and I'd progressed from war criminal to dangerous brute.

A stewardess came by to pick up the trays, closely followed by another handing out earphones for the movie. Just as well.

YOU HAVE A SHORT NIGHT WHEN YOU FLY TOWARD THE dawn at five hundred miles an hour. Stewardesses woke us from unsatisfactory dozes and dealt out skimpy breakfasts. The plane landed without event and we were fed into waiting busses which took us to the terminal of Barajas Airport. It was about seven-thirty in the morning, local time, and the day was clear and cool.

Going through immigration and customs in Spain made me see how much I'd been missing in previous trips to Europe. Nobody was waiting to carry me off for reaming and candling. Nobody could be induced to look at our bags. I admit it was a hassle getting the bags themselves. There was one baggage belt for all planes landing and everyone stood in a mass and hollered across a barrier at some overworked porters when he saw his particular suitcase or bundle, but outside of that no problem.

We drove into Madrid along a fancy turnpike. It was much like the approach to any large city, except the rows of small, large, and medium factories and warehouses we passed through seemed to be only a thin coating applied along the highway. In the spaces between you could see empty farmland running off to the horizon. The country was flat, so that horizon was far away.

It was only about twelve kilometers to Madrid. When we hit the city the traffic was like Buenos Aires on a busy day except possibly more careless. I noticed Susan making involuntary jumps and starts as we whistled around, cutting other cars out and being cut out ourselves.

"A bit hectic," I observed.

"Yes, it is." She flinched again. "I've been once to Italy and several times to France and although there isn't as much traffic overseas as in New York, one seems to notice it more."

I told her the *Guide Michelin* said that our hotel was less than a block from the Prado. That perked her up and diverted her mind from her worries. I wanted to see the Prado myself. I also wanted to see what Susan's reaction to paintings would be. I could probably gauge how expert she was from what she did in the Prado.

We arrived unscathed at the Palace Hotel and were quickly checked in. Plenty of willing bellhops, most of them smiling broadly, made the process easy. The man at the desk couldn't believe I spelled my name the way I did but he wasn't obstinate about it. He also courteously refrained from comment on discovering that I and the dolly I was traveling with were staying in separate rooms.

I suggested to Susan that we take naps and meet for lunch after which we'd go look at the Prado. I didn't smile, but by God she did. Not at me but at the prospect of the Prado.

The lunch hour in Spain being what it is—doesn't start until two—we didn't leave the hotel until well after three. We walked down one block and there as promised on the other side of a busy, wide tree-lined avenue was the Prado. It was a big, plain pile of bricks and I'd frankly expected more. Susan looked at it as a young nun might at the Vatican—maybe not a young nun these days.

We crossed the avenue, not without risk, and went toward the main entrance. Sitting on benches under the trees of the entrance court was a scruffy lot of young longhairs of both sexes, some with rucksacks and some without. I'd seen similar types in the States and in Paris, all looking alike and all not seeming to have much fun.

A slender girl in blue jeans and Indian beads came up to us and asked in American English if we'd give her some money. Not begging exactly, more counting on us to help. I drew in breath for a refusal but damned if Susan didn't dig a hundred pesetas out of her purse and pass them over. The girl said thanks and wandered off.

"What did you do that for?" I asked, walking a little faster before others came to try.

"I'm sorry for them," she said. "So many are so badly lost."

"Her family probably paid her way over here and would be happy to pay it back."

"You're not the type to be sympathetic to the young disaffected. We're losing a lot of potentially good people through not being sympathetic. Almost as many as we lost in Vietnam."

I intelligently dropped the subject.

Once inside the Prado, it became apparent I did have an expert adviser. Susan knew exactly what she wanted to see and even had a fair idea of how to get there. We went first to the Goyas, then to the El Grecos, and last to the Velázquezes. Some of those things of Goyas were hard even for me to look at and I was used to unpleasant sights. I couldn't help wishing that El Greco had paid a little more attention to his proportions but the light and color in his paintings simply felt great on the eyes. I had nothing to complain about with Velázquez, nothing at all.

Susan wasn't the chatty kind of connoisseur—the sort who feels constrained to tell you about impasto and composition and brush stroke. She simply enjoyed the paintings all

48

through herself. Technique interested her certainly; periodically she went to within a few inches of a picture to check something and she obviously understood what she saw. When she was doing that she reminded me of an old sergeant armorer I'd once had and the way he'd inspected weapons, with respect and an eye to where they might be susceptible to rust. If I hadn't asked questions I don't think she would have spoken to me but only because she was lost in what was before her.

When I asked about the history of a few of the pictures she knew in all but one case, and when I showed curiosity as to the care of paintings, she gave me brief instruction in that, pointing out a Velázquez that was overdo to be rebacked, and an El Greco that showed a trace of sag which possibly could be corrected by a new stretching. On another Velázquez—a portrait of Philip IV, an unpleasant-looking fellow—some underpainting was making its way to the surface; that she said could not be corrected by anybody except Velázquez. She said some of the Goyas needed cleaning.

I asked how the colors had stayed so fresh over the centuries. She smiled without true amusement. "Those men simply used good, natural pigments and oils and prepared their colors themselves and they wanted their work to last forever. These paintings here will still be fresh when ninety percent of the work being done today is cracked and crazed and all tint and tone lost."

We didn't leave until the closing bell sounded and the attendants began gently to chase everyone out. We walked across to the Ritz, which my *Michelin* said had a fine setting and a luxurious lounge bar. *Michelin* was right. We sat in a spacious rococo room with high ceilings and an immense chandelier. A calm, elderly waiter, whose uniform included tailcoat and white spats, took our order.

Susan sat back in her chair. She reminded me of women I'd seen after they'd risen from an agreeable time in bed. Satisfied and relaxed but willing to try again after a short rest.

She spoke first. "I haven't asked about your plans. Will you get in touch with the Conde de Quintinar tomorrow?"

"I'll call him this evening and make an appointment for day after tomorrow. There's another man Du Vigny wants me to see first. He's in Toledo. Or at least I hope he is. I'm going there tomorrow. I'd be very happy for you to come along, although I'll have to see this man alone. Du Vigny's instructions. Still, from what I've read there's a lot to see in Toledo and you wouldn't have any trouble amusing yourself."

"I'd like very much to come. I've always wanted to see *El Intierro del Conde de Orgaz*, and *El Espolio*."

She mispronounced the Spanish words slightly so I almost missed it. With a delayed reaction I said, "What!"

Her eyebrows went up. "I would like to see *El Intierro del Conde de Orgaz* and *El Espolio*."

I put my voice in normal. "What are *El Intierro del Conde de Orgaz* and *El Espolio*?"

She repeated the names, getting the accent right this time. "They're paintings by El Greco, and are generally accepted as his two master works. The *Conde de Orgaz* picture is in a little church in Toledo, and *El Espolio* is in the sacristy of the cathedral."

"In the cathedral. That's got a three-star rating in *Michelin*. Tell you what. I'll lay on a car. We'll drive down fairly early and I'd like to take a look around the cathedral. Then I'll hunt up this man I'm to see and we'll meet for a long lunch and come back here. How does that sound?"

She almost gave me a smile for myself. "That sounds fine."

We had another drink. I asked for details on what was

involved in rebacking a picture. She told me and it sounded complicated beyond all belief. I wasn't paying full attention, because in the back of my head I was remembering Du Vigny telling me he preferred "El Espolio" but didn't insist on it.

Susan had run down and was frowning at me. With her eyebrows she could put emphasis in a frown. "You really know hardly anything about art history or techniques of restoration, do you?" she asked.

"No, never claimed to."

"The way Philip talked the day before yesterday, I thought you were trying to be modest." Her face said, "trying to be modest and not doing well at it."

At the Palace Hotel, I called the Conde de Quintinar. He recognized my name immediately and said he'd received letters from Du Vigny and Hayden. I explained some other business would occupy me tomorrow and asked for an appointment the following day. He seemed slightly disappointed at even a day's delay, so I guessed he wanted Du Vigny's money. The French paintings were at the Conde's family place, located some twenty kilometers west of Quintinar de la Orden, and he hoped my adviser and I would be his guests there for as long as necessary. I thanked him and we were polite.

Susan and I didn't dine together. She almost tactfully said she preferred a light dinner in her room and early bed. With the aid of my invaluable *Michelin* I found and ate largely at a restaurant that specialized in sea food. One gets very little sea food in Paraguay.

Du Vigny couldn't possibly expect me to get a picture by El Greco out of the Cathedral of Toledo.

I read myself to sleep with my *Concise History* of Spain. It gave me the strong impression that for complicated turbulence, Spain was in a league by itself.

===================== *9*

THE SEDAN AND DRIVER I'D ORDERED WERE WAITING
when Susan and I came out of the hotel the next morning. The
driver was a man in his mid fifties, short and wiry with a long,
seamed face, which split in a wide smile when we walked up.
He greeted us in terrible English and said his name was Luis
Morillo. His relief was obvious when I answered in Spanish.

Luis drove with a bit more care than most of his
compatriots, which didn't mean he was a careful driver. From
Madrid almost to Toledo, the terrain we passed through was
flat to gently rolling. Although there were patches of green
crops, most of the land was brown and seemed to be in pasture
or simply lying fallow. The few trees were either olives set in
groves or clumps of poplars around the isolated farms and
scattered villages. The whole landscape had a hard bitten,
hard used, look to it. It was the opposite of lush.

The villages matched the land, seeming to have pushed
their way up from the soil. In every one, a towering brown
church, always huge in comparison with the settlement it
stood in, dominated the buildings clustered about its skirts.

Luis had asked me to say frankly if we wanted the usual
tourist chit-chat. He had a regular spiel, painfully learned and
thought to be mostly accurate, that he would be happy to
provide if we desired. I told him no thanks, but that if we did

pass something of more than ordinary interest we'd appreciate hearing about that.

He had nothing to offer until we were approaching a town about forty kilometers out of Madrid. He jerked his chin toward the looming church. "There is something interesting, señor. That church in this little town of Illescas is probably richer than many cathedrals."

"Oh?"

"This is true. The church has five El Grecos. They bought them for not very much money when El Greco was living all those years ago. Now those pictures are worth who can say? A friend told me that he heard the last El Greco sold cost over a million dollars. So the people of Illescas go to Mass and say their confessions surrounded by at least five million dollars. They are poor but it is a matter of satisfaction to them."

"These paintings are just on the walls of the church?"

"Yes, of course, they belong to the church." He chuckled and turned dangerously to look at me a moment. "The people I drive are often surprised by that. They say why doesn't the church sell the paintings and give the money to the poor? They do not understand but you who speak Spanish might. The poor would lose the money very quickly and then the people of Illescas, poor again, would no longer have the satisfaction of knowing how rich was their church. It would be just another church in a small town."

I repeated the conversation to Susan. Luis obviously checking from the front seat to be sure I translated correctly. Recognition showed on her face. "Oh, yes," she said, "Illescas. One of those Grecos is quite well known—it's a picture of the Virgin giving San Ildefonso a chasuble. It's one of the best of his last period." She eyed me. "Perhaps we might stop by on our way back?"

"Sure. Wonder how a church in this little town had the foresight to buy five El Grecos."

She shook her head. "It's not surprising. This is close to Toledo where El Greco spent most of his working life. He was a prolific painter and was anxious to sell his paintings to whoever had money to buy them. He didn't quite go door to door, but if he heard that the church at Illescas was in the market for some paintings he probably rode over with samples the first chance he got."

There was another question in the back of my mind. I went back to Spanish. "Luis, I should think the people of Illescas would be concerned about the safety of those paintings. If they are just on the walls of the church, couldn't someone steal them?"

"I've been asked that before, señor, and—ah, look ahead, señor, there is one of the reasons the paintings are not stolen."

I peered over his shoulder down the road. It ran straight and empty except for two figures. As we neared, I could see that they wore green uniforms and each carried a carbine slung over his shoulder. Their hats were odd affairs in patent leather, shaped like an old three-cornered hat with its front point sliced off right to the crown. Although they must have been together, they were walking along the road as if they were point men on a combat patrol. One was fifty yards ahead of the other. It would be hard to take those two out at the same time.

"The Guardia Civil?" I said. I'd heard of them.

"Yes, the Guardia Civil," repeated Luis. "Absolutely pitiless bastards." Pride and dislike were mingled in his tones. He bit his lip. "You are sure the señorita does not understand Spanish?"

"Not a word."

"Good. No Spaniard would steal from a church. We may

54

burn churches every now and again from exasperation, but we do not steal from them. If a foreigner were to take a painting from the church of Illescas, the Guardia would go after him very hard. Few things are efficient in Spain, but the Guardia Civil is first among those, and it is not in the habit of bringing someone to trial in a court. I would not like to be the man who stole from a church and was caught by the Guardia. Those men without shame from other countries who would consider stealing the El Grecos of Illescas would probably first take the pains to learn who protected them and thus would know of the Guardia and this would make them reconsider."

I was Irish and enough of my Catholic upbringing remained to make me pretty sure I wasn't going to steal from a church either. Luis's little speech about what would happen to a man who stole from the church in Illescas made me wonder what the Guardia Civil would do to a man who stole from a cathedral.

I told Susan what we'd been talking about. Being a liberated woman she theoretically shouldn't have minded my repeating Luis's description of the Guardia as "absolutely pitiless bastards," but Luis would have, so I merely said they were a tough bunch.

"They're a cruel band of mercenaries supporting a dictatorial regime," she said, with more vehemence than she had shown since telling me I was a brute who shouldn't be at large.

Trying to remind her Luis understood some English, I motioned at him. He must have caught the gesture in his mirror. "No, no, señor," he said. "The señorita is right and I am not offended. I have finally come to like Franco myself but that is because I am older and my children are making something a little better of themselves. God knows what will happen when the old man dies." He crossed himself. "Unfortunately, his is the only kind of government that can rule Spain. We are not a docile people. Now we are near Toledo." The last was spoken in English and I thought was a nice touch of diplomacy.

We came to the end of the plain we'd been traveling through, and the road began to drop steeply down through rugged ground. For the first time we saw groves of trees, thick and natural. This would be the north side of the Tagus valley.

We passed a group of roadside stands exhibiting wildly colored pottery. Luis jerked a thumb at the display. "There's one way to tell you are close to Toledo. These people would sell their grandmothers to anyone who wanted a souvenir."

"Where are you from, Luis?"

"I? I am from León. There is a city! Its cathedral has a beauty the poor one here cannot even approach. You must see the cathedral in León, señor. And in León, we are not vulgar batteners on the stranger."

We swept around the nose of a ridge and came into view of the city of Toledo. Susan gasped.

The city loomed there on another ridge that jutted out into the valley. It almost blended with the far Tagus cliffs for it and its encircling walls were built of the same grayish-brown rock. Toledo was like a galleon with the central tower of what had to be the cathedral reaching up for a mast, and a huge block-square edifice with spiky roofed turrets at each corner serving as the high poop. There was only a short stretch of road from which you could see the city plain, then it dipped again and we were in an undistinguished suburb.

We passed a bull ring which Luis said was small and poorly designed, and came out on an open park before a gate flanked by crenelated towers. Forty-foot walls ran off to either side as far as I could see. Behind, the city climbed in tiers toward the tower of the cathedral and the turreted mass of the great square building.

"The Bisagra Gate," said Luis. "Very old. Rather ugly." He pointed to the left. "Those are the Arabic walls, built on the remains of the Roman ones. The high walls on the other side of the gate are newer; they were built by Alfonso the Wise after he took back the city from the Moors in 1085. The big square building like a castle is the *alcazar*. That's the place Moscardo held so long against the Republicans in 1936. I could guide you through the town, señor, but the local guides would set up a terrible fuss. They have an association."

I told Luis we wanted to go to the cathedral and then walk around on our own. He approved and said we should have maps as it was easy to lose one's way in Toledo. We made a brief stop for Luis to pick up maps at a small building in the park where there was a tourist office and then continued on into the city.

Once inside the walls we went up a road that hung on the side of a cliff—part natural and part formed from layer after layer of old masonry—and then turned right into the city proper. The street we followed had two-way traffic but it shouldn't have. We passed an irregular square which Luis said was the Plaza Zocodover, the main plaza of Toledo. The longest side couldn't have been more than fifty or sixty yards. "They are jammed inside their walls here," said Luis. He shrugged. "They like it that way."

I'd thought the street by which we'd come to the square had been narrow. The deeper we went into the city the more I got the feeling the car was going to hit a point of no return, and we would be stuck like a cork in a bottle. Luis drove blithely along, honking at pedestrians and shooing them into taking refuge in doorways. At last, we popped out of the stone maze into a street that once more supported two-way traffic and was lined with shops. Some displayed items aimed at the tourist trade but most were selling groceries and hardware and what people needed to live.

Susan drew a deep breath. "I never thought we'd come out of that. I expected narrow streets but I didn't think they'd let cars drive through them."

We went a short distance and then finally found real space again. Not much but some. It was the plaza of the cathedral. There was a parking area crowded with vehicles. Luis halted and dismounted to open doors. Susan and I got out and stood staring at the massive façade of the cathedral. Its form was severe and simple but statues and carvings and gargoyles and strange domes and cupolas abounded to the point the whole immense structure seemed covered with stone flames.

The three of us looked at it for a while. Luis superciliously, Susan and I with awe. Luis pointed out a tiny entrance to one side. "One must go through there, señor, when there is no Mass. Entrance to the cathedral itself is of course free, but if you want to visit the treasury or the sacristy or other special places you must buy tickets. They sell them just inside."

A mass of people, nearly all festooned with cameras, emerged from a passage that opened into the plaza behind us. Luis gave them an expert eye. "One of the daily tours from Madrid," he said. "Those seem to be German, a bad sort, although the French can be worse."

Inside the entrance was a lovely cloister. To one side was a gaudy booth, very out of keeping, selling souvenirs and tickets. The German tour, thank God, seemed to have a group ticket, so I didn't have to stand in line.

The entrance to the cathedral proper was through a wide,

high arch. This didn't mean we could merely stroll through. The arch was filled with great wooden doors fitted with iron hinges thicker than my leg, and the only way in was by a small door set in one of the leaves of the great one. The Germans were still filing through that when I'd finished buying our tickets. We went after them.

The interior of the cathedral should have been breathtaking. Stained glass was brilliant in the walls and there were five enormous naves, their vaults supported by pillars which seemed light to the point of airiness until we walked near and realized how thick they were. But right in the middle of the central nave, blocking it entirely and making it impossible to get a full appreciation of the tremendous expanse enclosed beneath the more than hundred-foot high roof, was a great structure reaching almost to the roof itself.

I asked Susan, "What's that stuff in the middle? If I'd been the Spaniard in charge, I wouldn't have put that there."

She nodded. "Practically every Spanish cathedral has one of those. It's the *coro*. Some say that since there is so much light and so many sweeping vistas in Spain, when they came to build their cathedrals the Spanish wanted to make them more private than their sheer size permitted, so they broke up all the space by putting one of those in the center of each. That's where the choir and the organ are. It's a defect, but it's a very Spanish one."

"You've had training in architecture, too?"

"Not a great deal, but any art student gets some."

An all-around expert. "Let's go see *El Espolio*," I said. "It's in the sacristy, you say."

"Yes." I got a curious look.

A couple of faded signs on the wall guided us to the sacristy. A man at the door carefully tore a corner off our tickets. We went through a small vestibule into a brightly lit hall, thirty or forty yards long and less than half as wide. The ceiling was nearly as high as in the cathedral side nave. There was no mistaking *El Espolio*. It had the place of honor on the wall opposite the entrance. One look explained the title. It was of Christ at Golgotha, and the soldiers were taking His garments. The canvas was full of people and action. The figure and clothes of Christ glowed nearly as brightly as did the stained glass in the main cathedral walls. The soldiers in the picture weren't Roman, they were Spanish officers and pikemen of the 1500s, when the Tercios of Spain cleared every field in Europe. El Greco must have had to answer some questions about that.

We went down the hall to stand before it. Du Vigny couldn't have meant this. It was about six by ten feet. Setting aside his remarks about doing nothing dishonorable, nobody ever would be able to take this from the wall where it hung, tuck it under his arm, move through the Guardia Civil to some frontier, and make his way back to Paraguay.

I needed to call upon Don Jaime Pedro de García Mendoza y Zibaru.

"Susan," I said, "I have to go see that man I mentioned. Here's your ticket for the other things in the cathedral. I'll meet you back at the car around one. Okay?"

As I was leaving the main hall, I turned for a last look at *El Espolio*. Susan had turned herself and was staring after me. I waved at her and went on.

DON JAIME LIVED AT NUMBER 3 CALLE SAL, TO THE south of the cathedral. Map in hand, I entered a tangle of deep alleys. There was no chance of bringing anything larger than a motor scooter into this network. The alleys were exceptionally neat alleys. They were paved with wide, close-fitting flagstones, worn glossy by use and looking as if they'd been swept only an hour before. The houses on either side were three and four stories tall. Their fronts were severely plain, except many of the doorways had carved lintels and side pillars.

Plenty of people were bustling to and fro. Sometimes I got a curious glance. I guessed few foreigners penetrated this far from the shops and principal monuments. It was a good chance to see if anyone had decided to put me under surveillance, so I stopped from time to time and pretended to examine some of the ornate doorways. For anyone to follow me through that warren, he'd have to stay close. I didn't pick up any tail.

I was grateful for previous experience taking small infantry units through jungle. Street names were on large blue and white tiles set in the stone walls. I found one labeled Calle Pimienta and went along to where it split into Sal and Hierro. Pepper Street dividing into Salt and Iron. Halfway logical.

Number 3 Calle Sal had a doorway fancier than others I'd seen. Set above the lintel was a complicated coat of arms.

With all Don Jaime's names that was to be expected. There was a gleaming heavy brass knocker in the form of a hand suspended by the wrist on the right leaf of the double doors. I worked it up and down, producing resonant booms.

After a short wait one half of the double doors opened and a small, plump woman about sixty, in a black dress and white apron peered up at me. She had bright beady eyes set in a round, wrinkled face.

I said, "Buenos dias. Is Don Jaime in?"

"Buenos dias, señor. May I ask your name?"

I had a card all ready. It had been made by the best place in Asunción which meant the engraving had many curlicues and flourishes. Under my name I'd written in pencil, "From Paraguay."

The maid took the card and examined it carefully. She seemed to approve of the curlicues. "Please wait a moment, señor."

I stood in the narrow street. Four young boys ranging in age from nine to maybe twelve came running by making loud Spanish noises. It was hard to believe that children lived in the crevices of the pile of stone that was Toledo but of course they had to.

Perhaps two minutes passed, and the door opened again, this time widely. "Please enter, señor," said the woman. "Don Jaime is expecting you."

I walked through to an entry way that went on into a shady central patio full of plants in enormous pots. Some white flowers shone in the light filtering down from three stories above. Nodding and beckoning for me to follow, the maid led the way up a wide flight of stairs to a dim corridor with single doors on either side. She opened the first door on the right and bowed me through.

I was in a long, narrow room that ran the full width of the

patio below. The wall facing the patio was nearly all window; the other walls were all bookcases, jammed full of books, straight up or stacked on their sides or stuck into any nook or space that could be found for them. There were flowers on the low window sills, and a tiny fireplace tucked in one end wall. The desk, overflowing with books, and several scattered chairs were a tan wood that matched the bookcases. It was a light and airy room in barely controlled chaos.

A white-haired man was standing before the desk. Hot brown eyes, set wide in a smooth, ruddy face, examined me. He had a notable beak for a nose and his jaw stuck firmly forward. He was carefully dressed in a dark suit.

"Jaime de García Mendoza," he said, "para servirle, señor." His manner was stiffly formal.

I announced my name and we shook hands. Don Jaime said, "Consuelo is bringing wine. Please sit down. I have been wondering if someone would come. I'd hoped it might be before now."

"There were arrangements to make, señor. Du Vigny sends his best regards and I have a letter for you." I took it from my inside coat pocket and passed it to him.

He held the letter in his hands looking at it, making no move to open it. The expression on his face was hard to read. He was frowning slightly as if he were reasonably sure that inside the envelope he would find bad news.

The maid entered carrying a tray with several bottles and glasses. Some time was spent while Don Jaime decided which sherry would suit me best. The maid served us and left. We touched glasses and drank.

Don Jaime put down his wine, flicked the letter with a forefinger, and asked my pardon. He tore open the flap and took out three folded pages. From where I sat I could recognize Du Vigny's neat handwriting.

I sipped my sherry and waited, eaten with curiosity. Don Jaime read at a fair speed and with complete attention. Once he made a small noise in his throat. I couldn't say whether it was of distress or surprise. When he finished he leaned back, letting his hands holding the letter fall into his lap. For a good minute he stared ahead of him.

He roused himself. "Please forgive me, señor. This is the first direct communication I've had with your master in nearly three years, and we were very close once." He looked at me. "He says that you are a former army officer who has entered his service and that I am to trust you as I would him. Well, what about him? Did he go mad? Frenchmen do, and in unpredictable ways."

"I'm sure he's not insane, señor. I have known him long enough to be positive of that."

"He must have lost something, if not his mind, his balance or his judgment. I can't tell you how shocked I was to learn he'd stolen money. Not that I never believed him incapable of acts that others would view as crimes, but to steal money. It must have been a crisis of that sudden crushing boredom with life that the French call accidie. No matter, I owe him much—my life among other things—and a promise is a promise. What are your instructions?"

I shifted in my chair. My instructions were nothing to be proud of, but they were the only ones I had. "I am to report to you and act in my best judgment on the matter you will explain to me." I coughed. "I am also, if possible, to bring an item to Du Vigny. He would prefer *El Espolio* but doesn't insist on it."

A smile broke across Don Jaime's face. Natural good spirits seemed to be returning in him. "That is all your master told you?"

"All the instructions he gave me, señor. I carried to him

the message you passed to Pierre du Vigny in Paris, so I know that. And this morning I saw *El Espolio* in the sacristy of the cathedral."

His smile became broader. "And you were staggered at the thought your master wanted you to bring him one of the greatest El Grecos in the world?"

"Señor, I'm not sure what to think."

"Are you aware of how Du Vigny and I became friends?"

"It was during the Civil War when he was in the International Brigades but he went into no details."

"Are you familiar with the history of Domenico Teotoco- pulo, called El Greco?"

"No, señor. Only that he worked here in Toledo," I said.

"Yes, from 1575 to 1614, his most productive years. Let me fill your glass." He picked up a bottle. "It appears I'm going to have to tell you a rather long story."

DON JAIME REFILLED HIS OWN GLASS ALSO. "EL Greco was born in Crete, which explains both name and nickname. He was trained as an iconographer, or painter of those bizarre, portable triptychs the Orthodox put such store by. When a young man he went to Italy and was retrained there in a more normal style. Moved most probably by ambition, he left Rome and came here. At that time, the Spanish Empire was twice the size of ancient Rome's.

"His reputation grew and he had many commissions. The Marqués de Villena of this province was his first patron and then El Greco attracted the attention of the Alba family—the family who among their titles held that of Duque de Toledo. The most famous of the Alba's was the man who pacified the Netherlands so well for Philip II that bad little Dutch children are still frightened into good behavior by threats that the Gran Duque de Alba will come for them if they continue naughty. So El Greco flourished and became rich.

"His fame was such that the first historian of Spanish art, a man named Francisco Pacheco, visited him in 1611 to gather first-hand information for a book he was writing. The book is lamentably vague on certain points, but on one Pacheco is positive. For each of his major pictures, El Greco painted a small version on a thin, wooden panel using the techniques he had learned in his youth as a painter of icons. We don't know the size of these small versions except they can't have been large, because when Pacheco visited him, El Greco was near the end of his long life and all of his small copies were kept in only one cupboard.

"We also don't know clearly why El Greco painted these—let me call them miniatures; it's a convenient term if not quite accurate. It's possible he used them as preliminary studies for his large picture. It's possible he made them afterward as keepsakes. The reason isn't important. It is almost certain they existed—Pacheco is reliable—and it is certain that if they did exist they have been lost. All but possibly one. Have you been to the Prado?"

I started. I'd been listening too hard and the question caught me off balance. "Yes, señor, yesterday."

"Did you see the El Grecos?"

"Yes, but I don't remember a small one."

"Not surprising. The larger canvases around are overpowering. But in one corner of the middle El Greco room is a painting of the Annunciation in oil on a live oak panel. It measures twenty-five by twenty centimeters, considerably less than a foot square, and the wood is only half a centimeter thick, about a quarter of an inch. The records show only that the painting was acquired sometime in the late 1600s with no indication of where it came from. Nevertheless, it is unmistakably El Greco's work. And I am convinced it is one of the miniatures that unaccountably was separated from the rest. The larger version hangs today in the cathedral at Siguenza, and although there are minor differences there is no doubt that one is a copy of the other."

He smiled a trifle sheepishly. "Most men have some occupation or hobby which they use to distract their idle

67

moments, and sometimes to fill up moments which could be better devoted to more gainful work. Mine has long been the lost miniatures of El Greco.

"I am a historian. I used to teach, now I merely write books. Art is not my field, but I am Toledano and if I could determine what had happened to the miniatures I would gain a great name, especially here in my native town. In my younger years, right after the Civil War, I had little time for the miniatures as establishing and caring for my family took all my efforts. But by 1950 I was secure enough to be able to spend some time amusing myself.

"Around that same year, Franco mellowed to the point of recognizing the existence of historical monuments such as survivors from the International Brigades. Du Vigny could visit Spain and we picked up the threads of the friendship we had formed in our war.

"Naturally I told him of the miniatures. He was interested and joined the game. It was much better to have a friend taking part, especially as with his quick mind and French bias he quickly formed a theory of his own. We could argue for hours when we visited each other and write letters when we were apart and busily search for evidence to support or refute.

"Now, I must return to history. El Greco did not found a family. He had only one known child, an illegitimate son named Jorge Manuel. The son was trained as a painter, but he never approached his father's genius. He was also argumentative and belligerent; nevertheless, El Greco loved him dearly. Upon El Greco's death all his property, including all pictures, went to the son.

"Jorge Manuel was almost immediately involved in a long-drawn-out lawsuit with the Villenas, the family of El Greco's first patron. The quarrel was over El Greco's house which had belonged to the Villenas. They claimed it had been ceded to El Greco only for life. Jorge Manuel held it had been given with no such restriction and now belonged to him. Eventually there was a judgment against the son and not long afterward he died. The Villenas are known to have gained possession of several large El Greco paintings. I have always thought they got the miniatures also, but the surviving records are far from complete.

"From that point, events are too complicated to discuss in an afternoon, or even a week. The Villena family split and decayed, with some members going to other parts of Spain, or merely off adventuring. Eventually the Toledo Villenas died out completely and their lands and much of their possessions went to the Albas who still kept the title of Duque de Toledo in their family. Kept it and still have it. The Albas are today the greatest grandees of Spain.

"Spain itself in the next centuries split and decayed much like the Villenas. The Hapsburg line of kings rotted out and we acquired Bourbon rulers, which in theory we still have. But it is Napoleon who plays the next important role in the history of the miniatures as far as Du Vigny and my game is concerned.

"Shortly after he assumed the title of emperor, Napoleon decided to make his brother Joseph King of Spain. He sent him to Madrid in 1807 with an Army of Occupation. The country exploded. God knows why. We have been ruled by a foreign strain ever since Juana la Loca died and poor Joseph would have been an improvement on the king who reigned. We had no real armies, so we invented the guerilla. In the following six years, Spain consumed more French than Napoleon ever lost in Russia. Spain consumed itself in the process."

Don Jaime fell silent, staring abstractedly at nothing in the room. The Goyas I'd seen at the Prado gave me an idea of what he was looking at.

He took some wine and went on. "Du Vigny thought the

miniatures had been carried to France by some commander of Napoleon's. His favorite was Marshal Masséna, Napoleon's first military governor. The only one of the emperor's marshals who compared with his master as a battle captain, but also one of the greatest thieves in history. Masséna campaigned several times through the Albas' domains and there were always wagonloads of loot going north from where his divisions passed.

"I remained convinced the miniatures were still in Spain.

"So we each pursued our separate bents—Du Vigny in France and I in Spain. He tracked down the families of French marshals and generals who'd served in Spain, and I the branches of the Villenas and Albas. We were discreet, because our game would not have added lustre to either of our reputations, his as banker, mine as sober historian.

"Among the many lines that I investigated was that of Don Cristóbal de Villena, a younger son who went to the court at Madrid in 1666 and there ingratiated himself with the Queen Regent Mariana in the usual manner. For his skill, Don Cristóbal was granted a holding in Catalonia and the title of Marqués de Villasol. The family he founded went through only four generations before becoming extinct when the then Marqués de Villasol was executed for treason with the French in their last attempt to rape away Catalonia in 1765. The investigation into Don Cristóbal's line kept me busy for a year, but it came to nothing. All the family possessions had been forfeited to the crown because of the final treason, and then dispersed.

"I go into detail about Don Cristóbal, both to show you the way our game was played and because it is important to the rest of my story. Do you have any questions before I continue?"

"Only one, señor. Considering El Greco's name as a

painter, wouldn't people have been careful to keep track of over a hundred paintings of his all in one lot?"

"They might have, except for an artistic upheaval. El Greco's death coincided nearly to the year with the rise of Velázquez. The young Velázquez was famous in Seville by 1618 and went to Madrid to become court painter in 1620. His style is so different, his work so real and of the day in which he painted that almost overnight in the small world which bought and cared for paintings, El Greco became as old-fashioned as some once-admired Victorian painters are today. Velázquez and his imitators were the fashion. It wasn't until early in the last century that El Greco was appreciated again."

He rose and walked over to the crowded bookshelves. Without hesitating he pulled out a thick tome. Stuck in the book was a sheaf of papers; some of them were new and others obviously old.

Don Jaime returned to his chair. "I'm not quite through with history, but I am ready to explain what occasioned my visit to Paris and my bungled attempt to pass a message to Pierre du Vigny."

He enjoyed expounding, which was natural for a man who'd been a teacher. And I enjoyed listening to him.

"Have you heard of Simancas?" He asked.

"Only the single mention you made when you spoke to Pierre."

"It is an enormous old castle close to Valladolid, a long day's drive to the north. In it are housed the royal archives of Spain, running from the time of Philip II up to the year 1800. In that year, someone intelligently decided the best thing to do would be to go to another place and start anew. There are over ten million documents at Simancas, all in excellent condition, thanks to the loving care of a small group of devoted men and women. Unfortunately these documents are all meticulously filed according to the system devised around 1550 by the first man in charge.

"Most documents on receipt were neatly folded into a uniform rectangular shape and then tied into bundles of around a thousand. Once a bundle was complete it was given a number and stacked on one of hundreds of long, open shelves. Some of the shelves hold only army documents, others hold correspondence with ambassadors, others legal papers, and so on. The bundles are roughly in chronological order, but only roughly. Professional archivists have been known to weep on their first visit to Simancas." His voice held the same note of annoyance and pride that I'd heard in Luis's when he'd talked of the Guardia Civil.

"No one is exactly sure what is there, or even if it's known something is there, exactly where it is. A folder of sketches by Leonardo da Vinci was once mislaid for nearly a hundred years. Some scholars have devoted their lives to merely listing the contents of the bundles on several shelves.

"I tell you this so you'll understand the rest.

"As a historian, I have long been granted access to the archives. I am currently preparing a textbook for the University of Madrid on the reform of the Spanish courts under Carlos III, the best of our Bourbons which is not strong praise. I was toiling methodically along the shelves in Simancas which hold the papers of the Cortes Real and was at the section which approximated 1765. I remind you of the line of Villenas in Catalonia which ran out because of the treason of its last representative in that year.

"I opened a bundle and had leafed through a quarter of the documents when I found a report on the execution of Don José Jesus Villena y Sotomayor, Marqués de Villasol. Naturally the name caught my eye and I read the report in its entirety. The marqués had been properly hanged with gentlemen of appropriate rank officiating and three priests in attendance on the sixteenth of September 1765. He had died poorly, having to be carried to the gibbet, which was scandalous behavior in a Spanish grandee. His effects were being disposed of as directed by the ministers of the king.

"The remainder of that bundle and the next three were the documents found in the home of the marqués. They probably had been forwarded with the report of execution for examination to determine if any other nobleman should be accused of conspiring with the marqués. Whoever sent those papers had included every paper he could find. The earliest was dated 1618.

"I spent a week going through those papers one by one and ended with these four." He held up the older papers I'd seen him take from the book. "I borrowed them quietly from the archives and will see they are returned. Simancas now has a microfilm service but it is six months behind in its work."

He selected one of the old documents. "This is a copy of a receipt for certain goods and belongings deposited by Don Cristóbal Alfonso, son of the Conde de Villena, for safekeeping in a monastery while Don Cristóbal was in Madrid serving at the court. It is dated June 1666. Monasteries often served as trustworthy warehouses for the goods of those, principally the nobility, who had to travel and did not want to be encumbered with too much baggage."

He dropped that paper in his lap and took up another. "This is a copy of an acknowledgment by the representative of Don Cristóbal Alfonso Villena, Marqués de Villasol, that the monastery has returned to him certain goods and belongings left two years earlier."

A note of excitement had entered his voice. "Each of these two is a detailed list, but there are discrepancies between them. Items that were left and not returned. I can recite them:

'a leather bag of gunflints'; 'a carved ivory box'; 'a reliquary of San Ildefonso in worked silver'; and 'a chest of paintings held as surety for the judgment against Jorge Manuel Topcoi.' "

"Topcoi?" I said. El Greco's son had been Jorge Manuel.

"Yes. Some poor, not excessively literate monk who was inscribing the copies of the receipt would have had no trouble with the names Jorge and Manuel, but Teotocopulo would have been hard for him. He would have condensed and distorted."

Some of Don Jaime's excitement stirred in me. "Wouldn't the Marqués de Villasol have complained about some of his property being lost?" I asked.

"He did," said Don Jaime. He picked out two more old papers from those in his lap. "The marqués didn't keep copies of his letters, but these are replies from the prior of the monastery apologizing for the shortage and saying a thorough search and investigation were being made. From what the prior writes, the marqués seems to have been more annoyed by the disappearance of the reliquary than by the chest of paintings. No mention at all is made of the gun flints or the ivory box."

He regarded me for a space. "We now come to a hard point, Señor Clancy. Only small paintings would be put in a chest. Suppose the chest is what it seems and is still at that monastery. Suppose again the paintings within it are in good or merely fair condition. There could be between one and two hundred El Greco miniatures. Do you know what their value would be?"

"No, señor." Luis had said he'd heard that the last El Greco sold had gone for over a million dollars.

"Neither do I." Don Jaime gently pounded on the arm of his chair.

"Once late at night, my old friend and I made a bargain.

If I found the miniatures, I would do all possible to see that he received one for himself. If he found them, he would see that half of them came to Spain. You're here because I keep my bargains. Regulations and laws may have to be flouted if Du Vigny is to have *El Espolio* or another picture. That does not matter. What does matter is that if we find the paintings they must not be risked—either by rough handling or by passing through hands that might divert them."

The old gentleman did have a nice way of putting things. He could have said you come recommended only by my friend who has turned thief on a grand scale, prove to me that I can trust you.

He looked at me expectantly and I looked back with dismay on my face. His lips quirked. I hadn't figured on hearing anything like Don Jaime's story nor being handed the problem he'd just presented me.

"I have a proposal," he said. "I have made copies of the documents I found in Simancas." He picked out the new sheets from the papers he held and passed them to me. "The old hand is difficult to read for a person without experience. Take these and read them and then come and see me again. We'll talk more and decide how to proceed."

I thanked him. He'd been careful not to tell me the name of the monastery and I was sure any reference to it had been carefully censored out of the copies he'd made.

I thought a moment.

"Please let me have two or three days," I said. "There's a young lady with me who's an expert in the care and restoring of paintings. She's with me at the order of Du Vigny. I realize now why he wanted her to come. I'll study these copies and perhaps discuss the matter with her, and I'll do my best to devise some method of operation so that my employer may have *El Espolio* and at the same time the paintings are not endangered nor do we run foul of the authorities." I paused. That wouldn't be quite enough for him. "And, I hope a method such that we should not be ashamed if we're successful."

"Ah," said Don Jaime. "I want Du Vigny to get *El Espolio*, but I know he'll understand the limits that are upon us. If it cannot be done, you and I will go together to the monastery and astound the monks. Then at least, Du Vigny's name will be associated with any discovery through you, his representative. That should give him pleasure."

"Could you tell me one thing, señor? Is the monastery fairly close to Toledo?" It should be since the Villenas were from the province.

"It's less than fifty kilometers from here. There are several monasteries within fifty kilometers of here, you know."

I grinned at him. He grinned back. He said, "I don't know if the miniatures still exist, although I have more confidence than I have had for many years. I do know I am very glad I found those documents. I'd lost a lot of taste for our game since Du Vigny went to Paraguay, and as he says in his letter, he never knew what to write to me before. I felt the same. Now, an old zest and an old friendship is being restored for both of us, come what may."

WE TALKED FOR ANOTHER HALF AN HOUR. DON JAIME
had many questions about Du Vigny and Paraguay and I
answered all that I could. I learned that Don Jaime was a
widower with two sons and one daughter, all married, and four
grandchildren. None of his children had stayed in Toledo.
They had said living like mice in a museum was unbearable.
Don Jaime loved the city and found tourist watching to be
enlightening and amusing. Since the tourists mostly returned
to Madrid by four in the afternoon, he and his friends could
then enjoy their city, themselves.

Out of curiosity I asked if he knew León. He said he did
and that if I ever visited it I would see a cold city whose only
claim to notice was that certain historical events had occurred
there. It had a cathedral with some middling stained glass but
otherwise mediocre. It would never do to let Luis and Don
Jaime meet.

It was after twelve when I left Don Jaime's. I started
walking abstractedly toward the cathedral. Result was I
became thoroughly lost. It was impossible to see any land-
marks from the bottom of the slits that were the streets of
Toledo. Kind passers-by set me on the correct way.

I came out at the cathedral plaza. Across it, I could see
Luis in a knot of other drivers, all apparently discussing
weighty affairs. In the other corner was a tiny park with

hedges and benches. I sat on a bench by a stone stairway leading down to a terrace some thirty feet below where at a distance children were playing. Few people passed and it was a good place to do some thinking with faint child noises as an agreeable background.

I lit a cigarette and took out the censored copies of the documents Don Jaime had given me. It wasn't hard to locate the items on the first receipt that were missing on the second. They were all together in a clump: first a walnut chest, then the gunflints, the ivory box, the reliquary of San Ildefonso, and last the paintings of Jorge Manuel Topcoi.

In his two letters to the marqués, Don Cristóbal, the prior of the monastery was extremely apologetic and went on at length about the search made through the monastery for the missing articles. In both, he mentioned the unsettled times and the many members of the nobility who had thought it wise to avail themselves of the order's good offices to protect their valuables, thus creating a constant flow in and out of trunks and chests. He sympathized in the most profound degree with Don Cristóbal's emotion over the possible loss of the reliquary of San Ildefonso. Investigations were continuing.

I took another look at the first receipt. It listed fifteen chests or cases of various kinds, some of leather, most of different woods. Each mention of a chest was followed by several smaller items all suitable for putting in a chest. Right below the entry for the Topcoi paintings was an entry for another chest. I contemplated that for a while and made a deduction that wasn't hard to reach. The marqués had lost one chest containing all the other missing items. Don Jaime had made that, too, because he'd talked of a chest of paintings and the paintings were the last items listed as they would be if they were at the bottom of a chest and people were making an inventory of its contents in the order in which they were packed.

But from the way the prior was bleating in his letters, it seemed more than probable Don Cristóbal's chest had been picked up by mistake by some other family. If that had happened the damn chest could have gone anywhere in Spain. Had Don Jaime considered that? Of course he had. He was too smart not to have. He had some other reason for thinking that the chest hadn't left the monastery. Maybe he had another document he hadn't given me. If he did, he'd told me at least one lie, and he was not the kind of man to whom a lie would come easily.

In the message he'd passed to Pierre, Don Jaime had said he thought he knew "where they are now." He thought they were in the monastery. He'd probably explain why he felt so sure if he decided to trust me.

That brought up a point. Suppose I didn't settle Don Jaime's doubts, would Du Vigny give me the first fifty thousand bonus if all I did was walk beside Don Jaime while we went to the monastery and he announced to the monks they might have a chest tucked in a corner that could hold pictures worth upwards of a hundred million dollars? That last figure surprised me even though I'd thought it up myself. It wasn't a real figure, but it was an astonishing one. Hell, none of the figures I was thinking about was real.

I became aware that someone was standing in front of me. It was my art adviser, her strong eyebrows registering displeasure. "Do you know what time it is?" she demanded.

I stood hastily, looking at my watch. It was twenty after one. I tucked Don Jaime's papers in my inside pocket. "I'm sorry, Susan. I got to thinking. Please forgive."

"I'd never have found you if I hadn't gotten bored waiting in the car and started walking around."

Hanging about waiting on a male hadn't put her in a good frame of mind. I said heartily, "Let's see if Luis can recommend a good restaurant and we'll go have a couple of nips and a big lunch."

She stayed surly until we got to the restaurant. It was built into the north wall of the city. There was a wide patio shaded by high trees between the remnants of the Arab walls and the higher, tougher-looking walls the Spanish had built after retaking Toledo. There were square, metal tables covered with white linen cloths scattered under the trees. Gnarled geraniums, some over a yard high, bloomed violently from stone troughs and pots set by the old fortifications and the trees.

The surroundings were such that Susan had cheered up even before the drinks arrived, and by the time she was halfway through her martini she was talking amiably about what she'd seen while I'd been conversing with Don Jaime. Part of my mind listened to her and the rest considered what to do about her.

She was useless for scrounging around a monastery slyly peering into old chests. The monks would probably be happier to let in the devil, horns and all, than a dolly wearing a pants suit. On the other hand, she would come in handy with Don Jaime to show him I had someone who knew how to treat old paintings, and I would probably need her to handle anything I might pick up. Trouble was she might jibe when she learned I wanted to sneak away with one of whatever we might find.

Might find. That was an important phrase. There wasn't much point in being elaborately tricky when I'd need her help anyway if I were successful, and if I weren't successful all my effort would have been wasted. I could use a couple of levers on her. It would be wise to hold back on some parts of the story and on my designs on *El Espolio* but she'd still have to be cut in on most.

I put my full attention back on what she was saying. Nobody minds being listened to, and I wanted her in a good mood. We had second drinks and then ordered. Since the waiter's English was rudimentary, Susan had to depend on me. I waited until we'd finished our soup—crayfish bisque, tasty and hot—to start.

"Susan, please tell me something. Suppose you took some small paintings made with pure colors and oils on wood panels and put them away in a walnut chest. If you waited more than three hundred years and opened the chest, what would you find?" I would try to sneak up on my topic.

She bent her eyebrows at me. "Made on what kind of wood?"

I hadn't been using my memory course on Don Jaime's story but I dredged up what he'd said about the miniature in the Prado. "Most likely live oak."

"If the chest were in good condition, the paintings probably would be too. Tell me—oh, I don't know what to call you. I won't call you major, and I don't like using Patrick to you. I guess it's Clancy. Tell me, Clancy, has this got something to do with the lost small copies El Greco is supposed to have made?"

"Hell. Yes it does, but why do you ask?"

"Don't be silly. This is El Greco country. I've been looking at pictures of his all morning. And the way you've been behaving. You come with me to see *El Espolio* and go off with a strange expression to wherever you went. Then I find you brooding in the park. And now you start asking me about small paintings on wood that might be three hundred years old. It's a normal question for me to ask."

I frowned. "Would it be a normal question for anybody to ask?"

She pursed her lips. "Probably only someone who knows art and art history. What's gotten you interested in the lost El Grecos? Is somebody trying to sell you one? That's about on the level of selling the Brooklyn Bridge."

The waiter made a welcome diversion by arriving with the roast suckling pig he'd recommended. He served and poured the wine. I took a bite—found it a tad greasy but good—and decided I might as well empty the bag, keeping back only my hope to get Du Vigny his picture.

"Okay, Susan," I said, "nobody's trying to sell me anything. I've got a tale I think will interest you. You said on the plane you came on this trip because you were being well paid to practice your profession. You may get a bigger opportunity than you expected." I wanted to get that point over early. I told her the whole story Don Jaime had told me, reserving only my hopes for *El Espolio*.

I held her attention. Toward the end she forgot to eat, and scowled at me whenever I took a mouthful and interrupted the narrative. She scowled at me again when I'd finished.

"Too many people have looked for those pictures," she said. "How can your Don Jaime locate them just like that?"

"He didn't locate them just like that. He and Du Vigny did a lot of looking in wrong places before. And he hasn't really located them now. This may still be another wrong place."

"But simply to stumble across key documents. I don't believe it."

"According to Don Jaime, that's the way things happen in Spain. I do believe him. Enough to give it a try."

"It could be a swindle. You don't know the art business

the way I do. The tricks some people have pulled to plant forgeries are nearly incredible."

"You'd have a hard time selling me on Don Jaime and a monastery cooperating in a swindle."

"If it were successful, it could net him millions."

"Don Jaime doesn't stand to make a cent. I expect his name as a fast man in an archive will be increased, but he only wants the pictures found. I don't know who they'll belong to—the monks, or the Catholic Church, or the Spanish government—but I'm sure they won't belong to Don Jaime."

She sat back. "They can't have survived," she said, talking to herself. "Let me think."

I let her think, and finished my suckling pig. Hers went cold. I motioned to the waiter he could clear. He looked worried when he saw how little Susan had eaten. "The señorita didn't like her meal?" he asked me.

Susan darted the waiter one of her strict looks. I said, "She has things on her mind. Careful, friend." He tiptoed off to return with large bowls of small fresh strawberries and generous rations of fluffy whipped cream. He gave me a glance of sympathy as he served them.

Susan shook herself. "There's something crooked here. I don't know what but I know it's here." She started composedly to eat strawberries.

"What makes you jump to that conclusion, damn it?"

She made a nasal sound of disdain. "There you are, a mass murderer working for a mass embezzler and you tell me this fable about the lost El Greco copies. What did you expect me to say? 'Oooh, how thrilling! How can I contribute to the success of this unselfish endeavor you and your employer are engaged in?' Come off it, Clancy. There has to be some sort of trap or snapper or gimmick. What is it?"

She ate more strawberries while I wished that my art

adviser were slightly dumber or less well-qualified. "All right," I said at length. "It's not crooked, but it is bent." I reluctantly told her about Du Vigny and his hopes for *El Espolio*. I anticipated outrage. Instead an expression of understanding crossed her face—understanding followed almost instantly by another frown.

"Only one picture?" she said.

"Only one." I said crabbily.

A few more strawberries disappeared.

She said, "Let me phrase this so you will clearly understand. If I go along with you, what's in it for me?"

I couldn't complain. "Well, on my own, I'll offer five thousand more than your present contract, simply for your continued assistance and for keeping quiet. If we find the things there'll be a bonus, and if Du Vigny gets his picture, there'll be another, I'm sure. I can't commit Du Vigny without talking to him but he's no miser, that I can promise. And of course, even if we just find them and can't get a picture, you should know better than I do what the effect will be on your professional standing. Hell, I should think merely being one of the first to hear about the papers Don Jaime found would be worth something."

She nodded. "A well-calculated appeal to greed and anxiety for status, both of which I possess. I must say Don Jaime has made a believer of you. How do you propose to go about searching for these hypothetical paintings?"

"Right now, I don't have the vaguest idea. My God, I'd never heard of the things until this morning. I still don't know where the monastery is, or why Don Jaime for some reason seems damn sure the missing chest with the missing stuff should still be there. From the prior's letters you'd think the chest had been given by mistake to some other family. The old guy talks about writing to other people and the difficulty of sending letters and how important he realizes the reliquary is and—"

I fell dumb, my mouth hanging open. Susan looked at me with surprise. "Are you all right?" she asked.

"The reliquary! Son of a bi— Excuse me, Susan. Something's just occurred to me. Where's the waiter?"

At my signal the waiter came trotting over. He probably thought I'd bitten on a rock in the strawberries.

"Are you Toledanfl?" I asked him.

"Sí, señor."

"Please tell me, is there a Monastery of San Ildefonso near Toledo?" Don Jaime had said the monastery was within fifty kilometers.

He thought. Apparently I'd asked a reasonable question. "I think I've heard the name, señor," he said, "but I'm not sure. Let me ask the *maestre*." He went off.

"What's gotten into you?" Susan demanded.

"I may be on the way to knowing why Don Jaime is so confident the chest didn't get shipped out by mistake. Bear with me a couple of minutes."

The waiter and the maître d' came back together. The maître d' was positive. The Monastery of San Ildefonso lay about thirty kilometers to the southeast of Toledo. He said, "It's on the edge of the escarpment, señor, where the high land falls down to the plains of La Mancha."

I thanked everyone properly and turned back to Susan, feeling quite smug. "I believe I have discovered a malfeasance, three-hundred–odd years old. Cristóbal Villena put his stuff in the Monastery of San Ildefonso. In the chest with the paintings was a reliquary of San Ildefonso. Somebody in the monastery, most likely the prior, couldn't stand the temptation and took a leaf from the Jesuits. 'When the end is holy, the acts are blessed.' He kept the reliquary and to do so he had to keep the whole chest. His conscience wouldn't let him either destroy or disperse the other Villena goods, so he carefully lost that chest in some corner of the monastery."

I admired my astuteness.

"You mean you hope his conscience made him act that way. Are you a Catholic?"

"A lapsed one, but with my name, what else? In those days, a relic of San Ildefonso, the patron saint of the monastery, would have been the greatest thing in the world to those monks. Don Cristóbal wasn't very smart to give it to them for safe keeping."

She was silent a few seconds. "You may have a point," she conceded. "Will that help you make a plan?"

"I think it will. You'll excuse me if I don't discuss it with you until I hear your decision."

"You're rather transparent, Clancy. Either I go along or you'll freeze me out."

"I'd hate to do the last." That was true. Difficult she was, but also bright as hell, and she could be a big help.

"I'll let you know before the day's out."

"Fair enough."

We had coffee, and I paid the bill. "Okay," I said. "Let's head for Madrid."

"You said before that we'd stop in Illescas on the way back to see the El Grecos," she replied accusingly.

"We will! We will! I just forgot for a second."

We went out to where Luis was waiting. It was a silent ride to Illescas.

We turned aside from the main road and stopped in front of the church. It might be a church in a poor town, I thought, but it was large and looked well cared for. One reason became apparent when we went through the door. A little nun was at a table inside and she explained that when there was no mass, it was customary for those from outside the parish to contribute fifteen pesetas. This seemed more than reasonable.

The five El Grecos were as Luis had said. They were hung on the walls, probably just where they'd been put when they were first bought. Some special lights were arranged for them but that was all. There they were, protected by the little nun at the door. And the Guardia Civil beyond.

Susan looked at them the way she looked at paintings. I envied her what she got from a good painting. I liked paintings but I knew I'd never find in one what she did. When she'd seen them well, she said softly to me, "Let's go, Clancy."

As we went to the door, I stuffed a hundred peseta note in the poor box for luck. One of the pictures had been as Susan described on the trip down—a scene of the Virgin giving San Ildefonso some vestments. That I took to be a very good omen.

She stopped beyond the portico of the church. "All right, I'm in," she said. "For the extra five thousand and the promise of a bonus." One corner of her mouth went up. "And because I can't stand not being in."

"That's great, Susan." I didn't feel it was wise to say more.

When we were on the road again, I asked her if she knew who San Ildefonso was. It pleased her to be able to enlighten a Catholic. San Ildefonso had been bishop of Toledo in the thirteenth century. Most appropriate.

================ *13*

BACK AT THE HOTEL I ARRANGED WITH LUIS TO REMAIN in our service for the next few days. I had plenty of expense money, he was pleasant and drove better than the norm, and we'd probably be needing a car and driver. Luis was gratified.

I suggested a drink and Susan accepted. At the desk there was a cable from Du Vigny saying that he also wanted a Sisley from the Quintinar collection. I got a cable form from the concierge and filled it in, acknowledging his message and sending regards—which meant I was making good progress. I already knew about the Sisley. Du Vigny's cable had been sent simply to give me a good reason to reply.

As we started for the bar, I saw a man walking to intercept us. He was nearly as tall as I, and thick through the chest although slim at the hips. He had heavy black hair, brushed straight back and cut a bit shorter than the fashion. I made a small bet with myself.

"Mr. Clancy?" he said as we met.

I said I was.

"Good evening. I am Señor Ortega Crespo of our Department of National Security. Would this lady be Miss Allgood?" He spoke flawless English.

I said he was right again and collected my mental bet. Susan might have resented the Miss if it hadn't been for Ortega's announcement about his outfit. She got her hand kissed. My own hand was given a firm clasp. Señor Ortega asked if he might talk with us a moment.

"Of course," I said. "We were just going into the bar. Will you join us?"

"You're very kind. I regret I must say I have come to see you more or less in my official capacity."

"Please don't be concerned. I have more or less been expecting such a talk."

As we men let Susan precede us into the bar I noticed Ortega's eyes move up and down. He seemed to approve of her rear view. It wasn't bad. The pants of her suit fit tightly enough to give the observer a good idea as to what was inside.

We settled ourselves at a corner table and ordered, Ortega taking sherry. He brought out a small blue folder and passed it to me with a deprecatory "Sorry, but customary." It identified him unspecifically as "Oficial de la Seguridad Nacional de España."

Susan's eyes were round. I hadn't warned her about this. Just as well. If we were what we claimed, it would be normal for her to be flustered by the appearance of police, no matter how suave.

Ortega hoped we had enjoyed our trip to Toledo. I said that it was a lovely city, that we'd had a great lunch, and that I'd had a most pleasant chat with Don Jaime Pedro de García Mendoza y Zibaru, an old friend of my employer. Ortega let his eyes show appreciation, and he turned to talk with Susan about her day. She warily described what had impressed her most about Toledo. Ortega expressed his sincere gratitude for her kind words about one of the prides of Spain.

The waiter brought the drinks and Ortega went back to me. "I believe you will be in touch with the Conde de Quintinar?"

"Yes. My employer is interested in buying some pictures

from the Quintinar collection. I think Miss Allgood and I will be going down to his country place in a day or two to spend some time there."

"It's pleasant around Quintinar de la Orden. Very good hunting of all kinds. So you saw Señor Du Vigny's old friend Don Jaime?" Ortega smiled sardonically. It was the kind of smile I was getting used to seeing on Spanish faces. "Don Jaime is something of a miracle. Do you plan any business with him?"

"Not exactly. As you may know, he and Du Vigny are old friends from the International Brigades, and Du Vigny thinks Don Jaime might be of assistance to us in another project. Du Vigny would like to have some Spanish art, possibly a couple of fair examples of the Flemish school. Don Jaime said he'd be happy to help. I'll be seeing him again."

Ortega's expression became judicious. "Many paintings of the Flemish school have been declared national treasures, you know, Mr. Clancy. It is forbidden to take any of those out of the country."

"I quite understand. There are minor artists though whose work can still be exported and I am looking for those. This doesn't mean that Du Vigny might not be interested in a major work, but if he did buy one, it would be as an investment."

Comprehension flashed across Ortega's face. I hoped he'd come to the conclusion that Du Vigny was going through some complicated dodge in cleaning his money.

Ortega turned to Susan again and flirted a bit in a competent manner. The conversation turned general and social only.

He finished his sherry. "You've been very helpful, Mr. Clancy, and I thank you. You understand, we received a call from our French colleagues and of course we have to respond. I apologize for this intrusion."

"No apology is needed. You ought to see the way your French colleagues intrude."

He smiled like a wolf. "We can too if we have to, Mr. Clancy. If you'll excuse me, I must go." Susan let her hand be kissed again with as much evident pleasure as if she were offering it to be bitten, and Ortega took himself off.

"That man scared me," said Susan. "One of Franco's police—brrr!"

"You have absolutely nothing to worry about."

"Not yet, you mean." She worked thoughtfully at her drink. "I've never had any police of any kind come to see me before. I guess it's something to expect now that I'm working with a mass murderer and for a mass embezzler."

"Look, can you let that 'mass murderer' rest? How about 'hired killer'? Would you settle for that?"

"Why, I didn't think you were sensitive, Clancy. I suppose your employer isn't a mass embezzler?"

"He prefers to call himself a thief."

"A thief from widows and orphans and poor people."

"God damn it, that's not right either. Du Vigny set up some kind of investment scheme in France. Like a building and loan association, I think. It did great and there were lots of small accounts, including widows and orphans and poor people trying to put a little aside. Then the organization qualified for some sort of charter that meant the government insured the accounts up to a certain sum, same as in the U.S. As soon as that happened, Du Vigny scooped the till and went to Paraguay. The government had to pay up."

"How touching. I'm sure it's true."

"It is. You ought to see the way the French government

treats me when I come within reach. They were the ones flim-flammed and they resent hell out of it."

We'd finished our drinks. Without being asked, the waiter brought new ones. He whispered, "The gentleman who left hopes you'll be his guests, señor." I looked up at him. His face showed respect.

I told Susan about Ortega's hospitality. "They have a smoother type of cop in Spain. There's a French one lets me smoke one of my own cigarettes every now and then, but this is the first time a cop has bought me a couple of drinks."

"Do the French police want to arrest you?"

"They'd love to. Haven't been able to find a reason yet. It's fairly complicated. You see, Du Vigny has a son in France, and he's moving quite a bit of money back to France into the son's hands. I don't begin to understand how the hell he's doing this but I'm part of it. I carry messages back and forth between Du Vigny and his son and the French police hate that. Eventually the son is going to be quite rich. He leads a hell of a life, though. There's a cop on him wherever he goes, and he's had to install one of those electronic gimmicks that suppresses microphones in his apartment."

"That's terrible. Du Vigny must be a monster."

"No, he's not. He's different for sure, but personally he's rather a nice guy. And you should admire him for fighting on the side of democracy in the Spanish Civil War."

She glanced around us. The bar had filled up a little since we'd come in but no one was sitting close by. "You told me you'd discuss your plan after you heard my decision," she said. "I'm ready to discuss."

I hadn't been looking forward to this. "I may have misled you a bit. I don't have a plan so much as a line of action. Tomorrow we'll see the Conde de Quintinar and open negotiations with him. We should go down to his place the next day. It's in La Mancha, and could be a very handy base because it's fairly close to both the monastery and Toledo. I'll take you to meet Don Jaime and I hope you'll do your best to convince him of our general trustworthiness and dedication to art and so on. He can probably provide some pretext for me to visit the monastery. I'll go and see how the land lies and we'll take it from there."

She laughed briefly. "I'll say you don't have a plan. What do you mean get *you* into the monastery? What about me?"

"Susan, this is a monastery. Monasteries plain don't allow females to roam around inside. They probably have a visitors' room you could sit in, but that's all."

She didn't like that but was reasonable enough to accept the fact. "I don't know how you're going to use my skills."

"I'll give you full reports on what I find, and you'll give me advice. The main thing that worries me is getting inside with permission to grub around. Do you think the song and dance about looking for paintings of the Flemish school would work?"

"It should. I know one dealer who spends three or four months a year in Europe visiting village churches to see if they have anything to sell him. He doesn't find El Grecos but he turns up quite a lot of authentically old trash which he sells to Texans for large sums." She cocked her head. "He says the religious communities of the entire continent are becoming quite sophisticated and prices are rising continually."

"Hey, that's good news. Maybe the prior will have that outlook. We'll check with Don Jaime. So let's leave it that we'll go exploring and decide what to do according to what we find."

She sipped at her drink. "I'm a fool, but I have to admit

this gives me a fever, Clancy. It's so easy to become worked up about something you want to be true." She grimaced as if she tasted something sour.

"Care to meet for dinner tonight?"

"Thanks, Clancy, but we'll be seeing enough of each other over the next few weeks. Better we should take rests from each other when we can. And, to be honest, I'm still having some trouble accepting that my relation with you has changed from expert on contract to close semi-criminal collaborator." She regarded me thoughtfully. "I guess 'hired killer' does suit you better than 'mass murderer.' "

There was a difficult compliment to answer. I said. "Very kind. Let's meet tomorrow in the lobby at ten."

She agreed and finished her drink. I said I thought I'd have another so we wished each other good evening. I watched her walk away, noticing I wasn't the only male present who did so.

The door was by the mahogany bar which ran across one end of the room. As Susan left, I saw a man standing at the bar. He was turned so he could see me and his eyes met mine. He nodded as if I were someone he recognized but whose name he couldn't remember. The man drained a few drops from his glass, replaced it on the bar, and walked casually out.

That had been Arthur Grey, English tourist, last seen by me in the bar of the Hotel Guarani in Asunción when I'd gone to look him over at Izzy Meyer's behest.

I DROPPED A TIP ON THE TABLE AND WENT OUT and down the short curving corridor to the long lobby. No Arthur Grey in sight but an elevator door was just closing. I stood irresolute for a moment, then crossed to the concierge.

"By any chance has Mr. Arthur Grey registered yet?" I asked.

He consulted a card file. "Yes, sir. Mr. Grey checked in this morning. He's in room 920." He turned to look at a rack of keys. "I believe he's in. Do you wish to call him?"

"No, thanks. Only wanted to know if he'd arrived."

I returned to the bar and had another drink—a thoughtful drink. I followed that with a thoughtful dinner. Afterward I had ice and a bottle of Scotch sent to my room and did more thinking.

Coincidences do happen, but this wasn't one. The only questions were, what the hell was Grey, and what the hell was he after? There were many possible answers, a couple of which I liked better than others. One thing was plain—Grey wasn't being stealthy. I decided that I would continue to march and see what developed.

The next morning, I met Susan as arranged. She was all ready to call on the Conde de Quintinar, but I could see she had been doing some thinking of her own, and possibly a few second thoughts had surfaced. We found Luis waiting, and he looked even more pensive than Susan. There was an easy explanation for that.

I wished him good morning and gave him the address of the Conde's office. After we'd been driving a few minutes, I said, "Luis, did a Señor Ortega talk to you last night?"

He pulled the always disconcerting trick of turning around so he could meet my eyes. "Not him, señor, but yes, one of his men did."

I hastily said, "Don't worry about it, Luis."

He turned back and I went on. "I work for a gentleman in whom the police have interest. This gentleman lives in Paraguay and has sent me to Spain to buy pictures for him. Pictures are what I am after and nothing more. If the police want you to report on what I do, go right ahead and do not be ashamed. In fact, you will be doing me a favor."

He sighed with relief. "You make things easier for me, señor, even though it is repugnant to tell the police anything."

"One must make reasonable accommodations in life, Luis. Do we understand each other?"

"Sí, señor." The verve of his driving picked up. Perhaps I should have let him brood.

The Conde de Quintinar was Director General of an engineering firm called CONQUINSA, apparently the Spanish way of saying Construcciones Quintinar, Sociedad Anonima, or Quintinar Construction Company. Its offices were on the eighth floor of a big new-looking building in the northern part of the city. The large reception room was starkly furnished in plywood Danish and decorated with pictures of bridges, dams, and roads. A girl a few years younger than Susan sat at a desk. Her eyebrows were heavier than Susan's and her straight nose was ideal for looking down. Even so she wasn't bad.

I told the girl who we were. She smiled and her face

lightened considerably. We were expected. After a little chatter over an intercom another girl appeared and ushered us down a corridor formed by moveable glass partitions. To either side we could see people working at drafting tables, or doing paperwork or talking to each other. The set-up wasn't plush but it looked prosperous and busy.

The Conde's office rated solid walls, a bigger desk, and its own drafting table, but the furnishings were just as functional as in the rest of his outfit. He himself was something like Ortega only more so. He was tall and slim with jet black hair. He was only about thirty-five. His long face was narrow almost to being hatchet like and his nose was even more straight up and down than his receptionist's. The Conde's smile was friendly and he seemed genuinely glad to see us. When he found that Susan didn't speak Spanish he went to English, which he handled well enough.

He might have been a modern Spanish businessman but he had wine in a cupboard and insisted that we each take a glass, and we talked a little about how we found Spain and Madrid. Susan got some appreciative glances. Maybe heavy eyebrows meant something special in Spain.

Polite he was, but after five minutes he went to business. "Well, Mr. Clancy, I'm happy you have come. I need some extra capital in the next few months and I hope to get at least some of it from your employer. It will enable me to expand and to take advantage of a major opportunity. Rather late, Spain has decided to move into the twentieth century and I'm trying to help it. I was very pleased to learn that grandfather's paintings have so increased in value since he brought them back from Paris. I had a fellow who knows about these things go down to look at them and he made a most encouraging report."

The Conde might be frank and open about wanting money, but he was letting me know he had a good idea of what he had to sell.

I was frank and open in return and described Du Vigny's interests. The Conde seemed well aware that Du Vigny had the necessary capital to supply some of his needs and didn't seem to mind at all where it had come from.

He'd already warned his staff at the estate to expect various people, so we could go down whenever we wanted. "None of the family is there right now. My mother's with me here in Madrid and my younger brother and his wife will be in Switzerland until June, so I'm afraid there's only the major-domo, Claudio, to receive you but he'll make you comfortable." He made a small apologetic movement with his hands. "Some books call the place a palace but it's not at all that. Fairly big but a bit run down like everything in La Mancha. Take as long as you like."

I said we'd go down the next morning and he gave me directions and said he'd inform the major-domo. There'd be no trouble since there was a telephone and in the last few years the telephones of Spain had started to function properly. We made our farewells, I promising to give him some early word as to our decisions on the paintings.

I told Luis that we would be moving out of Madrid for a few days, and asked him if he could come along. I didn't want Ortega getting nervous about Susan and me wandering around with no one to report on us. Luis seemed sincerely touched that I should ask him. "Of course I can, señor. Wherever you want to go in Europe. I have an International license."

"Fine. You make arrangements with your company. If there's any problem have them call me at the hotel. We're going to a place near Quintinar de la Orden, and we'll be wanting to drive around the country side a bit—over towards Toledo."

Luis turned around. We were bowling along a busy street. "I'm afraid we'll need a different car, señor, like a Landrover."

"Yes! Yes! Whatever you say!"

He looked through the windshield again. "Once off the main roads, you will find a more versatile vehicle does better."

I knew the Landrover. That could be exactly what we might need. Luis said his company had several and he would get a new one. He left us at the hotel and went off well content.

"Is that all?" said Susan. "Are we through for the day?"

"Not quite. I have to send a cable to Du Vigny and then I need some more technical advice. It's nearly noon. Why don't you go into the bar and order drinks? A martini for me, please. I'll be right along."

I told Du Vigny we'd seen the Conde and were going to the Quintinar Palace. I mentioned that I'd run into Mr. Meyer's friend and ended with regards, meaning all still was well. Du Vigny would have no trouble with the reference to Izzy and if Grey were getting copies of my cables he might not catch it. If Du Vigny could find out anything about Grey, he'd arrange for it to get to me.

I joined Susan. My drink was waiting, and I thanked her. I said, "Susan, I don't know a hell of a lot about art itself and infinitely less about the art business. A couple of things you've said incline me to believe it's a rough racket. Would you care to amplify?"

"Ho!" she said. "It would take too long. The art business deals with beauty, but its methods are mostly nasty. Could you be more specific?"

"Yes. This guy Hayden. What kind of a bird is he?"

"Philip? Oh, he's an ethical dealer, which means he won't knowingly handle a forgery, but he will take any advantage he feels he can get away with." There was a hint in her tone that Hayden may have taken an advantage once or twice with her.

"How does he work? How does he locate prospects and things to sell them?"

"He's spent years building up a network of—I wouldn't call them friends. Associates, maybe—all over the world. They trade information back and forth for shares of commissions." She smiled wryly. "Philip was quite cross, I think, when he found that you were going to represent Du Vigny in this Quintinar purchase. If he'd been allowed to take a more active part, he would have made more money."

"Is he charging you a commission for arranging this job?"

She stiffened. "He is not! I won't have that sort of thing. I'm good and I don't have to pay to get work."

"Don't be mad. These are questions I need answers to. Has Hayden asked you to keep him informed about what we do in Spain?"

Comprehension showed in her face. "Yes, he has. That's normal. He'll use what I tell him to put someone else in his debt." She sighed. "And in a way, telling him what we do here is the commission I pay him for this job."

"Don't think I have to—"

She interrupted with some asperity. "You don't. I have no intention of ever saying anything to Philip about our other project."

"Good. There's only a little more. I'm sure Hayden was in touch with you about working for Du Vigny some good few days before we met. I know you're a Ms." I did my best with the pronunciation. "But do you have anyone you—well—confide in?"

"I am not married, nor have I been, nor am I planning on

being so, nor is there anyone I'm sleeping with regularly," she said coldly, her eyebrows prominent.

"But there must have been some others besides Hayden who knew you were going to Spain?"

"Of course. My landlord and a few friends, but they only know I was going to Spain. They don't know about the Quintinar pictures, and certainly not about your fantasy. I am more discreet than you seem to think."

I was in danger, and I had enough. The link almost had to be between Hayden and Grey. "All finished," I said. "Thanks a lot, Susan."

"What about you?" she said. She was going to get a little of her own back. "Are you married or do you have anyone you confide in?"

"I was married once. She left me a few years ago." In the middle of my second tour in the Nam. I didn't blame her. She hadn't liked never having much money and me being gone so long. "I don't have anyone I confide—" What she really meant was did I have someone like Nelida. I thought Susan had told the truth. I should do the same to her. "Well, you've been very open with me. Yeah, I have a friend in Paraguay."

"Some docile little Latin girl?"

In spite of myself, I laughed. "You don't know Paraguay and the women there. They had female lib long before the rest of the world even thought about it. Got it the hard way, right after our Civil War. Most of the male population was killed off in a war with Argentina, Brazil, and Uruguay. The Paraguayan women put the country together again and got mighty independent in the process."

That diverted her slightly. "You're very fond of the place, aren't you Clancy. How did you come to go there?"

"My father was in the army too, and when I was a kid from fifteen to eighteen he was chief of our army mission in

Asunción. I liked it then, and after I resigned from the army, I went back down." It was a place where I'd been happy, where I'd had my first girl, where I'd done considerable of my growing up—so I'd gone back to heal.

"And there you met Du Vigny and went to work for him?"

"Yeah, he'd come over on the run nearly a year before."

She shook her head. "And the Paraguayans simply accepted him?"

"You make the rest of the world too hot to hold you, chances are the Paraguayans will still let you in. Besides the country's poor. There's plenty to eat, but not many ways to make money. Du Vigny's built a cement plant and bought a river steamer and generally boosted the gross national product more than a couple of points. The French are still doggedly trying to extradite him but no luck. Every time they get the proceedings up to a high court, the Paraguayans find some technicality to throw everything out and make them start over. Du Vigny's a highly esteemed citizen."

"I can see how the country would suit you and him," she said wryly. For a moment, I thought Paraguay had made her forget our earlier conversation. No such luck. "Why were you so nosy about any relationships I might have?" she asked.

I took a breath. "This is nothing to worry about, but I saw an Englishman named Grey last night who I think has been smelling around Du Vigny's affairs before. Money in the quantity of Du Vigny's, acquired the way he got it, draws steady attention in certain circles. One's the cops, like Ortega. The other's the sharpies, of whom this guy may be one and your pal Hayden sounds like another. The sharpies stooge around hoping something will fall off Du Vigny's table that they can grab."

The news about Grey didn't disturb her half as much as

Ortega's visit. Her time in the art business must have opened her eyes to certain realities. "Hayden, you say. Do you think he has something to do with this Grey coming to Spain?"

"I'm pretty sure of it. Mainly because of the timing. Grey checked into the hotel the day after we did. He's got access to good information on our movements." And he'd come to Asunción right after Du Vigny had begun to work on the Quintinar paintings through Hayden. I didn't mention that. Susan was alert to Grey and that was all that was needed.

We had nearly finished our drinks and it was time to think of lunch. I raised my glass, "Here's to success, Susan. That everything will work out and that we'll have a good time to boot."

She drank to my toast, but there was coolness in her eye again when she put her glass down. "We're talking freely and getting along better than I frankly ever thought we would, but we should have one thing clear, Clancy. Do not feel impelled to come on all masculine and make passes. If I ever decide that I need someone to go to bed with and you'll do, I'll let you know. Understand?"

She wasn't being aggressive, she was stating a position. "Yes," I said, repressing some obvious retorts.

There were some other museums Susan wanted to see and some shopping she wanted to do, so we arranged to meet the next day and she excused herself.

That was a strange little girl there. I mused as to what I'd do if one day she were to say, "Okay, Clancy, I feel lusty. Let's hit the hay. Please help me with my zipper." I decided I'd jump at the chance.

After lunch I went back to the Prado and hunted down the little El Greco Don Jaime thought was one of the miniatures. Once I found it and looked at it close to, I was surprised that I'd missed it the first trip, even though tremendous canvases blazed all around.

WE ARRIVED AT THE PALACE OF THE CONDE DE Quintinar right at noon.

The drive from Madrid was dull, through much the same kind of terrain as between Madrid and Toledo. Going down the escarpment to La Mancha gave something to see because we passed a real castle and a couple of old watchtowers. La Mancha itself was flat as a flitter and almost as treeless. There were silvery green olive trees in abundance but these were pruned to the size of large bushes and confined in regular groves. There were also miles of vineyards. I'd always thought vines grew on trellises; here they too were brutally pruned and looked like small bushes.

We turned right at Quintinar de la Orden and ran twenty kilometers over a secondary road. I saw why Luis had recommended a Landrover. We found the tall, twin-stone pillars, each bearing a coat of arms, that marked the entrance to the Conde's land. There was no gate or lodge. We turned through and drove nearly half an hour past millions of olive trees and an equal number of vines before we reached the palace. The Conde had a sizeable spread.

The palace, set in an oasis of high poplars, was only two stories but it spread out a lot. The plain façade wall was over fifty yards long. Two tiers of high windows were regularly and monotonously spaced from end to end; their lines were broken only in the center by a tall ornate door. The walls were a faded pink stucco. The steps leading to the central door were of brown stone, warmer in color than the stone of Toledo. Where the stucco of the walls had flaked off in spots, the same brown stone showed through. The road ended in a circular drive around a pool with a central fountain that was sending a stream of water as thick as my arm ten feet into the air.

Luis stopped before the steps and Susan and I dismounted. There was nobody in sight.

"Cripes," I said.

"Yes," said Susan.

The tall doors at the head of the steps opened and three men came out. One was wearing dark trousers, a white shirt with a narrow black tie, and a yellow striped vest closed almost to his throat with brass buttons. The other two were dressed similarly but had no vest, which seemed to be a badge of office.

The vest wearer came up to me. He said, "Señor Clancy, Señorita Allgood?" Our names were barely recognizable.

I nodded. He went on. "I am Claudio, the major-domo to the Conde. You are welcome, señor." He glanced at the other servants getting bags from the car assisted by an awed Luis. "Your chauffeur will be lodged with us. Please follow me."

He led the way through the main door into a forty-foot square entrance hall whose ceiling had to be the main roof. A flight of stone steps was opposite. It went up to a landing and split to rise to facing balconies.

We climbed to the right balcony. From it a central corridor with doors on either side went straight to a big window in the distance. We walked toward the far away window, the servants with the bags bringing up the rear. Claudio halted between the last two doors. "You are on this side, señor, the señorita is there." As the man with Susan's bag opened the door to her room, a little plump rosy-cheeked girl, wearing a black dress and white apron, popped out.

"This is Carmen," said Claudio. "She will be the señorita's maid. Your *mozo* will be Domingo, but he is busy in the kitchen at the moment."

I translated for Susan who looked at Carmen with more concern than she had at the cop Ortega. "What will I do with a maid, Clancy?"

"I'll tell her to unpack and put away your things. She'll do any ironing or washing you might want her to, and she'll help you change clothes and like that," I said, pretending I was accustomed to dealing with ladies' maids. I gave Carmen instructions; she beamed and scurried into Susan's room.

"Lunch will be at two, señor. I'll come to announce it. Would you and the señorita like something after your trip?"

"Yes," I said, sincerely. "Very much. Please send ice, gin, and dry vermouth."

"Of course, señor. You want a martini on the rocks."

"That is true. How do you know martini on the rocks?"

"The Conde likes them. Señor, the toilet in the bathroom of your suite does not function. There is a connecting door into the next suite where the toilet is in fine condition, but the shower has no water. Is there anything else, señor?"

"No, thank you very much, Claudio." He bowed and went off down the corridor.

Susan was standing close to me as if I were her big brother and she were in a difficult situation. I took pity. "Go to your quarters and wash your face or whatever and then come on over and we'll have some drinks. I've sent for martinis."

She went through her door, looking over her shoulder. It was the first time she'd been out of her depth since I'd met her.

In my suite I found a sitting room, and beyond it a

bedroom and a bath. The furniture was vaguely French in style, and gave the impression of seedy elegance. I started hunting for the connecting door to the next suite where the plumbing worked. I had no luck in the bedroom, and was examining the walls of the sitting room—covered in a dim, red-gold patterned damask cloth—when Susan bounded in.

"There's a Zurbarán in my room!" she announced. Her tone was such that I envisioned a diamond-backed Zurbarán in a corner, all coiled to strike. She looked over my shoulder and said, "My God, there's another."

I whirled ready for combat. There was a big painting of some vaguely Biblical scene on the dividing wall between my bedroom and sitting room. In my search for the door giving access to the latrine, I hadn't noticed it. It was a handsome picture and the colors were bright and sweet, but it was still the kind I could overlook when my attention was on something else.

Susan was staring at me. "Two Zurbaráns," she said. "Just put on the walls to cover space. These can't even be rooms the family uses all the time."

A small procession arrived to interrupt any conversation. First came my valet, Domingo, an eager young man wearing the lower ranking servant's uniform of dark trousers, white shirt, and black tie. He was closely followed by two maids carrying trays with ice, glasses and the requirements for martinis. I had Domingo show me the door giving access to the working toilet. Blasted door was covered with the same red damask as the walls and the small brass handle blended right in with the pattern. It would be hell to find in the dark. I sent Domingo to unpack for me and excused myself to Susan.

When I returned, Susan, martini in hand, was taking a closer look at my Zurbarán. "Needs cleaning," she told it severely as if it were the picture's fault.

Domingo reported out of the bedroom to say my unpacking had been completed and ask for other instructions. I had none. He pointed out the bell that would summon him and left us alone.

"This place unnerves me," Susan said. "All these servants and Zurbaráns hung casually around."

And the plumbing doesn't work quite right, and the upholstery is threadbare, I thought as I fixed a drink for me. Don Jaime would probably proudly declare it to be very Spanish. "The Conde said that there were pictures here the government wouldn't let him sell out of the country," I said. "You ought to have a field day."

"Oh dear," she said, "I've been in New York too long to be happy in feudal times. I've never in my life had a maid all my own, especially one named Carmen."

"Where are you from, Susan?"

"Upstate New York. My father is a country banker in a small town."

"Where'd you go to school?"

"Vassar," she said defensively.

"Great school. I dragged a couple of girls from Vassar when I was at the Point. Did you ever go over there to hops?"

"Yes," she said, blushing, as if she were confessing to unnatural practices. "Not often."

I changed the subject. "How long do you think it will take us to look over the French pictures and figure out an offer."

"Depends on what your Du Vigny has told you. I shouldn't need more than this afternoon to pick out the paintings to try for, and then you must have instructions about price. I'm not an expert on dickering for a picture. Putting a price on a painting is the worst part of the art business."

"I hope we can string out our stay for a few days. Toledo is only around ninety kilometers away, and our monastery less than seventy. We'll look at the French pictures this afternoon and I'll call the Conde. I'll make him a good offer. Not my top one but one I hope will interest him. There should be some other pictures that Du Vigny might want. You can tip me which are the best. I'll tell the Conde that I'll need to refer to my chief. He should invite us to stay on."

"Very sly."

"Then tomorrow we'll go see Don Jaime and do our damndest to show how trustworthy and bright we are."

"Ha. You'll look pretty silly if the monastery is really called Saint Peter's or something. God. I never dreamed I'd end up in this kind of delirium."

She fixed herself another drink and invited me over to see her Zurbarán. I went, small prurient hopes stirring, but all I did was see her Zurbarán. For one thing, her little maid was sitting patiently in a straight chair, waiting for someone to tell her to go away.

Susan was horrified. I modified her comments in translation so that Carmen left cheerily. Susan's Zurbarán was enough like mine to make me think they'd been made as a pair. Back in my room, Susan became chatty and told me a few stories of skullduggery in the art business which confirmed her remarks about its methods being often nasty.

Claudio came on the dot of two and guided us the long distance to the dining room on the first floor. It was as large as I expected and there was a Velázquez portrait hung in the center of an end wall.

We were subdued while we ate our lunch under the eyes of the Velázquez grandee, the two of us huddled like survivors at one end of a table that would seat forty, served by Claudio and two menservants.

Afterward, Claudio took us to a row of three small connecting sitting rooms where the pictures collected by the syphilitic grandfather were hung. I recognized some because the Impressionists were painters I liked and had read about, but most were bright and lovely and nothing more.

Susan first went around looking at the paintings for herself, then made some unkind remarks about the Quintinar's keeping them for decades in a place where no one saw or appreciated them, and then finally got to work. She walked back and forth between the Monets and Pissarros and eventually picked one of each for purchase. "They're not their greatest work but they're good and very representative. How much are you authorized to spend for these?"

"Up to one hundred and fifty thousand each."

"That might be a shade high."

"How about offering two fifty for the two?"

"Worth a try. If you want to propose buying anything else to your boss, there are four Morisots that are as good as any I've ever seen."

"Who was Morisot? Never heard of him."

"Her. My God. One of the few Frenchwomen who was painting in the 1890s. I should think you might get those for twenty-five thousand dollars apiece. She's an unappreciated artist but no one's ever painted women in a manner better calculated to please men. I expect the grandfather bought those paintings for the models." I looked at the ones she indicated and had to admit that the subjects all had a merry, eager look in their eyes.

She also recommended a Sisley which apparently had no excuse to be with the others, Sisley being a highly respectable man who lived in the country.

"Maybe he just saw it and liked it," I said, but Susan wouldn't give the grandfather the benefit of any doubt.

There were three Toulouse-Lautrec portraits which I thought sketchily done and which Susan agreed were not the artist's best. Still, she said, if the price could be kept below fifty thousand one of them would be worth it.

I made a list of pictures to sound out the Conde about and rang for Claudio who took us to the telephone. It was in a small library next to the main hall. At my request, Claudio put a call through to the Conde with the ease of practice and left us alone.

I passed on the offer for the Monet and Pissarro. The Conde said he would have to give the matter thought but would let me know as soon as possible. I explained that Du Vigny might also be interested in one or more of the Morisots and Lautrecs and quite possibly in the Sisley, but that I would need some guidance before I could make an offer. The Conde warmed up noticeably. I wondered how much capital he needed.

"Excuse me for doing this on the phone," I said, "but we'll be moving on to Toledo tomorrow to scout around for some Flemish things and I—"

"There's no need at all for you to move to Toledo," interrupted the Conde. "It's just over an hour's drive and you'll be much more comfortable at the palace, I assure you. I'd be happy if you'd stay as long as you'd like. And frankly I think there's an advantage to me if you'd remain on the spot until we've brought this business to a conclusion one way or another. You are certainly better placed to answer any questions Señor Du Vigny may have."

We arranged to talk again and hung up. I told Susan nonchalantly that everything had worked out as expected.

Having watched and listened to Claudio, I placed the call to Don Jaime myself. Don Jaime said he would be happy to see us tomorrow at ten. There was a slight emptiness under my ribs when I hung up. The sums of money I had been tossing around in conversation with Susan and the Conde weren't real to me, any more than the bonuses promised by Du Vigny, but the El Grecos that might or might not be in the monastery— those were becoming realer to me the more I thought of them. There was no justification for this.

Susan went to her room to take a nap and I prepared a cable for Du Vigny. Claudio had said a man went into Quintinar every day and he could send it. Then I had a nap of my own.

That evening after dinner, it developed that Susan could play cribbage. Claudio came up with cards and a board. Susan went happy to bed with nearly five hundred of my pesetas.

I stayed up an hour more, studying Don Jaime's copies and getting my points in order. It reminded me of times I'd spent before important briefings when I'd been on staff duty.

16

ON THE DRIVE THE NEXT MORNING TO TOLEDO, WE
ran for half an hour over the dead level land of La Mancha and
then climbed steeply up through the tumbling rugged edge of
the escarpment. I saw two watchtowers sited far apart at high
points for best observation toward the south. On the plateau
behind we passed a castle on an outcrop of rock. The
watchtowers and castle were dilapidated but they looked
tough and defensible. I would have loved to see how they'd
been fought when they were in the front of the southern
march of Castile against the Arabs.

Once we passed the old frontier zone, the rest of the trip
ran through undulating semi-barren land. There were no fields
in crops but a good bit of the time there was a remote white
flat puff of a flock of sheep somewhere in sight. A couple of
flocks close enough to look over were each attended by a
shepherd and two or three dogs.

We dropped down the south side of the valley of the
Tagus and crossed the river to Toledo on a high stone bridge
that my *Michelin* said had been built by the Romans and
restored by the Arabs. We hadn't seen it the first trip because
we'd come in from the north. Susan and I gaped up at the city,
which was even more spectacular from this approach. Luis
sniffed and muttered about León.

At the cathedral plaza we left Luis with the Landrover,

and I led Susan into the maze to the south of the great pile of the cathedral, my map handy. She wanted to stop every now and then to look at a doorway. I didn't mind, once again as it gave me a chance to see if we were being followed. There were a fair number of people moving up and down the alleys, none taking more than a casual interest in us.

We found the Calle Sal and started down its short length. At the far end was an incongruous note. A pair of flower children were leaning against the wall in a patch of sun that had managed to find its way down. The male was playing a recorder. He wasn't bad.

I stopped at Don Jaime's door and worked the big brass knocker. While we waited, the recorder music stopped and I glanced around to see the hippie couple ambling in our direction. They hadn't quite reached us when the old maid opened the door and smiled in recognition. She said, "Don Jaime told me you were coming, señor. Please enter."

I stood back to let Susan go in, but she was watching the hippies pass. The male was wearing grubby blue jeans speckled with multi-colored patches and a long, fringed, buckskin vest open over a grayish tee shirt. Several bead necklaces with round metal pendants hung down his front and he carried a shoulder bag. The female wore the same uniform. Both had long half-blond hair. The female's hair was lank and the male's was frizzy, and the male had the usual straggly beard. They went by, not looking at us, their shoulders hunched slightly forward as if their chests hurt them. They couldn't have been much above twenty and they weren't tall and they didn't look very strong. The girl was singing something gently.

"What's up?" I asked Susan in a low voice.

She turned to me. "I swear that's the girl who asked us for money the other day in Madrid."

I looked up the Calle Sal. The pair had nearly reached the corner. Don Jaime's maid stepped out and looked after them. "Those sad, shameless ones," she said. "They come to the city and do little and buy less. Simply sit in the Plazas or in corners and talk to each other. Those two have been all morning against the wall there making their music. They are bad for the children to see." She ducked inside and motioned invitingly for us to enter.

I met Susan's eyes and shrugged. "We'll talk later." I added my own gesture of invitation to the maid's.

We were taken to Don Jaime's work room and library.

Susan's presence seemed to put an extra sparkle in Don Jaime's eyes. He was disappointed to find she didn't speak Spanish so he did his best with English. His was that of a man who could read the language well but had hardly any chance to speak it. The words were all right and the pronunciation terrible. Susan for sure had her effect on Spanish gentlemen.

There was the expected to-do about serving wine with almonds and small cakes added for Susan's benefit. After five minutes of small talk, Don Jaime excused himself to Susan at some length and shifted to Spanish. "Have you told this young lady of the miniatures?" he asked me.

"Sí, señor. If M. Du Vigny is to have his picture, she will have to help. I believe she's discreet and I'm sure she's expert. For one thing, she's quite familiar with the story of the miniatures. She's not very optimistic that they've survived."

"That is as it may be. Have you any ideas about how we should go on from here?"

I took a deep breath. I'd had time to study, now I was in for an examination. "Sí, señor. I believe Don Cristóbal deposited his goods with the monastery of San Ildefonso—the one on the edge of the escarpment about thirty kilometers southeast of here. The walnut chest which was not returned contained not only the miniatures, but also the gunflints, the ivory box, and the reliquary of San Ildefonso. The prior tried to convince Don Cristóbal that the chest must have been given to another family by mistake, but what really happened was the prior sequestered the chest so as to retain the reliquary where it would be properly venerated."

I watched him carefully. I'd expected some astonishment at either my cleverness or stupidity but all I could read on Don Jaime's face was polite attention. I continued doggedly, "When it was safe to do so, the prior, or more probably his successor, would have surfaced the reliquary, but the chest with the other items would have been tucked away somewhere and the story behind its presence would have been forgotten as soon as possible. This is all theory, but if we could find out whether the monastery had a worked silver reliquary of San Ildefonso, we'd have fair confirmation of what happened back there in the late seventeenth century."

"How would you propose to find this out?"

"I'd ask you to write me a letter of introduction to the present prior of the monastery explaining that I am in the service of an old friend of yours who wishes to buy some examples of Flemish art and that you would be grateful for any assistance he might give me. Señorita Allgood assures me that there are American dealers and agents who do visit religious institutions to see if they have anything of interest to dispose of. I'd look for such art and I'd buy some, too, but at the same time I'd look around, first for a reliquary and then for the miniatures. I can't say what chance of success I might have until I visit the monastery at least a couple of times. I'd be careful to keep you fully informed of developments."

I shut up. I could have talked more, but I didn't have anything else to offer.

Don Jaime smiled warmly, and I relaxed. He said, "Not

bad, my young friend, not bad at all. My theory as to what took place back there, three centuries past, agrees completely with yours and I had the name of the monastery from the first. You are, of course, Catholic."

"Well, a rather lapsed one."

"So am I. So are most Spanish males over fifty. Now, if you do find the paintings, how will you get one for Du Vigny?"

"I don't know, señor. I give you my word I would not do anything to risk the paintings. If you talk with Miss Allgood, I think you'll see that she wouldn't either."

His brow wrinkled. "I would not like to steal from the monks."

"Considering the way they got the paintings in the first place, it would be difficult to say whether we'd be stealing from the monks or from whoever survives of the Villena family."

Don Jaime's eyebrows raised. "You know I hadn't thought of that." Enthusiasm entered his voice. "And all property of the line of Villenas who held the miniatures was forfeited to the king when the Marqués de Villasol was hanged, so we'd really only be stealing from Spain's present vacant throne. Magnificent! Let me fill your glass."

That was apparently the best point I'd made. Don Jaime chuckled to himself like Father Christmas for a good minute. "All right," he said. "I agree. I'll not only write, I'll call the prior. I know him slightly. He comes to Toledo for some of the principal events of the year, such as the Fiesta of Corpus Christi or when there is a change of military or civilian governors and so on. Being a notable of the city, I am also on the dais or at the head table and we talk. His name is Father Fermin."

He eyed me. "He is a discerning man, Father Fermin. I would not try any crude deception, if I were you."

"I won't, señor."

"I don't think you will. You've shown me intelligence. From the throne! I should have realized that. Please ask the señorita to excuse me for a few minutes while I write your letter."

"Sí, señor."

He rose and went to his desk. I summed up the conversation for Susan. She said, "I don't know if I can stand you being smug, Clancy." There was no sting in her voice. "You didn't say anything to me about those paintings belonging to the throne instead of the monks." She cocked an eyebrow at me.

"Been saving it," I lied.

"Uh-huh."

Don Jaime rejoined us and read his letter aloud. It started with a fancy salutation and then hoped that aid could be extended to Señor Don Patricio Clancy and his associate Señorita Doña Susan Allgood who were in Spain on matters which might be of benefit to the Monastery of San Ildefonso. There was an equally fancy close. He said it would be better to give the details about his old friend Du Vigny to the prior on the telephone.

I thanked him. There was one other bit of information I wanted. I asked, "Is it possible that this chest might bear the Villena arms?"

"Certainly. Give me another moment." He went to a shelf and brought back a big tome. He hunted until he found a page he showed us. The Villena arms weren't overly complicated. There were things that resembled PFC stripes in the corner and a small diamond and tower in the center. I started to ask for paper and pencil to make a tracing, but Susan beat me to it. Don Jaime gave them to her, and she whipped out a freehand copy that I couldn't distinguish from the plate in the book. It was an ability in her that I should have expected.

Our business was concluded but Don Jaime still wanted to chat. He shifted to his difficult English and asked Susan a few questions about what she thought of Spain. For all that the language gave him problems, he was deft with it. He steered her onto the topic of the miniatures and they got a pretty good discussion going about the little painting in the Prado. I learned that an El Greco altar piece had been discovered in 1937 in a gallery in Modena, Italy; it showed the same techniques, oils on wood, as the Prado picture, and it had been in excellent condition. It was believed to have been painted before El Greco came to Spain.

When a lull came, I tried to learn about Don Jaime's service in the Civil War. I said in English. "Sir, Du Vigny told me he met you in the International Brigades. Didn't you have trouble after Franco won?"

He laughed. "He didn't tell you the full story of my war?"

"No, sir."

"My sympathies were with the army when most of it rose against the ridiculously inefficient Republic we had in 1936. Like many people of Toledo, I went to the troops who were holding the *alcazar* in the name of the rebels. I was young and able-bodied and was given a rifle and made a part of the garrison. You are familiar with the siege of the *alcazar* of Toledo?"

"Yes, sir. You held the place from late July until late September under constant heavy attack, until General Franco could bring up the Army of Africa to relieve you. It was a great feat of arms."

Don Jaime agreed with me whole-heartedly. "It was indeed. The government forces even brought fire engines from

Madrid to spray gasoline on us before setting the building alight, and they mined and blew down all four towers. The *alcazar* was rubble before we were relieved, but we held it and brought nearly five hundred women and children alive through the siege in the cellars. I am proud to have been one of the garrison of the *alcazar*."

He shrugged. "Afterward, I saw things that made me feel the Republic, ludicrous though it was, had some merit after all. So I deserted from Franco and went to the government side. They didn't quite know what to do with me, but since I spoke French, I was made one of the liaison officers with the International Brigades. That was how I met Du Vigny.

"We fought together until the Brigades were smashed along the Ebro in our last campaigns. Franco had taken Barcelona and our army was an exhausted rabble. Du Vigny was so sure I would be shot he begged me to come north with him."

"I can see they didn't shoot you," I ventured.

"Of course not. The logical French would have shot me as a deserter, but I fell into the hands of Spanish. Shoot a hero of the *alcazar* of Toledo? Impossible. Franco's government simply pretended I wasn't there. It suited me."

He glanced at Susan and then eyed me quizzically. When he spoke it was in Spanish. "Permit me a personal inquiry. I sense your interest in this affair is more than simple dedication to the wishes of your employer?"

"Si, señor. I've been promised a sizeable reward if I do no more than bring it to what he terms 'a successful conclusion.' If I bring him a picture, I will get another hundred thousand dollars." It was best not to try to hide the obvious from Don Jaime.

"A strong incentive, Señor Clancy." Unspoken was the hope that it wouldn't incite me out of my head.

He returned to English to invite us to lunch, but I begged off and he didn't insist. He gave me directions as to how we could reach San Ildefonso from the Quintinar Palace. The best way went partly by a still used old Roman road. Old things seemed to hang on in Spain.

When Don Jaime saw us to the door, he said he looked forward to hearing from me the next day. There were no hippies in sight when we took our leave.

17

AS WE WALKED AWAY I ASKED SUSAN, "WHAT MADE YOU think that girl hippie was the same one who was panhandling in Madrid? All that tribe look as much alike as Chinamen to me."

"I'm surprised you didn't say gooks. You probably don't look at people who don't interest you. Not only did I more or less recognize her, but I remembered a necklace she was wearing with a very nicely done peace-symbol pendant. Navajo work, I think. Silver set with polished turquoise."

I was figuring out an answer when we turned into the Calle Hierro and I saw I wouldn't have to. The hippie pair were waiting there, sitting side by side on a doorsill some yards up the passage.

Susan's pace faltered. I'd have walked by them, but the male rose as we neared. He said, "Hey, how are you? My name's Dick. You Major Clancy?" The spin he put on "major" was like a splinter under my thumbnail. "You Mizz Allgood?" he said to Susan. Dick had a reedy voice.

"I'm Clancy," I said.

The girl joined her friend. "I'm Elaine. Nice to see you again," she said. Susan nodded.

Dick smiled. "There's this man who'd like to buy you a drink, you know. Over to the Plaza Zocodover." His pronunciation of the Spanish name was good. "That okay with you, Major?"

He was six inches shorter than I and looked brittle. I said, "I don't use the 'Major.' I suggest you don't either."

"Got him mad," Dick said happily to Elaine. "Told you I could."

Elaine said, "Now stop the shit, Dickie. Will you go to the Zocodover?" Her pale blue eyes could have been made of glass.

"Yeah," I said. "Love to."

"Neat-o." Dickie was back in charge. "You just walk up there and sit in any of the cafés. The man will be right along. Bye-bye." He and Elaine stepped aside.

Susan and I continued on our way. "You could have been more patient with those two," said Susan.

"We all have our little failings."

"Who is this man we're going to have a drink with?"

"Grey."

"What makes you so sure?"

"If it isn't Grey, a complicated situation is going to become intricate, and I don't like to think about it."

The walk to the Plaza Zocodover took less than ten minutes. A large, official-looking structure occupied all of one side of the plaza and tiny shops and cafés the other sides. Groups of men of varying ages stood around in the paved center portion of the plaza, talking and smoking and often waving their arms. The few stone benches were occupied by older men doing the same thing. The central fountain and its round pedestal seemed to be a hippie preserve. About twenty were roosting there, ignored by the natives. Some were chatting, two were playing a quiet guitar duet while others listened. Nobody was smoking anything suspicious which I expect was wise from what I'd heard about the attitude of the Spanish police toward marijuana.

I steered Susan to a table against a pillar at the café with the brightest awning. We both ordered beer. I didn't see Grey or anyone else I knew.

"What did you think of Don Jaime?" I asked Susan.

"There's another male chauvinist pig," she said, looking at me, "but he carries it well. I liked him. I have to admit I think you convinced him you're trustworthy."

"It may be hard to swallow, but I am reasonably trustworthy."

"You're not quite what I expected when I first heard about this job."

"You don't fit the mental picture I formed, either."

Her brow creased slightly. "Did you think I'd be some fat bull dyke?"

I tried not to wince. She was amused. "Just testing, Clancy. You're hopeless. I saw your face when Elaine told her Dickie to stop the shit. I'm afraid there's no way of ever making clear to you what an intelligent woman has to go through. It's not only being patronized and underpaid and lunged at, it's the male surprise and dismay when we do something that doesn't fit the lace-and-perfume frame of reference, unless we happen to be whores or Lesbians."

She smiled again. Dratted girl was having fun.

"Don't be nervous," she said. "I won't keep it up." Her eyes went to the plaza. "Look, there are Elaine and Dick."

The two were sitting by the guitar players at the fountain. Dick took his recorder from his shoulder bag and joined in the music which was sad and unmelodic and inexplicably easy on the ear.

Grey came from the mouth of a passage across the Zocodover. He paused to get his bearing and then crossed toward us. I watched him approach until he stood before our table.

He said, "Major Clancy, Miss Allgood? I'm Arthur Grey. May I join you?"

"Sure," I said. "Please sit down."

Speaking fluent Spanish, Grey ordered beer for himself and new bottles for Susan and me. "Very good lager they have in this country," he said. While we were waiting for it to arrive, he told Susan, "Major Clancy and I don't formally know each other, but our paths have crossed. Isn't that right?" The last was to me.

I said, "I've explained that to Miss Allgood."

"Oh, you have? Well, that's fine, isn't it."

Susan regarded him suspiciously.

Back in Asunción I'd thought Grey about forty. Now that I'd seen him close, I revised that estimate upward five years. Whatever his age, he was in fine physical shape. He was wearing gray trousers and a blue blazer with brass buttons. His narrow tie was mostly black with thin red diagonal stripes. It looked like an English school or regimental tie.

The waiter served the beer. "Cheers," said Grey, and took a healthy gulp. "Hope you don't mind me rather barging in, but I reckon a short talk now could be to our common advantage. Not in any hurry, are you?"

"No, we have lots of time."

"Good. Excellent." He pulled a thin wallet from his inside pocket and took out a card. "Business card," he said apologetically, handing it to me. "Arthur James Grey" was engraved in the center, and "Inquiry Agent" in the lower right corner.

"Private detective, you call it in the States," he said. "Been at it a few years."

His accent and bearing weren't what I would have expected in a private detective. He paused a few seconds as if giving me a chance to speak, then went on. "A shade unethical perhaps, or at any rate rather pushy, but it has occurred to me that you might be able to use my services. I have quite a few contacts on the Continent. Know my way around this country and France, too. Could be you might need my kind of help, so I thought I'd let you know I was about and available."

"You're free at the moment?" I asked.

"You might say that. Actually, I have a project in hand, but it's more personal than anything else. Nothing I couldn't drop. Think we might do each other a bit of good."

I said, "Do you know a man in New York named Hayden?"

His eyes flickered. Hayden wouldn't be happy to have his connection with Grey known to Du Vigny.

Grey nodded, and sacrificed Hayden for whatever he was after. "Yes, I do. Know a fellow in Paris, too. Policeman named Raspière. Think he's another mutual acquaintance, isn't he?"

"Yeah."

Grey chuckled. "Got a terrible down on you, he does. I've known old Raspière a long time. Met him first when I was in Singapore during our trouble in Malaya and the French were having their Indochina war. He was in the Sureté in Saigon. We did some reciprocal backscratching and I helped him turn up a bunch of Indonesians running in arms to the Viet Minh. We became quite pals, although I'm the first to admit he's a very peculiar chap. Not a man to worry much about methods if you understand me." He looked at me questioningly.

I understood him, so I nodded.

"Old Raspière let me see your dossier once," he went on. "Your boss Du Vigny's too. Very thick Du Vigny's is, although yours is nothing to be ashamed of. Anyway, when Hayden mentioned that you were coming to Spain on Du Vigny's affairs, I thought there might be something I could do."

"Hayden didn't send you then?"

"No, no. Please don't get the wrong idea. Philip knows me, yes. I did a job of work for him once a year or two ago. Had to do with some very posh snuffboxes of all things. I was in New York on another commission a couple of weeks past and Philip mentioned he was concerned that you might run into unfamiliar problems. So I did a little scouting around as you can easily realize, and here I am."

Here he certainly was. "That's kind of you," I said. "So far we've run into no problems."

"Glad to hear that. To tell the truth, I'm not sure what kinds of problems you might encounter. Philip was sketchy as to what you had underway here."

"Nothing very hard. We're buying some French paintings from a Spaniard."

"Heard about that, of course. Would you be buying anything from Don Jaime de García Mendoza? When Don Jaime showed up in Paris, Raspière got most excited. Did his best to put a big flea in the ear of the Spanish police but they weren't terribly interested. No joy for poor Raspière but easier for you, I reckon."

"We're not buying anything from Don Jaime."

"That so? Perhaps you won't need me, but one never knows. In case anything comes up, give the word and I'll be around. I'm sure fees could be arranged to suit circumstances. I'm high, but I generally give satisfaction."

"How would I get in touch with you?"

"There's a number on the back of that card." He drank beer.

I looked over at the fountain. The music session was still in progress. I said, "That's a real pair of charmers, you have there. Been working for you long?"

Grey was mildly indignant. "Normally I wouldn't have

them as a gift. Still, one has to make do with what's at hand and they're all right for sitting and watching a place and the like. One advantage is that that kind are all over the lot like sparrows and nobody pays them much more attention."

"They've got a vague, used-up look to them."

. He agreed. "Yes, not a healthy young couple. Seen worse, though, and in England, too. Very sad."

He dug out a cigarette case and lighter. Susan took a cigarette but I declined. "I think we've bored this pretty lady long enough," he said. "Are you enjoying Spain?" he asked her.

Susan bridled but returned a civil answer. Damned if Grey didn't give her some advice—good advice it sounded—on other things in Toledo that someone in the art business might want to see. He was a polished article.

After five minutes of that sort of talk, he called the waiter over and paid him. "Pleasant talking to you, but I must get on. Look forward to seeing you again."

We thanked him for the beer and I rose to shake hands. We watched him cross the plaza to leave by the passage from which he'd entered. Dick and Elaine got up and slowly followed him.

"How much do you think he knows?" asked Susan.

"Not a hell of a lot more than Hayden. He told us a couple of lies. About Hayden for one—that guy pointed Grey at us—and that business about Raspière for another. Grey may have some sort of contacts in the French police—that would be normal, I guess, in his business—but I bet all he has is someone who gave him the dope on the Du Vigny case. Grey is just not Raspière's cup of tea."

"And who is Raspière?"

"He's a mean French cop who would love to plug me into a high voltage electric circuit."

She stared. "To make you talk?"

"Yeah. The way he tells it, I think it would work, too. Luckily, French cops seem to have gotten the same sort of fits from their liberals about police brutality as our own have. It's hard being a cop these days. Very limited scope."

"My cultural horizons are being broadened in a way I never expected. Why did Grey want to talk to us? Can he make trouble?"

"Susan, no one can make trouble for us right now. Grey can huff and puff and we can ignore him. As for the police, we could call in Ortega and tell him exactly what we've done and most of what we're planning to do and all he could do would be applaud. It's only if we find the prize package that we're going to be vulnerable to guys like Ortega or Grey. This chat today was a fishing expedition. Grey let us know—"

I stopped short, and bent to look under the table. Too late. There it was, stuck to the underside of the top near the edge where Grey had been sitting. A black box smaller than a pack of cigarettes. I had to pull hard to get it loose. There was a sheet of plastic adhesive on one side holding it to the table. The ends and other side of the box were pierced with fine holes.

I straightened and showed it to Susan, simultaneously putting my finger to my lips. I poured some of my beer into Grey's empty glass and immersed the thing.

"Goddamn my eyes," I said. "I apologize, Susan." With my experience in Paris I should have known better. The Spanish police might be content with merely putting Luis to reporting on our movements but a sharpie like Grey would have tricks.

"Is that what I think it is?" She was looking at the box in the beer as if it were a tarantula.

"I'm afraid so. He probably stuck it there while fiddling

with his cigarettes. Damn things can send conversations up to half a mile. Only cost about a hundred bucks. Mass production has brought down the price."

"Good God, Clancy. Did we say anything important?"

"We didn't blow any major gaff, but I said enough to stir friend Grey's interest to a higher pitch."

"You didn't say anything about finding pic—"

"Ssh! Pierre du Vigny swears once those things get wet they don't work, but let's not take chances."

Grey had made it plain he doubted that all Susan and I were doing was buying French paintings. Now his doubts were confirmed. We'd have Grey with us from now on.

"The hell with it," I said. "Let's go to that place we were the first time and have lunch."

18

AS SOON AS WE RETURNED TO THE QUINTINAR PALACE, I wrote out a cable for Du Vigny. It was harder to put together than the others I'd sent him. The code phrases he'd given me didn't cover all eventualities. I toiled until I had something that I thought would make it clear that we were still making progress but Grey was making a nuisance of himself and I wanted Patricio and one of his cousins. Those two would be on the next plane out of Asunción. They'd reach Madrid in a day where they'd hole up in a Hotel Gondomar and wait for my call.

I hadn't heard from Du Vigny since we left Madrid so when I gave Claudio my cable to be taken to the telegraph office in Quintinar de la Orden, I stressed that whoever took it should ask if there were anything for me.

As a result of her experience with a bugged café table, Susan would have liked us to sit in a corner and write each other notes.

"Calm down," I said. "To bug this place properly would cost a fortune, even if Grey could get past the servants. Let's not chatter indiscriminately in front of the help but otherwise we should be able to talk freely." I told her about sending for a couple of troops.

She went all tense. "You're not going to kill Grey, are you?"

"Jesus. That's not a bad thought, but this is for just in case."

The man who took my cable to send brought nothing back.

After dinner, Susan and I went into one of the rooms with the French paintings. Claudio had put out drinks and the cribbage equipment without being told.

"Look, Susan," I said, "tell me about this Flemish school whose pictures I'm going to be looking for. In case the prior asks me a question, I would like to be able to make a halfway sensible answer."

I learned to my surprise that there really wasn't much of a Flemish school except in Spain. Philip II had been fond of Bosch and Breughel and had picked up many of their paintings in Flanders—often by having his troops pull them off a wall. The Spanish nobility had followed their king's tastes and Flemish and Spanish painters had done their best to fill the demand. Then along had come Remembrandt and Velázquez and broken the mold. El Greco didn't fit anywhere.

We spent an hour on that before I cried uncle. I had more than my memory tricks could hold.

Susan although reconciled wasn't pleased that I'd be going alone to the monastery. Partly because she knew so much more than I did and, although she didn't say so, partly because any female, liberated or not, likes to root in other people's closets. "All right," she said, "let's assume the monastery has the reliquary of San Ildefonso. You start looking in chests and open one and there find a hundred and fifty El Grecos. What will you do?"

"Probably scream and run."

Her eyebrows came down. She was not in the mood for banter. I said hastily, "No, I wouldn't do that. Anyway, I can't believe those things will be lying in an odd chest in a corner like a bunch of old postcards. If they've survived this long, they're not in an easy to find place or the monks would surely have turned them up by now. Let me look around the monastery first. The job may be hopeless. If it is, I'll give up on doing anything alone and go tell Don Jaime and we won't pretend anymore."

"No bonuses."

"No big bonuses. We'll still get satisfactory tips."

She ran her fingers through her hair. "I know you're right, but I would so love to find those pictures and you just keep chattering about looking things over and seeing how the land lies. Very frustrating, Clancy."

I cast around for a new subject. "You've impressed firmly on me that you know art backward and forward. How come you took up restoring instead of painting yourself?"

"Because I'm not a good painter. I'm not bad but all I have is a knack—no true talent. Since restoring is the quickest way for a woman to get started in the art business, I specialized in that. But I like the work and I'm very good at it and I generally find it very satisfying." She looked at me curiously. "Was it satisfying to you being a soldier?"

"Yeah, most of the time."

"You liked killing people?"

"How about some cribbage?"

"Don't weasel. I really want to know."

"Oh, dear. The truth is I didn't spend all my time in the army cruising around in a Huey, hunting Cong. I've done a lot of things, and I liked most of them. As for killing people, I didn't get any raunchy blood lust thrill out of killing a man, but, yeah, I got satisfaction out of being good at what I was paid for, same as you."

"Why did you resign if you liked the army so much?"

"Because it looked as if there wasn't going to be much to

like in the future. You said once the army whitewashed me and General Jonas. They honest-to-God didn't. When our leaders found they couldn't court-martial us, they decided to show the newspapers and Congress that at least they didn't approve of us. Didn't change anybody's mind, but the general was sent to a busy-work job in the Reserves and I was ordered to a records holding detachment—me, a combat jump infantry officer. That's the same as putting you to restoring kindergarten finger paintings. So I resigned."

"Resigned and went to Paraguay and hired yourself out to Du Vigny."

"That's right."

She sat silent for a few moments. "Sometimes talking to you is like talking to a Martian. I'll play some cribbage now."

I hit lucky and won fifty pesetas. She was still way ahead but her good night was curt.

19

LUIS AND I LEFT RIGHT AFTER BREAKFAST. SUSAN came as far as the big hall to see me off but not in the worshipful spirit of a maiden seeing her knight sally forth against dragons. She was an almost visible green.

We followed the road to Toledo until we'd climbed the escarpment. Then we turned left and picked up a ruler-straight, one-lane road that took us through the gently rolling country directly to the monastery. The Roman road that Don Jaime had mentioned. In a few places, grass and time had taken it, but mostly the tight-packed gravel surface was in fine shape. We saw several flocks of sheep and met one other car, but otherwise we could have been crossing part of the moon.

The monastery loomed on the skyline while we were still several kilometers away. It was a single, square, three-story building made of the same gray-brown stone as the city of Toledo. There was a cluster of low stone out-buildings to the rear. The monastery itself would have dwarfed the palace of the Quintinars. It was a block, completely plain except for triple lines of windows, and one statue set in a niche over the only door in view.

San Ildefonso was sited on a broad nose projecting from the level of the high land south of the Tagus into and through the broken tumble of the escarpment falling down to the plain of La Mancha. The location was eminently defensible which seems to have been a factor considered by anyone building anything in Spain up until recent times.

Luis halted on a gravel oblong to one side of the simple entrance, and jumped out to open the door for me. He looked respectfully up at the plain mass.

I went to the monastery door and saw a bright brass knob set in a stone socket. I pulled.

The door was opened quickly by a bent old man wearing a dusty brown robe, belted at the waist by a rope and a twined rosary. He had sandals on his gnarled feet. "And what brings you to San Ildefonso?" he asked, tilting his head up at me.

I explained that I'd like to talk to the prior, if it were convenient, and that I had a letter to introduce me. I passed over Don Jaime's letter. The monk fished a pair of steel rimmed spectacles from some recess in his robe and peered at the address on the envelope.

"Well, come in, come in," he said beckoning me through the door.

The stark entry hall had a high flat ceiling. The walls were bone-white plaster, the floor close-fitting flagstones like those in the streets of Toledo. A wide arch opened into a dim transverse corridor. To the right was a carved holy water font with a plain black crucifix above, to the left was a half-open dark wooden door.

Almost automatically I dipped my fingers in the font and crossed myself. It was a long time since I'd done that, but in that place the grip of old lost customs took me without my noticing. The old monk smiled approvingly, showing he lacked a few good teeth.

He pointed to the door at the left. "Step in there and wait, young man, if you please. I won't be more than five minutes." He started off down the corridor as I went through the door.

I was obviously in the visitors' room. It held a plain table with several magazines and books, all religious, and severe chairs and other furnishings. A single bare electric bulb hung from the ceiling. There were several religious pictures on the walls. A couple of sweetly garish prints and a couple that looked old and interesting. And in each of the two window bays that pierced the thick walls was a large wooden chest.

I made for the chests. It was stupid, I knew, but a thrill moved under my ribs. The lid of the first had a central round carving with a cross and laurel leaves that certainly weren't the Villena arms. The other bore a worn circular bas-relief that looked like an oval with three stubby spikes shooting out of it—even more remote from the shield, chevrons, and central diamond of the Villenas. Both chests were of a dark yellow wood whose grain showed knots and waves. Both were unlocked and absolutely empty.

I may have drawn blank my first try but at last I was actively searching. That was a step in the right direction.

The old gatekeeper opened the door to the visitors' room and said the prior would be happy to see me. I followed him out through the arch into the long corridor. On the interior side, the wall was broken only by doors. What little light there was came from deep window bays between the rooms on the outer side. As we walked along, I could see there was a chest under each of the windows.

It was a fair walk to the prior's office. Down half one side to a right angle turn and then down half of that side. We passed several monks of all ages, including a couple who looked no more than sixteen. They must have been novices. All examined me with profound interest.

"Here's the prior's study," my guide said in Spanish as we finally neared an imposing metal studded door set in a rounded archway. "Now, he's in major orders, so you must call him

Father Fermin." He opened the door and ceremoniously ushered me into the prior's presence.

The room was large and more austerely furnished than the visitors' room although there was a beautifully carved crucifix between the two windows. Behind the prior's chair and table was a large bookcase. The only note of color in the room came from the few books with bright covers. A small door in a far corner probably gave into the prior's bedroom. The few light fixtures at least had glass shades. Electricity seemed to have come late to San Ildefonso, and it didn't fit well. A telephone on the table was an even more incongruous note.

The prior rose and came to greet me. Father Fermin was nearly as tall as I, but couldn't have weighed half as much. His cropped hair was thick and white. He took my hand as I said my name and it was like gripping a fine mail gauntlet. His face was bony and deeply lined and when he smiled, most of the lines deepened. There was little of the solemn about him.

"Thank you, Anselmo," he said to the doorkeeper. "Did you ask for the wine?"

"Sí, Padre. Con su permiso." He left as Father Fermin conducted me to a chair by his table.

I said, "You're very kind to receive me, Father."

"I am happy to do so, Señor Clancy. Don Jaime called me yesterday and quite stimulated my hopes."

The door to the corridor opened and a young novice entered, carrying a tray. He put it on the table between Father Fermin and myself, staring at me in fascination as he did so. The tray bore a wide mouthed earthenware pitcher and two glazed pottery beakers.

Father Fermin thanked the novice and told him that was all. The novice withdrew as the prior deftly poured the beakers full of a dark red wine. "Salud, my son," he said.

I raised my beaker with him and drank. The wine was faintly harsh and satisfying. I said honestly, "This is very good, Father."

"It's not bad. We make it ourselves. Both for our own use and to sell. It's a type of Valdepeñas and our main source of cash. Many years ago we used to have much land in La Mancha and we raised our own grapes. Now the country people down the escarpment bring their grapes to us and we all share in the profits."

"May I smoke, Father," I asked.

"Of course." He moved an ash tray forward. I offered him a cigarette which he took contentedly, saying, "So you represent one of these legendary collectors and are searching for items of interest to him."

"Yes, Father." The prior got to business quicker than any Spaniard I'd spoken to yet.

"I hope that we have something you will want and we can sell. I spoke to our *Intendente*—he is the member of our community in charge of the practical side of our life—and he is quite excited. He badly wants a new wine press. Don Jaime says your master is interested in paintings?"

"Yes, Father. Paintings and old furniture, such as those chests I have seen." That wasn't a lie and I hoped I wouldn't have to tell one.

"You understand that although we ourselves might be anxious to realize some money on our possessions, before we actually sold anything we would have to obtain the approval of our Provincial General in Seville?"

"No, I didn't, Father, but that sounds wise."

"It's to prevent us from unknowingly disposing of a treasure for a pittance. This has happened through ignorance in the past. Although to tell you the truth, I'm not sure we have anything your master will find of interest. We are a recent house, founded in 1609 and have never been heavily patronized by the great families. Still, we have hopes. Our parent house at Uclés has sold some of its minor possessions for handsome sums." He smiled. "Don Jaime said your master can well afford to pay as much as we can reasonably charge."

"Yes, Father, he can."

"Excellent. Don Jaime is a much respected man in Toledo, and I have confidence in him. I should tell you that we have had some visits from the fine arts people in the Ministry of Tourism to see if we had anything that would warrant our being designated a historical monument, but they regretfully decided we didn't. I mention this so your hopes won't be unduly stirred."

"Father, if the monastery were a historical monument, I don't think I could expect to buy anything for my employer."

"There's that. How do you propose to determine if there is anything of interest to you here?"

I had what I hoped was an answer. "I would appreciate being allowed to look at your pictures and at your other possessions whenever I wouldn't interfere with the activities of the community. You understand I'm sure, that sometimes there are items, forgotten or even unwanted, that have a higher value than one might expect. There's a young lady with me who is an expert in artistic matters. Perhaps she could come to the visitors' room and inspect whatever I might select as possible purchases?"

"Don Jaime spoke to me of her, and mentioned her in his letter. It's a pity she can't enter to help you but she would be welcome in the visitors' room. You'll need someone to show you around. The best man would be our librarian. In our community, he has wider responsibilities than in others." He vigorously rang a small hand bell. The door was opened almost instantly by the young novice. Father Fermin said, "Juan, please ask Brother Fernando to come here if he is not busy."

"Sí, Padre," said Juan and disappeared as if some giant invisible hand had snatched him out by the tail of his robe.

Father Fermin looked after him wryly. "The novices will be gossiping like hens after Complines."

"You have many novices, Father?"

He shook his head. "Only twelve. At our peak, in the early 1700s, we had over four hundred brothers and lay brothers and always at least fifty novices. We are now less than a hundred in all and several of those are infirm. We've closed the entire top floor. This century has not been good to monastics."

While we were waiting for Brother Fernando, I asked about the interior economy and operation of San Ildefonso. The prior explained that the monastery was self-sustaining and that the order although not contemplative or closed such as the Cistercians or Trappists was also not a teaching order. "We're a community for the glory of God and we take in the tired wayfarer. When the old Roman road outside was one of the main ways to Seville and Cadiz, we were very busy," he said. "Now there are not many travelers who pass. Only shepherds come every now and again to hear Mass with us. But we're still a refuge for the tired in body or in soul, and a home for those who wish to dedicate their life to God."

There was a knock and a short, plump monk entered at the prior's cell. Brother Fernando was completely bald and resembled an owl. The thick glasses he wore emphasized the last. His round face lightened considerably when he smiled. It was quickly apparent he'd already known I was coming. He told Father Fermin he had a small tour planned for me for the rest of the day. "But it will take much more than a day to look over all of San Ildefonso," he said to me.

"I have a couple of weeks if necessary," I said.

"You'll have lunch with us in the refectory then?" said Father Fermin.

"Thank you, Father, I'd like to. I have a driver outside."

"We'll take care of him. Tell me—Anselmo, the door-keeper, said you are Catholic?"

"Yes, Father, I am, but not a good one."

"We hope for the good ones but we'll settle for any kind." He smiled. "I will see you in the refectory."

20

BROTHER FERNANDO GUIDED ME DOWN THE CORRIDOR THAT ran outside the prior's study. Every window bay we passed had a dratted chest in it. Beyond the turning, I followed him through a wide door in the interior wall into the library. It was spacious and airy, long enough to have six windows looking into the porch of the interior cloister. Each of those windows had another chest.

Tall glass-fronted bookcases took up nearly all the wall space, and in the center was a table as big as the one in the Conde's dining room. Looking very small at the huge table, a young novice sat copying some document onto a clean page. He saw us and lost all interest in his task.

Fernando hissed and the novice went instantly to scribbling again. A narrow door in the corner gave into Fernando's office. This was about the same size as the prior's, but except for a crucifix was furnished differently. There was a big desk in the center, and beautifully made multidrawered wooden cabinets went all the way around the room. One group contained the small drawers most libraries have for card catalogs; the others held large, square drawers. Several green-shaded electric lights hung from the ceiling and an old but bright lamp stood on the desk.

Brother Fernando waved a proud hand. "Here are the catalogs of the library and the treasury and most of the records of San Ildefonso," he said. "The librarian is responsible for the archives as well as the books and valuables of the monastery. Not only that, we have a fine catalog of the pictures. That should be of interest to you."

"A catalog of pictures?" For sure I was interested. Fernando pulled out one of the small drawers and brought it to the desk. The drawer was an example of fine joinery. It held between three and four hundred cards, each for a separate painting, all filed in alphabetical order by artist with a short description of the picture and a pencil notation as to where it was located. All entries were written in a copperplate hand so fine as to look engraved.

I flipped rapidly through. No cards for El Greco or for Teotocopulo either. Over a third were listed under "artist unknown."

"This is marvelous," I said to Fernando. "I compliment you."

"It is marvelous," he agreed, "but not my work. My predecessor did this."

"Do you know there is a young lady art expert who is working with me?"

"The prior told me something about her. I never heard of a woman art expert before."

"Could I make a list of the painters whose works are listed here to take to her for study? She could pick out those whose pictures she thinks would be most likely to interest my principal. I could look at them and then perhaps she could come to the visitors' room to make a final selection."

Fernando nodded vigorously. "A fine idea. But you won't have to make a list yourself. That's what novices are for." He carried the drawer out to the big room and I heard him giving quick instructions.

"I told him to copy all entries on all cards, that will be

better," he said on returning. "He's quick and should have much done before you leave today, and he'll finish by tomorrow." I felt guilty at causing the poor little guy to be set at such a labor, but Fernando seemed to think the task was fitting.

He fished a fat round watch out of his robe. "We have time to go around perhaps half the first floor anyway." He regarded me with a mixture of irony and rue. "You'll find we have much and are still poor." He opened the bottom drawer of his desk and pulled out a large ring loaded with keys the size of a child's hand.

The tour consisted of simply going clockwise from the library around the first floor of the monastery. I saw a workroom where some monks were weaving at looms while one read aloud from a book on theology, and a carpenter shop where more monks were busy at benches, unread to. We stopped at the monastery chapel, a huge, bare hall, whose only decoration beside the small altar and the stations of the cross was the delicate tracery of the ceiling vaulting. Although there was no distracting ornamentation, the plain, straight benches were deep and solid with padded kneeling rails, so San Ildefonso didn't seem to go in for needless mortification of the flesh.

In the rear corridor, three monks were replastering a wall. Fernando explained that all monks, regardless of their principal job in the monastery, did a certain amount of weekly work on the repair and upkeep of the building as long as they were physically able. He mentioned offhandedly that he himself was a better than fair gardener and helped take care of the roses in the central cloister.

Quite a few rooms were locked. Fernando said a few were storerooms but most simply weren't being used any more. For all the organized activity going on, San Ildefonso had something about it of an old, complicated clock that gently and with dignity was slowly running down.

There were chests and paintings all over the lot except in the bare chapel. The paintings as might be expected were uniformly of religious scenes and as uniformly would have given Susan a fit. Even I could see they all badly needed cleaning. Some were mere brown blurs shot with faint, hidden color.

At length we came to a stout, wooden door with a massive lock. Fernando said, "This is our treasury. There is nothing here we could think of selling, but by seeing our treasures you may have a better idea of how valuable the rest of our possessions may be." He smiled wryly. "We have never been a worldly house and you'll not see much silver and less gold."

The lock needed two keys. A sensible security precaution except that both were on the single ring Fernando had dug out of his bottom drawer. Once inside he made a circuit with his keys, opening the doors which lined the walls to display what was ranged on the shelves behind. He'd been right about shortage of silver and gold.

Fernando took me around pointing out items of interest, his tone of voice slightly defensive. I saw that every item on the shelves had a small card tacked in front of it bearing a number and a short description. The writing was in the same meticulous hand as in the card catalog of paintings.

I pointed at one of the cards. "Is this your predecessor's work also?"

"Yes. Now, here is a very nice coral cross donated by the Alba family in 1783. They have always encouraged the religious houses near their lands." Fernando spoke as if he hoped the Albas would come across again. If their last present was in 1783, they were overdue.

In the next cabinet I saw a shelf with about twenty small

boxes and cases in a row, most of silver, one of what appeared to be gold.

"These are reliquaries, aren't they?" I asked, keeping my voice casual.

Fernando nodded. I bent to examine the boxes closely. Thank God, whoever had made up the cards had been careful to include the names of the saints whose bones or blood were supposedly contained within. I read each card. No San Ildefonso was represented. I felt cheated.

I made a try. "I'm surprised that you have no relic of your patron."

"Oh," said Fernando. "You've touched on one of our small mysteries. That reliquary is over there." He gestured across toward an opposite cabinet.

I strolled over to it. There was an item that had a shelf to itself. The card tacked before it said "Relicuario en plata y cristal. San Ildefonso (?)" The case was as described. Below the oval of clear crystal in the silver lid and tied to a purple satin backing was a two-inch length of straight bone, probably from one of the smaller bones of San Ildefonso's forearm. My own arm twinged sympathetically.

Crowded scenes were carved in the silver sides and the corners of the top. One resembled the El Greco in Illescas in which the Virgin was giving a priest a vestment. The workmanship was so good I felt that if the box were magnified a hundred times I'd be looking at clear, lively man-sized statues.

"Why is this a mystery?" I asked.

"Because we don't know where it came from. The first mention of it in our records is in an inventory of the treasury made in 1684. Before that, nothing. Now, San Ildefonso is our patron. If this had come to us from our mother house or as a gift we would have some papers, but we don't. Brother

Bernardo who was the librarian before me and who made those cards and the catalog, not only searched here but went to the archives of the Provincial General in Seville. Brother Bernardo was thorough and tireless, yet he could find no trace." Fernando sighed. "We doubt its validity, as you can see by the question mark."

"But that case? No one but a fine artist could have done that."

"We don't doubt the authenticity of the case, Señor Clancy, we doubt the relic it holds. That is very sad."

"I don't understand."

"The case is sixteenth-century work. Brother Bernardo thought it was Italian. A reliquary that fine if it held the true bone of San Ildefonso should have some documents with it." He shrugged. "You are Catholic. You may know that the counterfeiting of relics has been an industry from the early days of the church until recent times."

"Couldn't you accept it on faith?"

He turned severe on me. "One of the great problems of the Church is the nearly pagan desire of the less educated faithful to believe in wonders. Right here we have had cases of novices and lay brothers tending toward idolatry. This must be resisted. The Vatican has decided that even authentic relics are not to be—how shall I say?—overly worshiped."

I had no further interest in the treasury but I dutifully looked at all that Fernando wanted to show me. As we left, a heavy bell tolled. "Ah," he said. "Let us go to the refectory." There was anticipation in his voice. For a monk, the day's meals were probably the major available sinless pleasures.

I had a fine lunch in the refectory—a big bowl of lamb stew, supplemented with a hefty salad, several chunks of crusty bread, a slab of white, tangy cheese, and plenty of the same wine Father Fermin had given me. The refectory was about four times too large for the number of monks who ate there. I sat with the prior and the higher-ranking monks at a slightly raised table and felt like something on exhibit. My presence was obviously the subject of much comment at all the tables, and the monks with me were as curious as crows about where I was from and what I was doing. I answered their questions as well as I could. The *Intendente*, the man who was eager for a new wine press, wanted to know if I'd found anything yet, and looked frustrated when I said I'd just started.

Father Fermin asked only one question and it was a hard one. "I've been wondering, Señor Clancy, have you been to other monasteries in your search?" he said.

"No, Father. San Ildefonso is the first."

"Was there any special reason for picking us?"

I had an answer that wasn't quite a lie. "Don Jaime was sure no one had come here before, so he thought it probable I might find something of value and interest."

He nodded to himself. "We hope you do."

The *Intendente* had been listening. He agreed strongly and told me about wine presses for ten minutes.

After lunch, Brother Fernando and I went back to his office. He suggested that I might like to look through the records he kept. He took me around the ranked cabinets, naming what was in each of them as he went. The first twelve were the historical archives of San Ildefonso. Then came several holding religious documents from higher headquarters, annual reports from the *Intendente*, and the like.

He smiled when he reached the last four. "These will be of interest to you, Señor Clancy. They hold the inventories of our property over the years. Priors every now and then have had lists of our goods prepared. Not on a regular basis by any manner of means, more like once every forty or fifty years, but these could help fix the age of anything you might discover."

Fernando then explained he would like to catch up on his work. It appeared he was engaged in translating the writings of St. Thomas Aquinas from Latin into Spanish. "Not the *Summa*," he said apologetically. "The Jesuits did that long ago, but all his other works."

"That must be quite a task."

"I've been working on it since 1935 and am close to half through. St. Thomas was a prolific writer."

He withdrew to his desk and did work for a while, but soon fell into a contented doze, which I expect was a feature of his afternoons and might have been part of the reason he'd invited me to inspect the records.

I pulled out the first drawer in the historical section and immediately saw evidence of the organizing talents of Brother Bernardo. All the heavy hand-cut folders therein were titled in his easy-to-recognize writing. I spent an hour grubbing happily around in the archives for the 1600s, confirming Don Jaime's statement that the old hand was hard to read, and finding no trace of any correspondence with Don Cristóbal, Marqués de Villasol. The old prior had probably burned those letters as they'd arrived, saying a good Act of Contrition as he did so and sending for his confessor immediately after to be on the safe side.

When I moved to the cabinets holding the inventories, I wasn't long in finding a surprise. I looked over at Fernando, who had straightened up and was active again at his desk. "Brother Fernando," I said, "I see that Brother Bernardo made one of the monastery inventories himself. Wasn't that rather odd work for the librarian?"

Fernando turned in his chair. "Yes, but he'd finished cataloguing the library and the pictures and the treasury and putting the records in order, so he decided that it was time a proper inventory of San Ildefonso was made." His voice was fond. "If you look under your chair you'll find it has a number put there by Bernardo. He was exhaustive."

"Exhaustive! His inventory must take up nearly two of these four cabinets."

"Yes, and he didn't even finish it. He was still working on it when we lost him." A twinge of sorrow and regret passed over Fernando's round face.

"He died?"

"He must have. He disappeared. It was a bad time. The month of September 1936. The government was besieging the *alcazar* in Toledo and General Franco was coming north with the Army of Africa. There was fighting all through the province. Bernardo was accustomed to taking walks around the monastery to meditate and pray. He refused to change his habits and he went out one evening and was never seen again."

"You think he was killed?"

"Certainly he was killed." Fernando spoke firmly. "There were Red patrols about and they were not respectful of religious people. And the Army of Africa was mostly made up of the Foreign Legion and Moorish troops. Those were not respectful of any one or any thing. We never did find his body, but he must have been killed by some soldiers."

"You became librarian then?"

He nodded. "I'd been Bernardo's apprentice as Diego out there is mine." He motioned toward the main room where the novice worked. "I took my final vows in 1934 and became his assistant. He was a man of deep knowledge and kindness."

"He seems to have had a great sense of order."

"It would be more accurate to say he was very strongly against disorder. Would you like to see more of the monastery?"

I had plenty to think about. "Thank you, but I should be

leaving. I'll be back tomorrow. You have been very kind to me and I'm grateful."

He said. "And you are a welcome visitor. It is exciting to have you here, Señor Clancy. You're a major event in our quiet lives."

The industrious Diego had finished copying out over half the cards in the catalog, so I took what he'd done when I left. His writing was nowhere near as clear as Brother Bernardo's, but it was legible.

21

"THIS HAS BEEN A MISERABLE DAY," SUSAN TOLD ME the second I walked through the palace door. "I've found another Velázquez and two Goyas and three more Zurbaráns plus a whole crowd of Italians. After that there was nothing to do but read and walk around the garden."

"I'm sorry," I said insincerely. "Let's have a drink with the French pictures. I've quite a bit to tell you."

When Claudio led a maid carrying a drink tray out to us, he said the Conde had telephoned and asked that I return his call about eight. Claudio also brought a long cable from Du Vigny picked up by the daily messenger into Quintinar.

Susan growled but allowed me to read the cable. She even mixed the drinks to save time.

After I finished, I said, "Du Vigny's willing to offer a hundred thousand for the Sisley and fifty thousand for two Morisots. He's not interested in the Lautrec portraits. Hope the Conde won't be disappointed, but we're still paying a fat rent for our accommodation."

"All right. Now what—"

"Wait. Not quite finished. Two men I know named Patricio and Ricardo are probably arriving in Madrid right now and will be on call if we need them. Du Vigny's put an outfit in England to checking on Grey. So far all they've reported is that they've had no success, which implies he's not a legitimate private detective."

"I don't think I ever thought he was. Now, dammit, talk."

"Okay. First, the silver reliquary of San Ildefonso is there. According to the librarian, Brother Fernando, it seems to have just appeared in the monastery, showing up in the records for the first time in the late 1600s. Because it doesn't have the proper pedigree and certificates, the monks now think it's a fake. I mean that the bone inside is a fake. The case of the thing is beautiful work."

"Why that fits! Even that the case was nice work. No wonder Cristóbal was angry over losing it."

"Yeah, it fits. Looks almost certain the old prior kept the chest. But, boy, that place is huge and chests are something it's got a lot of. Somebody seems to have gone around sticking one in every window bay as a kind of decoration, and there are others in odd corners."

I went through a detailed description of San Ildefonso and of my visit there.

Susan shook her head. "That sounds discouraging. Could you search those chests without the monks wondering what you were up to?"

"I doubt it, but I don't think there's much point in trying. If we turn up those paintings, I'm sure they're not going to be in any chest that's out in plain sight. I just can't swallow that they'd have sat there for maybe three hundred years without some monk peeking in and getting curious."

She didn't agree. "The paintings would certainly have been wrapped up in some sort of protection. That chest was carried from Toledo to the monastery. If a monk looked in and only saw something in a bundle he might not have even bothered to unwrap it."

"Susan, we've got to limit the area of search to a size we

can cope with in a reasonable time. Now, there's something else that's going to help there. The librarian before Fernando was a guy named Brother Bernardo. He must have spent most of his waking moments organizing everything he could lay his hands on. He catalogued the library and the treasury and the pictures, and put all the archives and records of the monastery into neat, logical files. Then one day, bless his heart, he decided to make a full inventory of the whole place and to do it in proper style."

"Had no one made an inventory before?"

"Oh, yes, but not the kind that would have satisfied this guy. Those other inventories are about what you'd expect when some not terribly interested monk went around writing down what he saw—the novices' classroom has twelve benches, twelve tables, one teacher's stand, one blackboard. Entries like that. Not Brother Bernardo. In his inventory each item is given a sort of serial number and listed separately, together with its measurements, its general condition, and so on. His inventory alone takes up as much file space as all the others ever made in the history of the monastery."

She frowned. "I don't see why you sound so pleased about that. If this Bernardo were so thorough and the pictures were there, why didn't he find them?"

"Ah! Because he didn't finish."

Her face cleared. "Oh, so you think you can eliminate the part of the monastery that Bernardo went through."

"I do." I took a pull at my drink. "That may be easier said than done, and besides the monastery closed off the top floor some time gone which should mean stuff has been shifted. Still, Bernardo broke his inventory down by rooms and, heaven rest his precise soul, he dated the sections he did, so I should be able to figure it out. And Fernando doesn't seem to mind if I nose around the records."

"Why didn't Bernardo finish? Did he die?"

"Something got the poor guy. It was back in September of 1936, when Franco was fighting up from the south to relieve the *alcazar* in Toledo. Where Don Jaime was, remember?"

She nodded.

"Bernardo, who seems to have been somewhat pigheaded in addition to being a great record keeper, insisted on taking one of his regular walks and never came back. Fernando thinks either a Red patrol or some of Franco's soldiers killed him. All of those were tough characters."

"The men you call 'Red' were the defenders of a legally elected government under reactionary fascist attack."

"Oops. Sorry. It just slipped out." I remembered Diego's list and took it from my inside pocket. "Here's something you might like to see." I told her what it was and she leafed through it.

"I can see three names that could be interesting," she said. "Doesn't *desconocido* mean unknown?"

"Yes."

"The paintings by the unknowns would be interesting to look at," she said wistfully. "There's always the chance of finding something there."

"Well, we're going to buy at least some of those pictures. Enough to pay for a wine press, anyway. So please pick out some possibles. I'll take a look at them and anything halfway decent I'll have set aside. The monks are planning a special show for you in the visitors' room."

"They know about me?"

"Yeah. They're impressed to their sandals to know that I have a lady art adviser."

"Watch it, Clancy."

She went through the list of paintings again, much more carefully. I helped from time to time by translating the Spanish descriptions. There were sixteen she thought might be worth consideration. Since Diego had copied the full entries from the cards including the present location of the pictures, I noticed one thing when I looked over the items she'd checked.

"I guess the monks have too many pictures for their walls," I said. "Over half of these must be in storage. See, they're shown as being in either *Almacén* One or *Almacén* Two. *Almacén* means storeroom. That could be helpful. Those storerooms are places I want to get into."

"Better see if your friend Bernardo got into them first."

"Yeah. Well, how about a little cribbage?" I would offer her some diversion after her dull day while I'd been circulating around meeting people and seeing sights.

"I don't suppose you play chess?"

"The hell I don't. Let's see if Claudio can provide a set."

"There's one in a room across the big hall. I found it today. A very nice set that could be Chinese work. I'll get it."

I beat the pants off her two straight games and although she wasn't bored, I don't think she was thrilled by the experience. After the second game I excused myself to call the Conde.

When I returned she was still hunched over the board with the pieces as they'd been placed for my last mating attack. She was regarding them as if they were small furry animals, hitherto friendly, that had turned and snapped at her.

"Just bought two pictures," I said off-handedly.

"The Monet and Pissarro?"

"Yup. Had to go a little bit higher, but still got them for $275,000, so I guess I've saved Du Vigny twenty-five grand."

"Will Du Vigny look at the pictures?"

"Every day. He's almost as hard a picture-looker-at as you are. I made the offer on the Sisley and the two Morisots too. The Conde was intrigued."

"Sometimes I'm jealous of the rich," she sighed.

"I'm that way most of the time. Look, I should go to Madrid tomorrow to arrange about the money being shifted. Why don't we both leave here early and run up there? Then we'll pass by Toledo and drop you off. I'd appreciate it if you'd see Don Jaime and give him a progress report. Bet he'll give you lunch, and even if he doesn't there's more to keep you happy in Toledo than here. Luis can take me on to the monastery and come back to Toledo for you and the two of you can pick me up at San Ildefonso around five. Okay?"

"Why, that would be very nice. Thanks, Clancy, I'd like to do that."

"Good. I'll go give Don Jaime a call and let him know."

I whomped her once more at chess before dinner was served. She switched to cribbage after dinner and went right for my jugular. The experience cost me over nine hundred pesetas. Maybe it wasn't such a smart thing to beat her at chess.

WE MADE IT TO MADRID BY NINE-TWENTY AND I WAS first in line when the branch of the Banco de Zurich opened its doors. I displayed my credentials to a cool little man at a front desk and was wafted to an icy little man in a back office. It took fifteen minutes to set up a transfer of $275,000. I was told that the financial transaction would require a week and that the bank would then take care of packing, crating, shipping, and insuring the pictures. Damned if they didn't have a commercial agent in Asunción, although what with all the smuggling money in that town, I should have expected that.

I left wondering if the Swiss had taken over the world while no one was watching and feeling let down. A man moving $275,000 should have been offered a drink or something. The Spanish were much more careful about matters like that.

We left Susan in the cathedral plaza in Toledo. Luis would return to wait for her as soon as he delivered me to San Ildefonso. She had a map and seemed sure she could find her way around.

At the monastery I apologized to Brother Fernando for being slightly late and set about creating a spirit of benevolence toward myself. Diego had already finished copying out the rest of the cards in the picture catalog, and I showed Fernando the first part with the ones Susan had checked. "We are interested in sixteen pictures on this list," I said. "If even half are in reasonable condition, I can promise you we'll pay a price for them that the Provincial General in Seville will agree is very fair and that will probably cover a wine press."

Fernando beamed at me. "The *Intendente* will say a Mass for you. We will look at them." He leafed through the list. "We might as well go to the storerooms first. Diego will help."

On the way, I commented that quite a few paintings were in storage and Fernando said, "Most of our paintings have come as gifts to the monastery." He smiled at me. "The donors were often getting rid in a nice way of paintings they didn't want. Sometimes the paintings they sent us were not entirely suitable for exposure in a monastery so they were accepted, thanks were given, and they were tucked away out of sight."

The first storeroom made it easy to see why Fernando had brought Diego along. The place was not dusted regularly. It was a long, narrow room, lit only by a couple of high naked light bulbs supplemented by a few narrow windows. There were several cupboards around but most of the wall space was covered with open shelving made from unplaned lumber. The uprights were sapling trunks, still with the bark on. That shelving could have been made from wood left over from the scaffolding when the monastery was built. The shelves bore irregular bundles, rolled up rugs or cloths, piles of anonymous junk, and at least ten chests I could see. It was a halfway orderly mess.

Fernando opened the cupboards. Three of them held quantities of paintings, stacked face out on the bottom and a single mid-shelf. Fernando didn't seem to think the pictures would have a noxious effect on Diego if he were only exposed to short doses, because at his direction the novice began to work through the cupboards calling out the numbers that were on the frames. Brother Bernardo's doing again.

I took advantage of this activity to look at a couple of nearby chests. One was so damaged I could see right through it. It was empty, and bore no carvings. The other was sound and also carved but with nothing resembling the Villena arms. There were other appealing chests farther away. It shouldn't be hard to figure out an excuse to come back, preferably alone.

The smudged Diego eventually surfaced with the five paintings listed for this storeroom. The colors of all were brighter than those hung out in the monastery, probably because they had been stored away. Three were vaguely classical with undraped goddesses, but the other two were country landscapes, one showing little figures busily harvesting in fields of wheat. Those two wouldn't have induced lascivious thoughts in anyone but might have made for homesickness in novices not long from farms. I told Fernando that the landscapes and one of the others were good, definitely pictures my expert would want to see.

Diego carried the three into the corridor and we went around to the other storeroom. It was almost a duplicate of the first; there I had four pictures set aside.

We left Diego to clean up the frames of the selected paintings and cart them back to the library while Fernando took me to look at those paintings Susan had checked that were out on view. They were all so dim I had doubts that it would be wise to expose her to them for fear of a scene, but I picked two of the clearest anyway. They both had religious themes as best I could tell. I told Fernando they could stay on the walls until we set up Susan's show.

There was half an hour before lunch so we went back to the library. I asked, "Do you know how far along Brother Bernardo was in his inventory when the monastery lost him?"

"You're asking about many years ago." He was silent a moment. "I helped him from time to time but mostly I stayed here in the library keeping up with the daily tasks and working on my Aquinas. He had started at the top floor and worked down. He was on the first floor, and was going around it methodically as he did everything, when he disappeared. He was probably close to or in the first storeroom we visited this morning. Does that help?"

"Yes. Quite frankly, I don't believe that San Ildefonso is harboring any great unrecognized treasure in any room of which Brother Bernardo made an inventory."

"You are right there, Señor Clancy." Fernando smiled indulgently. "Brother Bernardo was always extremely thorough, and besides knowing paintings well he knew quite a bit about antiquities. Let's see if we can't find out where he stopped." He went to the cases that held the inventories.

"Nobody ever finished his work then?"

"No." Fernando stood motionless a few seconds, his back toward me. "I thought about it, but no." He pulled out the first of the drawers that held Bernardo's work. "Although he worked from the top floor down, he put the inventory together in the files in a different system, but he made an index. Here it is."

That I hadn't seen the day before. It was a folder with a plan of each floor of the monastery on a fold-out sheet of fine paper. Each room was labeled in a combination of letters and figures. There was a small red dot in the corner of each room block on the plan for the top two floors and in about half of the ones of the first. The draftsmanship and lettering were characteristic of Bernardo.

Fernando peered at the plan of the first floor. "You can see the rooms he'd finished—the ones with the red dots. I was right, he had reached that storeroom. What is it's label? AL 1-I." He turned to the cabinets again. "Yes. AL 1-I. It will be in here." He pulled out a thick folder and carried it to his desk.

He separated a sheaf of long sheets pinned at the corner "Díos mío," he said. "I remember now. I put these papers in there thirty-six years ago when I cleared his desk." He passed them to me.

The top sheet was headed "Almacén Numero Uno, Primer Piso (AL 1-I)." Underneath that was the notation "Desde 17 de setiembre, 1936 hasta _____." Then the list went down the unruled page. Bernardo had never filled in the blank for the date when he'd finished inventorying Storeroom Number One on the first floor.

I turned to the last page and looked at the bottom of the column. The last two entries were:

"AL 1-I-3487, Cajon, nogal 1,20 × 50 × 50. Trabajado en el superior. Muy buena condicion.

"AL 1-I-3488, Cajita de carton de piedritas. Muestras minerilogicas (?)"

That is, a walnut chest measuring 120 by 50 by 50 centimeters, carved on the lid and in good condition, and a little cardboard box of small stones which would be mineral specimens. There was nothing more. A pencil notation had been made by the entry for the chest and then erased. I held the sheet to catch the light and thought I could make out the words "Sala de visitas."

I wanted to get back into that storeroom. Very badly, I wanted to get back there. What in hell could that box of stones be?

"How long did it take Brother Bernardo to do as much as he did on this inventory?" I asked.

"Over three years," said Fernando. He was staring at the open folder before him. "I don't believe more than two people have consulted it besides myself and you since we lost him." He shifted his eyes to his own translation of Aquinas. "But monks work for the task and for the glory of God."

The big bell tolled to call the community to the refectory. Again, there was a place for me at the high table. I'd rather have gone to *Almacén* one than eat, but appearances had to be maintained. Fernando's announcement that I wanted to spend much money to buy certain pictures I'd selected sent my popularity sky high with the *Intendente*. I parroted a few of the phrases Susan had taught me about the Flemish school until I saw the prior smiling and I stopped.

As we were finishing the meal, I said to the prior, "I have been astonished at the completeness of the records of the monastery. Brother Bernardo did an extraordinary job while he was librarian."

"Yes, he did. Has Brother Fernando spoken much of him?"

"No, not a great deal, but I've seen enough of Brother Bernardo's work to know that he was a remarkable man."

"He was that," said the prior. He regarded me with some amusement. "You have probably formed in your mind an idea as to what he was like."

"Well, yes, Father, I have." I thought Bernardo must have been of middle height, slim or even skinny, with a pale face and black eyes and hair. He probably wore glasses. I was sure that he was always careful that any paper he was working on was lined up exactly square with the edges of his desk and that to him a picture a few degrees askew was a sight unbearable. I couldn't decide whether I would have liked him or not. Yet the few times that Fernando had spoken of him affection had been strong in his voice.

Father Fermin tapped the table gently with his forefinger, still eying me. "Would you come to my study after we rise for a short talk?"

"Of course, Father."

He looked around and stood. All of us rose with him for the closing grace.

The prior told Fernando he'd send me back to the library and I walked beside him to his study. We sat at the two straight chairs by his table.

"I can see you are curious about Brother Bernardo," said the prior. "I'm not surprised. It would be better perhaps that I talk to you of him. It was a heavy blow for Fernando when Bernardo disappeared."

He paused in thought. "In truth, Brother Bernardo was mad," he said.

"MAD? YOU MEAN INSANE?" I ASKED.

He nodded. "Yes, precisely. He was a gentle, lovable madman." The prior's voice reminded me of Fernando's when he spoke of Bernardo. "You shouldn't be shocked by that. The Church has never disdained to take madmen into her service, or broken men, or hurt men. I don't mean raving madmen, although she'll try to care for that kind, but those who have only a few visions or hear voices only every now and again she'll do her best to put to toil for the good of their souls and the glory of God. Send them to convert heathen or some fitting task.

"Brother Bernardo was at least two people. One was a serene man who liked to play chess and was well-educated and kind and thoughtful. Then there was the other who when he talked to you would pick a bit of lint from your robe, who counted things and made lists of them, who wanted a picture hung in the center of a wall even if it couldn't be seen there—a man who wanted balance and system and order above all else. But even this fussy man was kind. He could be persistent beyond all credence, but it was the mild persistence of long, soft rains that eventually wear down mountains.

"We had a wise prior here when Bernardo came. He gave one man the records to set in order and let both be examples in our community of brothers."

"Were you here when he came, Father?"

"No, I came to San Ildefonso in 1928 after I'd been ordained. In our order, there are always three or four priests in each house to say mass and hear confessions. I'd taken my novitiate in the mother house and then gone to the seminary. Bernardo had come some years before."

"What was he like physically, Father?"

"He was a big man, nearly as tall as you and more thickly built. He was very strong and one of the best stone masons in the monastery. Like many large men, he had a low, quiet voice."

So much for my accuracy at reconstructing Bernardo by looking at his work.

"And no trace of him was ever found?"

"No. Those were bad days. Bernardo liked to take walks in the countryside and went out nearly every day for an hour or two, no matter what the weather. He said he could pray better solitary and he liked to talk to the shepherds, who being much alone themselves were always glad to see him. When the siege of the *alcazar* in Toledo started it was risky to leave our walls but that never stopped Bernardo. Then one evening he was here and the next morning he was not. Our door is never locked. We searched for days but found nothing. That, you see, is why Brother Fernando suffered so.

"I don't quite understand."

"There was always the chance that Bernardo had simply left us." The corner of his mouth lifted. "It's been known to happen. Monks have unobtrusively fled from their monasteries for one reason or another. There were some here who feared Bernardo might have done that. Poor Fernando, who had been trained by Bernardo and who loved him dearly, never believed it, but that others should think so distressed him deeply. You may find this surprising, but some of the brothers thought

Bernardo had gone to join Franco's Army of Africa as a soldier."

"As a soldier!"

"By his own lights, he could have done that without peril to his soul. He never took final vows, but stayed a lay brother all of his time with us. And there was an incident a few days before which many thought important.

"The government of the Republic was not fond of the Church, from cardinals down to poor monks. Parties of government soldiers came by the monastery requisitioning food and wine. Less than a week before Bernardo disappeared, a last party came by. They took all our animals and the rest of the wine and all the food they could carry. These were not the rather apologetic soldiers who had been recruited in the province; these were Anarchist Assault Guards who had been brought down from Barcelona. They were not gentle in their manner. It was the only time I ever saw Bernardo in a rage. He was controlled but he was white and his face was hard as bone. He talked to the Guards in Catalan—the language they speak up there—until I feared they would kill him. But our prior ordered him to his cell and for a wonder he obeyed."

"Bernardo spoke Catalan?"

"Yes. In theory, we abandon all ties to the world when we enter here." He shrugged. "Actually, we all know very well indeed from the way we talk, some of the things we say, the turns of phrase we use, more or less from where each of us comes and much about the way we lived when we were young. Bernardo was from Catalonia and almost certainly from Barcelona. And something very bad had happened to him there before he came to the monastery. Do you know Catalonia?"

"Only from a map, Father."

"It's next to France and there's French blood in the people. The cool French mind seems to have mixed with the hot Spanish one to neither's advantage. They are hard workers and great businessmen up there and can be brutally violent. There were bad times in Barcelona when Bernardo was young. One year—1909 or thereabouts—more than forty churches were burned in Barcelona. And in 1921 the people did it again. Burned churches, sacked convents, killed priests, raped nuns, and probably did their Easter duty later. I always thought that last outbreak may have been what sent Bernardo to San Ildefonso."

"Then you think he may have gone to the Army of Africa?"

"No." The prior was definite. "I was Bernardo's confessor, and I am sure he didn't leave us of his own will. I cannot go into my reasons because of the seal, but I am sure. And I told Fernando so, but the doubts of the other brothers nagged at him."

The prior's knowing eyes met mine. "I hope I have gratified your curiosity, Señor Clancy. Will you gratify mine?"

"Yes, Father."

"Are you searching for something specific here in San Ildefonso?"

I cleared my throat. There were a lot of answers to that question. "Yes, Father." I couldn't have managed any other.

He said nothing, but sat looking steadily at me.

"Right now I'm not at liberty to tell you exactly what," I went on, "but I promise you that if I find what I am searching for I will tell you everything, and I am truly going to buy those pictures I have selected with Fernando's help."

He clasped his hands in his lap. "All right, my son, I think you've been careful not to lie to me—in fact it was the care with which you phrased several of the things I've heard you say which made me wonder—and I trust Don Jaime. I will trust you."

"Thank you, Father. It will only be a few days more."

He smiled and rose. "We must talk again and about less serious things."

I stood to take my leave. His hand started to move in what might have been a blessing but he smoothly caught himself and merely extended it to shake mine. I thought over the conversation on my way back to the library. He'd said that San Ildefonso had had a wise prior when Bernardo came. San Ildefonso still did.

Fernando was in the first stages of his afternoon nap but woke without protest when I stood by his desk and coughed. He thought it would be fine if I went back to *almacén* one to look at some of the pictures by unknown painters. He gave me the keys and sent Diego with me to help.

Diego was enchanted to be allowed to go with me and grub around a dusty storeroom. He was as eager to please as a puppy. We soon set up a routine. I had the full list of pictures, and when I found one by an unknown painter that was given as being in *almacén* one, I'd tell Diego the number and he'd hunt for it. While he burrowed in the cupboards, I sauntered into the recesses of the storeroom and looked at what was on the shelves, with priority to chests. At intervals of looking at what Diego produced, I worked down one side of the room and partway down the other. The light was awful, but as far as I could tell by a semi-Braille method, there was no chest bearing the Villena arms nor anything interesting in those that were open. I swore to bring a flashlight the next day.

I had a few qualms about groping in a chest and finding a rat but none turned up. There were no signs of them and hardly any of insects. There were cobwebs up high on the walls and nothing else. The thick walls and the lack of much to eat would keep most vermin away. I worried about things that ate wood because one chest seemed to be full of worm holes, but it was the only one.

I selected two more paintings, both landscapes, for Susan to see. I'd have to get something for Diego—a rosary or a missal or whatever the prior would let me give him. A novice monk wasn't the easiest person in the world to shop for.

As I moved slowly along a stretch of shelving that was barren of chests, an object that didn't fit caught my eye. In the shadow of an upright was a small block of yellowish white. "An ivory box!" shrilled so loudly in my head Diego should have heard it.

I picked it up. Ivory, hell. It was a white cardboard box, brown in spots with age, its top covered with dust. A label pasted at one end read "Clavos de la Primera Calidad." Below that legend Bernardo had written the number "AL 1-I-3488." The box at one time had contained top quality nails, but when Bernardo had put it down in his inventory it had contained putative mineral specimens. I held the last item listed for *almacén* one on the first floor. The box was heavy and rattled when I shook it.

I opened it. Inside were a bunch of small chunks of a substance that looked like grayish brown wax. I picked one out and held it where I could see better. It was a piece of hard, almost glassy stone, chipped into a flattened wedge about an inch long. There was an Ordnance Museum at the Point that had been a refuge for me when I was a plebe. This was a box of stones for flintlock guns.

I picked out another, then closed the box and replaced it. I dropped the two stones into my side pocket as I walked back to join Diego at his labors. There had been no chest near the box of gunstones.

Diego and I looked at two more pictures by unknowns and then I called it a day. I wanted to talk to Fernando. Diego was agreeable, but made it clear he was perfectly willing to get dirtier than he was. I thanked him as profoundly as I could without embarrassing him.

I left Diego to close up and bring along the two paintings I'd picked. I found Fernando full awake at his desk, writing in a notebook with several thick volumes open in front of him. I told him about the two pictures and said I'd like to look in the archives again.

"Certainly," Fernando said. "Are you interested in anything in particular?"

What I wanted was more information on Bernardo's disappearance but after my talk with the prior I hesitated to ask Fernando about it baldly. "In a particular period, yes. From the time the Civil War started until the relief of the *alcazar*. I know that has nothing to do with pictures, but I've heard much about that time since I've come to Spain and—well, I'm interested."

Fernando might not have been the prior, but he was smart in his own right. He gave me a shrewd look. "Then there are two parts of the archives that will interest you. One is our correspondence during those months and the other is our annals."

"Your annals?"

"Yes. One of the duties of the librarian is to write a summary of each week's events in the monastery. All those together make up our annals."

"Did Brother Bernardo start those?" I couldn't keep back the question.

"No, though you will find the section he kept by far the most voluminous and exact. Our annals were started in 1720 and have been kept ever since." He rose and started for the cabinets that held the archives.

Brother Anselmo, the doorkeeper, came in, a cross expression on his knobby face. He said "Señor Clancy, here's a note for you from a person in the visitors' room," and passed me a folded small piece of paper. I read:

Clancy—

No crisis, but something's come up so I had to leave Toledo early. Could we please go back to the palace now?

Susan A.

I looked at my watch. It wasn't quite four. Dammit, I could have had an hour in the Annals of San Ildefonso According to Brother Bernardo. They would have to wait until the next day. I told Anselmo I'd be right out and he went off, muttering.

Fernando was intrigued to hear that my art adviser was in the monastery visiting room. He said he'd come along when I left if I didn't mind. I asked if I'd be allowed to give Diego a small present such as a rosary or the like, and he said such things were permitted but it should be plain.

When we neared the portal, Brother Anselmo was waiting, probably on guard to make sure Susan didn't escape into the monastery to wreak havoc. He directed a sardonic glance at Fernando who bristled but remained silent.

Susan was sitting in one of the straight chairs in the visitors' room when we entered. Her note had said "no crisis," but her appearance belied that. It wasn't that she seemed frightened or worried, but her eyes were wide and shining and at the same time her face was tense. If anything, I'd have said she was happy and trying to hide it.

I introduced Fernando who if made prey to evil thoughts concealed it well. With me translating, he exchanged a few remarks with Susan, mostly to the effect that he hoped suitable pictures would be found that the monastery could dispose of in conscience. Susan's replies were polite but short, and I began to feel impatience radiating from her. As soon as I could do so in courtesy, I asked Fernando to excuse us.

He came to the door. I dipped my hand in the holy water font and crossed myself as we passed. Susan stared at that.

Luis was waiting outside with the Landrover. As we walked toward it, I asked Susan in a low voice, "What brought you early away from Toledo?"

"Early from Toledo?"

"Yes. You're over an hour ahead of time. You said 'no crisis' in your note, but—"

"Oh! Well, nothing much really, but I did see that man Grey again—"

"What do you mean nothing much!"

"Ssh! I'll tell you when we get to the palace. Have you ever been in that visitors' room?"

"Sure. Where did you—"

"I thought you had." Her expression was clearer now. It was one of triumph. "I'll explain all about it at the palace. You might tell Luis we're in a hurry."

IT WAS A SILENT RIDE BACK TO THE PALACE OF the Quintinar's. We both wanted to talk but there was Luis. Although we made good time by my watch, it was long inside my head. Susan had seen Grey and then something had happened to make her all but forget that gentleman.

Claudio opened the door as we pulled up in front. Susan said, "Let's go to your sitting room. Please have drinks sent there."

I relayed the order and we went upstairs. She went into her quarters saying she'd be right over. I stood in my door, fuming. Under what the hell kind of circumstances had Grey reappeared? I hadn't thought of him for nearly a day.

Susan came out of her room carrying her kit bag, her purse still under her arm. I stood aside to let her in and saw a maid bringing the drink tray up the corridor. We went into my sitting room and waited until the maid had done her duty and left.

"All right, Susan, what's going on?"

Her eyes, brighter than before, met mine. "Just be patient a little bit longer, Clancy."

I growled and went to the drink tray. It was a bit early for martinis, but, feeling the need for one, I fixed a couple anyway.

Susan went to sit at a table by the window. From her kit

bag she took some bits of glass and small bottles and finicky little tools like the ones dentists dig at you with, and finally one of those sets of magnifying eyeglasses on stalks that watchmakers use. She arranged all these in some order logical to her and picked up her purse. From that she carefully extracted a tightly folded piece of paper that looked to have been torn from a pocket notebook.

I put her glass down within reach but she paid no attention to it. She donned her watchmaker's spectacles, unfolded the bit of notebook paper, and manipulated something invisible to me from the paper onto a square of glass. She repeated the operation with a second square of glass. The next step involved the little bottles and two fine rods. Tiny drops of colorless liquid were placed on the two glass squares.

She settled into rapt contemplation of her squares. I resisted a temptation to pour my martini down her neck.

After a couple of minutes, she sat straight and took off her fancy eyeglasses. With a rag from her kit bag, she set to wiping and polishing things and putting them back in their places. Then she lit a cigarette and stared out the window.

"All right," I said. "Jesus, Mary and Joseph. I am a patient man, but what are you up to?"

She started. For the first time she seemed to see her martini. She picked it up, took a large gulp, and said huskily, "Clancy, you've been in the visitors' room at the monastery. Did you notice the chests in the window bays?"

"Yeah. First thing I did."

"And the carving on them?"

"Of course. Nothing on either one is anything like the Villena arms."

"No, but the carving on the lid of the right chest is a skeleton diagram of the way El Greco signed some of his pictures. An interlaced Greek delta and theta. He didn't use it often but enough so that it's accepted as one of his normal ways of authenticating his work." She gave me her triumphant look again. "I must say the carving isn't clear and I might not have recognized it if I didn't have El Greco on my mind, but while I was waiting for you I looked around to pass the time and I saw it. I saw it right away."

So what I'd thought was a spiky oval had been El Greco's monogram. The moral here, of course, was that if I'd had sense enough to bring her the day before we'd be that much further along.

"Jesus," I said.

"Right. Clancy, those papers from Simancas said just a chest. Nothing was said about it being the Villenas' chest. It was El Greco's chest they left."

"The damn thing's empty. I looked."

"Not quite. There's some dust. I scraped up as much as I could."

I looked at her kit bag. "What were you doing with that gear of yours?"

"There are some chips of paint in the dust from the chest. I ran a couple of simple tests that can be done with quite small samples. One showed that the paint was oil based, and the other that there was no zinc in the white. Since about the early 1700s all white paints have had zinc compounds in their base. So there is a chest with El Greco's sign carved on the lid and chips of paint of the kind he would have used still in it." She finished her martini and held the empty glass out to me.

"Clancy," she said as she took the refill, "those paintings were there. They must still be somewhere in the monastery."

I wasn't so sure about that. "You've done damn well, Susan." I lifted my glass to her. "Your health."

Damned if she didn't blush. It became her.

Before I went through my own show and tell act, I

wanted to hear about Grey. I asked her, "Now, where did you see Grey and why did you leave Toledo early?"

The pride and contentment in her face were replaced by concern. "I've been so excited that he didn't seem important," she said. "A real chest that El Greco used." She took a deep breath and launched into the story of her time in Toledo.

She had seen no one she recognized while sightseeing or when she'd walked to Don Jaime's house. Don Jaime had been cordial and as anticipated had asked her to lunch. He had listened to everything she had to say with the greatest of interest. The two had enjoyed an excellent meal marred only by some dark looks from the little old maidservant who evidently suspected Susan's motives toward Don Jaime. Don Jaime himself had been gallant but not obtrusively so and had entertained her with stories of the history of Toledo. She'd left the house about three, well-fed and in a cheerful frame of mind, intending to do some more sightseeing before leaving to pick me up at the monastery.

The flower children, Dick and Elaine, had been waiting in the cathedral plaza. Elaine had come up to Susan and in a friendly manner said Mr. Grey would like to talk. Susan had considered saying she didn't want to talk to Mr. Grey who treacherously scattered electronic bugs around but had decided it would be smart to hear what he had to say. Elaine led Susan to a small, pleasant bar not far from the cathedral and Grey was at a table.

"He couldn't have been more polite," she said, "but he came through strongly as to how disappointed he was at not hearing from you by now. He asked me to explain that without someone who knew his way around to help, you might run into trouble." She made a face and dipped into her drink.

"Did he say what kind of trouble?"

"No. He just talked about problems that might arise because of your unfamiliarity with Spain. He gave me another card with the number he said you could reach him at. He suggests you call at your earliest convenience."

I took the card she dug out of her purse. "He's still trying to muscle in. Since our hands are stainless and our hearts reasonably pure, he doesn't stand a hope. Did you ask him how the hell he knew you were at Don Jaime's?"

She bit her lip. "No, I didn't think to."

"That's all right." She may not have noticed Dick and Elaine hanging around when she got out at the plaza, or they may have wandered by and seen the Landrover. I didn't like it that they'd been waiting when she left Don Jaime's.

She said, "What you say about our hands being stainless is true, but if we find those paintings we plan on getting them a little dirty and then Grey could make us trouble. Suppose he went to Ortega?"

"You've got a point, but we still have to find them."

"They have to be in San Ildefonso, Clancy. Somebody must have taken the paintings from the chest and just put them somewhere when the chest was moved out to the visitors' room. It's only there, as you said, as a decoration. The paintings would have been wrapped, remember, and they're probably on a shelf somewhere now."

"Where'd the chips of paint come from if the paintings were wrapped?"

"El Greco was a hardworking painter. There were probably chips of paint all over his house and in everything he owned. Those chips didn't have to come from the miniatures." She finished her martini and asked for another. I got it for her.

"Let me tell you about my day," I said. I went through it all, including my talk with the prior, the unfinished inventory of Storeroom Number One and my finding the gunstones there. As I finished I took one from my pocket and passed it to her. She took it as if it might break.

"My God!" she said. "We've found everything that Cristóbal Villena lost except the ivory box."

"And the paintings. Don't forget those."

"You know what I mean. You think Bernardo found those, don't you?"

"I sure do. He was making his inventory, counting things and putting numbers on them and writing them down and he came to the El Greco chest. The reliquary had been taken to the treasury a couple of centuries before, so the first thing he took out was a leather bag of gunstones that came apart in his hands because the leather would have dried out. So he put the stones in the first empty box he could find, and they are the last item on his inventory."

"Then maybe he never got to the paintings."

"I don't know. Normally, I'd say he found the paintings, regained his senses, and took off with them. How much would they have been worth back in 1936?"

"Nowhere near as much as today, but still millions. I don't think that Bernardo would have done that. He doesn't sound like the kind."

"You and the prior and Fernando. Tomorrow, I'm going through the annals of the monastery for that time. There's a strong chance Bernardo hid the paintings somewhere else because some Red—I mean government foraging parties—had been coming by picking up food and wine and he could have been wary they'd take the paintings."

She re-examined the small stone she held, then made as if to return it to me.

"No," I said. "Keep it. I've another and I thought you might like one."

"Keep it? I can keep it?"

"Sure. Sort of a souvenir. It may not look like much but it's probably spent close to three hundred years in company with a lot of El Greco pictures. I figured it would have associations for you."

"You got it for me?"

"Yeah. And although I didn't know it at the time, you have sure earned it. Your recognizing the carving on that chest gives us a big piece in this puzzle."

She stared at her gunstone as if it had turned into an emerald. "Thank you," she said, and sniffed. She looked over at me. Her eyes were still bright but in a different way. She took another healthy pull at her martini. "It was very nice of you to bring me this."

I chuckled. She looked better happy. Not prettier or anything, simply better. She knocked back her drink as I watched. She was also beginning to look a little tight, which didn't stop her from peering hopefully over her glass. I made us both new drinks.

She took a couple of sips at hers in silence, then in a tone of merely wanting to know, she asked, "Why did you cross yourself when you left the monastery?"

I raised my eyebrows. "As I've said, I was brought up a Catholic and it's good manners."

"You're not a Catholic any more?"

"I'm sure as hell not a Protestant."

"You can't believe that mumbo-jumbo. All that about putting little bits of saints in boxes and holy water and all."

"Matter of fact I don't, but I don't know of another outfit that's got a better pitch. What's biting you?"

"It disturbs me when you cross yourself. And these men—the prior and Brother Fernando and the little one you say you're going to get a rosary for. I think you're afraid of them. I can hear it when you talk about them. You, and what you are, you're afraid of them. That disturbs me too. You're not afraid of Grey or Ortega but you're afraid of those monks in that monastery."

She wasn't tight, she was drunk as a hoot-owl. Sometimes drunk doesn't come entirely from alcohol. She'd had a lot handed her in a short time mixed with about six or eight rapid ounces of gin. There didn't seem to be a prayer that she'd make it to dinner at the big table beneath the gaze of the Velázquez grandee. The only question was whether to feed her another drink to make sure she rested peacefully. I considered her clinically. Wouldn't do to make her sick. I decided she could have another small one. She thought so, too. She took it and drank it without much chatter and said she believed she'd lie down for a while.

She could get up without help but hit both sides of the door going through. I followed her over to her quarters. She sat down on her bed and regarded me semi-alertly, her gunstone still clutched in her hand. I pressed the bell by her side table.

She opened her hand and looked at the stone. She said, "Keep this for me will you, Clancy?"

"Sure. Don't fall asleep for a bit. Carmen's on the way."

She sat patiently until Carmen bustled in, then docilely put herself in the latter's hands.

As I turned to leave, Susan said, "Bye, bye, brute," but she was smiling.

25 ═══════

SHE WASN'T SMILING THE NEXT TIME I SAW HER.

It was about ten-thirty. After a solitary dinner, I was sitting in one of the rooms with the French pictures—two of which now belonged to Du Vigny—and rereading about the beginning of the Civil War in my history of Spain, when Susan came in, wearing one of her other pants suits.

"There you are," she said, as if she'd caught me trying to hide. "Damn it, I can't find that stone."

"I've got it right in my pocket, keeping it safe," I replied sweetly. "Feeling a little nervous?"

"Oh, shut up."

I offered her the small stone. "Temper won't help a hangover."

She glared at me, grabbed her stone, and went to sit across the room. "That was a nasty trick, Clancy," she said. "Feeding me four or five or God knows how many martinis."

"Now just a minute here. I didn't so much feed them to you as you snatched them out of my hand. I didn't realize how things were going until after your third and by then it was goodbye, Susan. Do you remember what we talked about?"

"More or less."

"You were a little over-excited," I said in a magnanimous tone.

"I don't remember how I got to bed." Her tone was far from magnanimous.

I stared at her for a few seconds and then laughed like a jackal. Not for long. Her eyes became nearly incandescent. "Not me," I said, forcing down hiccups. "Honest to God, not me. It was your loyal little Carmen who tucked you in. I sent for her. So help me. Ask her."

"You know I can't ask her anything."

"Act it out like charades. You can do it with a little ingenuity."

Her face tightened for an instant and turned more normal. She ran a hand through her hair. "Things sort of blacked out, and the next thing I knew, it was dark and I was in bed with my nightgown on backwards. I thought—well—"

"Tch-tch. I've never taken liberties with a drunk girl in my life." True, except on occasions when I'd happened to be equally drunk which balanced out in my book.

She managed half a smile. "All right, Clancy. I—I'm sorry."

That was some sort of milestone. "Nothing to be sorry about." I said kindly. "Care for something to eat? They're keeping a snack for you in the kitchen."

She nodded. I rang the bell, hoping that some food would continue to improve her mood.

Claudio and a maid set her a place at one of the small tables and brought her what looked to be a fine, nourishing soup, some paté, and toast. Claudio tried to pour her wine, but she wasn't having any of that. She didn't eat with any pleasure, still she ate it all. I read in my history, trying to keep straight all the political parties that grew like weeds under the Republican government.

I glanced over at her a few times as she ate. Once I met

her eyes. She dropped them hastily as if I'd caught her doing something she shouldn't.

When she'd finished and the servants had cleared away, she lit a cigarette. I waited for her to finish. As she stubbed it out, I closed my book. "Susan, I've been thinking about what we found today. We've nailed the paintings to Bernardo, but in a way we're worse off than we were before. If he didn't simply scamper off with them, he could have put them anywhere in the monastery. Before I was thinking that—"

"Clancy, I'll be more receptive to theoretical discussion in the morning." Her voice was neutral. She seemed recovered from her minor binge.

"Okay." I was slightly hurt, and picked up my book again. I'd only read a couple of pages when I felt uneasy and looked up to see that I was on the receiving end of an unmerited scowl. I wondered helplessly what I'd done now.

"Want to play some cribbage?" I asked placatingly.

"No, thanks."

"Chess?"

"No." Her voice was sharp.

"I have the rest of the list of pictures. Care to look that over?"

"I certainly do not."

I frowned myself. "What's biting you?"

"I'm bored," she said.

"Bored? You haven't been up long and you sure had a full day. What—"

She made a growl of exasperation, got up, crossed the room, and kicked me in the ankle. "Clancy, you can be terribly stupid."

A great, white light broke upon me. "But, Jesus Christ, less than thirty minutes ago you were accusing—"

"That was thirty minutes ago. I'm changeable."

"Wow! I'll say!" I stood and pulled her to me. For a short space, I looked into her dark blue eyes. "You have very nice eyes," I said and kissed her mouth lightly and then each of her eyes. "Do you want to go to my place or yours?"

"I've never been in your bedroom."

"I've been wanting to show it to you."

The cool part of my mind tried to send me an urgent message about this dolly being hard enough to handle on a strictly business basis. The rest of my mind shouted the cool part down.

I asked Susan to walk up the stairs before me, saying, truly, that I liked to watch the way she moved. That went over well, and she made something of a production of the climb up to our floor.

In my bedroom, I flipped back the covers on the big square bed. She undressed while I watched. Then she lay on the bed and watched me undress. I wasn't anywhere near as graceful as she'd been. I was in a hurry. I left the light on. She raised her arms as I went to her. She was firm and warm and responsive.

Both of us were too aroused for matters to take long. A few minutes later we lay together, full of the comforting knowledge of the next time.

"I'm glad I stumbled on to the key to your affections," I said.

"What do you mean?" Her voice was as soft as I'd ever heard it, soft and close to my ear.

"The secret seems to be that one should keep you busy and occupied, give you an impressive present, get you drunk, and then refrain from toying with your unconscious body. Follow that program and you'll come over and coquettishly kick a man. It's not an approach that would have occurred to me in the normal course of events."

She laughed down in her throat. "I must admit that when you gave me that stone after I'd showed off over finding the chest, you nearly broke me up. Then I got so mad at what I thought you'd done. After I decided you hadn't, I realized one of the reasons for my being mad was that something might have happened without my taking part and I didn't like having missed it."

"That must be a pretty tough crowd you run with back in New York for you to leap to the conclusion you did."

She stirred in my arms. "You see, it did happen to me once."

"Somebody got you drunk and—uh—took liberties?"

"Yes. An art dealer I'd done some work for, and who seemed clever and thoughtful. I went to his place for a drink at noon—at noon for heaven's sake. We were supposed to be going out for lunch later. I don't think I was just drunk, I think he put something in my drinks, too. I passed out and woke up naked on some cushions on the floor of his bedroom."

"My God, that's rape!"

"Not quite. Technically, I'm fairly sure I wasn't raped. This is a sick story. I don't think he could rape anyone. He's kinky. He had a camera with a delay device and he'd taken pictures of himself doing things to me."

"Was he trying to blackmail you?"

She laughed without mirth. "I'd have been better able to blackmail him. He was in all the pictures. No, he only wanted them for his collection. I wasn't the first he'd done it to. He said he'd only keep the one copy of each picture although he'd make prints for me if I wanted. He swore he never showed his collection to anybody else. He hoped I'd be sympathetic since he couldn't help being the way he was."

"What did you do?"

"Nothing. What could I do? I or any of those other girls—what could we do?" She moved closer. "I felt dirty for a long time."

"You feel all right to me," I said, maybe a bit roughly.

"Are you angry?"

"Yeah, I'm angry." I held her more tightly. "When this is over, why don't we go by New York together and I'll have a talk with your collector."

"You'd hurt him?"

"I would and I'd burn his collection. Probably on his stomach. Nobody pulls stunts like that on a lady friend of mine."

"I don't want him hurt, although I would like those pictures destroyed." She drew away so she could look into my eyes. "But don't think you have to do anything because we've made love. I wouldn't have told you about him, if you hadn't said what you did about a tough crowd. You understand?"

"Lady, I don't hardly understand nothing, but I'm certainly not complaining." I bent and nibbled softly at the handiest nipple. "Let's not forget what we're here for."

She sighed with contentment and began to stroke me.

Later on when we were quiet again, she said that this night was the first time she'd made love since her experience with the collector. Then she cried a little, but only easy painless tears and drifted off to sleep.

I carefully disengaged myself and found my cigarettes. I lit one and sat by the bed contemplating her. Her figure was as good as I'd thought from only seeing her fully clothed. Firm, wide spaced breasts, slender waist, and just enough hips. She lay peacefully on her side, her lips parted slightly, and her face that of a girl ten years younger. Her eyebrows no longer seemed heavy when she slept.

I felt much as I had once when an Armored Personnel Carrier I'd been in had rolled over a medium-sized mine. Three others had been killed, but I'd crawled out of the tipped over vehicle unhurt except for being temporarily deaf as a stump.

It was the same as then. I was surprised but I knew what had happened and my surroundings were suddenly and queerly altered.

It was hard to figure out whether I was a dashing ladies' man or some kind of therapy. She was a complicated girl, with a sweeter, more vulnerable side to her than I had imagined.

The memory of Nelida came to me. That offered complications I didn't want to cope with.

26

SUSAN WAS GONE WHEN FROM LONG HABIT I WOKE AT six. I regretted her absence to the point of considering stealing across the hall but decided that could be pushing my luck too far. So I lay in bed until breakfast time and thought about other matters—mainly Brother Bernardo and Grey. It still bothered me that Grey had known Susan had visited Don Jaime.

Susan came into the dining room when I was on my second cup of coffee. I stood while Claudio seated her. She smiled and wished me a cheerful good morning but there was no little kiss or squeeze of the hand. "That was a nice night, Clancy," she remarked casually.

"It was. Very."

"Would you please tell Claudio that I'd like some scrambled eggs and toast in addition to the usual? I'm a little hungry this morning."

I did as asked. "You're a disconcerting girl," I told her.

"I intend to be."

She waited until her orange juice had been served before speaking again. "Yes, that was a nice night, and I for one hope it's not the last, but—"

"You are not alone in that sentiment," I said quickly, wanting to get that on the record.

She laughed ruefully. "Sometimes I think I need a keeper. After experiencing a sick-headed do-it-yourself dirty picture collector I take up with the likes of you. It's been propinquity and special circumstances and your not being completely awful the way you should have been. Yes, for some damn reason I like you and I liked going to bed with you and I will again, but I want to make one thing plain. I stay my own person with my own beliefs and ideas."

I had a stroke of inspiration. "You mean, you stay Mizz Allgood? That's fine by me." The sight of her composedly drinking orange juice against the memories of the night disposed me to go along with damn near anything.

She narrowed her eyes at me. "I don't think for a second you really mean that, but you said so and you'll remember it. I believe you stand by what you say whether you mean it or not."

Claudio entered and served her eggs. It occurred to me she was right. I did pay attention to the literal letter of what I promised or said.

"What's on the program for today?" she asked.

"I think you'd better plan on looking at pictures in the visitors' room this afternoon. I'll set up this show I've been promising the monks. Come along with me this morning. I'll get out at San Ildefonso; you go on to Toledo and see Don Jaime again. Give him a full report and ask him if the Spanish Army has good archives and if so could he get into them. Specifically I need to know if he could see the files of the operation reports of the Army of Africa when it was getting close to relieving the *alcazar* in September of 1936."

"You're wondering if any of those will mention finding a monk near San Ildefonso?"

"Something like that. If Franco's troops killed a monk I

doubt they'd have reported it, but they might report a dead one that somebody else killed. For that matter, ask Don Jaime if the Republican Army records are still in existence, too."

"This sounds as if you're snatching at straws, Clancy."

"I'll know better after I look at the annals and see if I can get Fernando to talk. Come back to the monastery around three and I'll have all sorts of pictures for you to be expert about in the visitors' room. You'll have a lovely time."

She gave a small, amused snort. "What do I do if I run into Grey or Dick and Elaine?"

"If they have anything to say, listen. Tell them you passed Grey's message to me and that I may be in touch. But be careful. Stick to busy streets and don't let anybody take you to see some sights the tourists usually miss."

"Oh, come now."

"It's possible, Susan. This damn Grey could try something. He heard enough over that blasted bug at the café to whet his appetite and he won't know that we're sort of floundering at the moment."

"I'm not so sure we're floundering. I'm hopeful."

"Hold the thought."

I excused myself before she finished, saying we'd meet at the car, and went out to where Luis waited with the Landrover by the fountain before the main door. The morning was bright and cool. There were a few puffs of good-weather cumulus in the sky—the sky that was nearly the other worldly blue as the skies in some of the El Grecos we'd seen in the Prado.

Luis wished me a warm "Buenos dias," as I came up. I returned the greetings in kind.

"Luis," I said. "There's one thing I need to know. How do you report to Señor Ortega?"

Embarrassment showed on his mobile face. "I telephone, señor. The man who saw me in Madrid gave me a telephone number to call there, and when I told them we were coming here and would probably be going to Toledo, they gave me another number in Toledo."

"Did the man who talked to you in Madrid show you any identification?"

"Sí, señor. He had a police card."

"When you telephone, do you talk to Señor Ortega?"

"Oh, no. One of his men only. The Seguridad Nacional has many men."

"Did you make a report yesterday when you went to Toledo?"

"Sí, señor. As soon as I returned to the city from taking you to the monastery. Señor, you said I should make these reports."

"I did and I meant it. Would you make a late report for me?"

He frowned. "I'm not sure I understand."

"Today, you'll take me to San Ildefonso and then go again to Toledo with the señorita. You'll probably leave Toledo around two-thirty. Don't call until just before then. Tell them everything but say you were unable to call earlier for some reason or other. Will you do this?"

He grinned. "Certainly, señor. With the greatest of pleasure." Luis had no compunctions about making a late report to the police.

"Thanks very much, Luis. No need to mention anything to the señorita."

I hadn't told her that Luis was supposed to be reporting to Ortega's police with my full knowledge and approval. I sure as hell wasn't going to tell her that I had a strong hunch those reports were going to Grey and not Ortega. It could be I had overestimated the importance Ortega would place on keeping track of our movements for his French colleagues. It also could be I didn't have the talents needed for this kind of work.

27

NOT HAVING GOTTEN AROUND TO IT THE NIGHT
before what with one thing and another, during the ride to the
monastery Susan went hastily through the remainder of the list
of San Ildefonso pictures and checked another ten prospects. I
told her I'd pick out five to add to the others for her
consideration and tactfully expressed a profound hope she
wouldn't abuse anyone when she saw the condition of some of
the paintings. She said she wouldn't. "Suppose none of them is
worth buying?" she asked.

"We'll take between eight and ten no matter what, and
pay ten thousand. A couple or three really look pretty good to
me, but I admit the rest aren't great art, so just pick the least
bad. It isn't so much that we're buying pictures as we are a
wine press. According to a man who should know, those run
about eight thousand and up."

"You're pretty careless with your employer's money."

"I saved him twenty-five thousand on the Monet and
Pissarro, so he shouldn't be too cross."

At the monastery she bade me a cheery goodbye and
waved as she and Luis drove off. I looked after them several
seconds, scratched my head, and walked to the portal.

Fernando, Diego, and I checked out the paintings Susan
had marked and I picked five as planned. We discussed the
staging of the show for Susan and Fernando made Diego

responsible for cleaning frames and carrying all pictures to the visitors' room and dubiously told him that he would assist as picture mover when the big moment came. After Diego scurried off, bright pink with excitement, Fernando said, "I hadn't the heart not to let him help, but his confessor is probably going to be plagued with tales of evil thoughts. Well, his devotion should be tested."

There was over an hour before lunch. "May I look in the annals, Fernando?" I asked.

"Of course." He showed me the proper drawers and left me to it.

The annals weren't quite what I expected. They were merely summaries of events, written every Friday and covering the previous week. I started back before Bernardo came to San Ildefonso to get the feel of what was usually written. I found bald, concise accounts of how many travelers passed and were fed and housed—at that time the Roman road must still have been heavily used—and what the weather was like. If an important visitor came by or if a monk took his vows or died that too was mentioned.

When Bernardo took over, as might be expected the weekly summaries became longer and more detailed. Sick monks, not just the ones who died, were now mentioned together with their probable ailment, and in many cases the names and home towns of the now few travelers were given. But it was still an unembroidered story of events important only to San Ildefonso.

I skipped to 1936. In the first months, the annals continued in the same homely vein, with no reference to anything outside the monastery until in early April when there was a remark about new government restrictions on religious houses. Then for the last week in that month there was a line that because of the riots in Madrid when four churches had been sacked by a mob, all week the prior had led the community in prayer that the misled people of Madrid should abandon the Devil's work.

During May, June, and early July the outside world continued to intrude into the annals with several notes of some new government decrees about Church lands or schools or monasteries.

There was a special entry for 18 July, the first entry made for a single day that I'd seen. "A crusade has started," it said. Just that and nothing more. That was the day the generals led over half the Spanish Army into rebellion and the Civil War began. It wasn't hard to see which side Bernardo favored.

There was another single-day entry on the next to last day of August. The first government foraging party had come by and taken some wine and stored food for the government troops besieging the *alcazar*. Bernardo made no direct editorial comment, but he did add a statement that one of the soldiers had said gasoline was being sprayed on the *alcazar* to burn out "the brave defenders."

For the week ending 5 September, Bernardo made the second statement about the war that had no relation to San Ildefonso. After the usual summary, he'd written, "We hear the soldiers of the Cross are in Talavera de la Reina, only seventy kilometers away." Calling Franco's Foreign Legion and Moorish troops, "soldiers of the Cross" seemed to be stretching things, but I could sympathize with poor Bernardo.

In the next weekly summaries, more foraging parties were described.

Finally, on 20 September there was another single-day entry. "Anarchist Assault Guards came and took all of our draft animals and cows, all of the wine, and most of the food. Their leader threatened to take the holy objects and our few treasures because there was not enough wine. The Spirit of

Barcelona has come to San Ildefonso." The word Barcelona was blotted. Bernardo's beautiful handwriting had failed him for the first time. It was the last entry he made in the annals.

The next was for 3 October and began by stating that the annals had not been written the previous week due to "the loss of Brother Bernardo." The writing was freer, still easy to read but with nothing of Bernardo's penmanship. There was no mention of the relief of the *alcazar* which had taken place on September 26. Brother Fernando had taken over as librarian.

I went rapidly through another couple of months. There was no further mention of Bernardo or any reference to the war. I restored the folders to their drawer and leaned back in the chair I'd pulled up to the cabinet.

Fernando spoke from his desk behind me. "Did you find what you were looking for, Señor Clancy?"

"Partly," I said, twisting my chair around so I could see him. He was looking more owlish than the norm. "Would you tell me about Brother Bernardo?"

He smiled sadly. "That's what I thought you were looking for. The prior told me that he'd talked with you of Bernardo."

I pointed around at the cabinets. "I can't help wondering about the man who did what I've seen here."

"He was a very fine man who had suffered a deep wound, not in his flesh. That wound had crippled him for life in the greater world but within these walls it didn't hamper him. It even may have made him a better brother to us all. He was odd, yes, and he so wanted to have all things neatly ordered, but he was also kind and good." His eyes went to the cabinets that held the inventory. "I have no doubt that he has gently badgered someone—one of the Archangels probably—into allowing him to make a proper inventory of Heaven and he is contentedly working on it now, putting numbers on everything, and seeing that there is a chest for every window and all the pictures are straight on the walls."

"A chest for every window?"

He chuckled. "Yes, it was very typical of Bernardo. You've certainly seen the many chests in the monastery. Most of them were placed by Bernardo. Of course, before him there had been chests around, some to keep things in, some simply because once they'd been put down they just were never moved. In the main hall there was a chest in every window bay but three. Bernardo was as bothered as if there'd been three of his teeth missing, so he found three chests and put them in the empty bays. That got him started on finding suitable chests for all the other windows. We used to tease him about it. That was one of his projects I did finish for him."

"You mean you put chests in the rest of the window bays?"

"There weren't many left unfilled, and it didn't seem right for me to work on his inventory."

Fernando was the one who'd moved the El Greco chest to the visitors' room and he had surely moved it empty.

"I can see you were fond of Bernardo," I said.

Fernando nodded. "I spent five years with him when I was young and will not forget him." He regarded me appraisingly. "The prior said that he thought your life had inclined you to discipline and to following and setting an example."

I coughed. "I was a soldier until not too long ago."

"That would be it."

"The prior told me that some of the monks here thought Bernardo might have gone to join Franco's Army," I ventured.

Fernando shook his head. "They were mistaken. I know he intended to come back. You see, he'd given me something and then had to take it back."

"Given you something?"

"Yes. The afternoon of the day he disappeared, I was working in the library on my translation when he came in and gave me a very nice box. As monks we don't own anything, but each of us has some things to use while he lives. Bernardo joked that I always had a clutter of pens and pencils around me when I worked and the box would do well to keep them in and make the library neater."

I licked my lips. "What kind of a box was it?"

"It was something he'd found while working on his inventory. It looked like ivory but carved in such a way you might have thought it was woven straw. Well, later that same day after Compline he came to me and asked if he might have it back for a while. He'd forgotten to measure it and put a label on it for his inventory. I went and got it, of course, and he smiled and thanked me and that was the last I saw of it or him." He sighed. "Since you first asked me about Bernardo, I've been casting back in my memory. I'm sure he meant to return the box to me."

"Did you tell the others about the box?"

"Oh, yes, but they said he hadn't been really himself for several days. Some Assault Guards had come and taken our animals and wine and most of our food. You probably read that in the annals."

"I did."

"Well, he was upset by that visit, but he kept on with his work and went for his walks and was nearly as cheerful as ever. If it hadn't been for one of the burros disappearing the same night as Bernardo, no one would have thought that nonsense of him going to the Army of Africa."

That was news. I asked, "One of the burros? The Assault Guards didn't take those?"

"They tried, but there mustn't have been enough of them

to control all the animals. Some of the burros wandered home a day or so later."

"Did the burro that was missing at the same time as Bernardo ever come back?"

"No, nor did we find any trace of it."

"Did Bernardo have any favorite places he went on his walks?"

Fernando shrugged. "He may have. He always went alone, so we don't know. The shepherds all knew him and they've said they would meet him almost anywhere within as much as seven or eight kilometers of San Ildefonso. We searched as well as we could. Not only was there much space to cover, but we weren't very strong. We had little food, you know. Eventually, we had to eat most of the poor burros who returned to us." He looked down at his ample form. "You would never believe how slender I was then."

"Thanks for telling me this. I am grateful, Fernando."

I had to work at being amiable during lunch. Those miniatures had gone out in the night with Bernardo and they could be damn near anywhere.

After lunch there was a final flurry of preparation for Susan's show. You'd have thought she was a visiting bishop. Fernando, Diego, the *Intendente* and I were all on hand to greet her when she and Luis drove up in the Landrover a little before three. Brother Anselmo was in the background, looking very black. Diego was sent to advise the prior of her arrival. He returned, panting, almost instantly and said the prior was on his way.

The prior arrived and welcomed Susan to San Ildefonso in stilted English which he abandoned as soon as the formalities were over. I served as interpreter for the rest of the ceremonies. I must say Susan did us proud. Even though the end result was a foregone conclusion, she went over those paintings as if they were being considered for the Prado. She even deployed her test gear on a few and did something to minuscule chips of paint carefully and imperceptibly excised from an edge of the canvas. Finally she picked eight as agreed and kept a straight face while I sat down and wrote a check on the Swiss account where most of Du Vigny's expense money was deposited. I started to give it to the prior but the *Intendente* neatly shortstopped it. He raised his eyebrows. "This is for the full amount, Señor Clancy. A much lesser sum would be a fine deposit. We still must get the permission of the Provincial General before we can turn over the paintings. That may take some time."

"I expected that. But if I pay all now, there'll be no need to worry about moving funds later. You might as well deposit the check. Any interest will be a contribution of my employer to San Ildefonso."

The prior gave me a look as close to the sardonic Spanish norm as I'd ever seen from him. Fernando carefully marked the backs of my purchases with a red crayon. Everybody but Diego, who was too shy, complimented and thanked Susan and me. Susan gracefully congratulated them on their collection and said she was looking forward to seeing more of the paintings since there could yet be items of value among them.

I told Fernando I'd be in Toledo on business the next day, so I might not be back to the monastery until the day following.

As Susan and I left, everybody in the group came to wave, including Anselmo. In the vehicle, Susan said, "There are as much as two thousand dollars worth of paintings in that lot. You got a great bargain."

28

AT THE PALACE I HAD THE DRINK TRAY SENT UP TO my room again. My afternoon conference with Susan was beginning to have the feel of a tradition.

I made us both long gin and tonics. As I handed Susan hers, I gave her a quick kiss on the forehead. First time I'd touched her that day, or anyway that day since very early in the morning.

"I must say you're not a clutcher," she observed.

"Yeah, I am. I just want to talk a while first."

"I suppose this restraint is one of your weapons."

"Us experts call them gambits."

"To hell with you, Clancy." She was smiling. "Why are you so gloomy?"

"Because I'm sure now those damn miniatures aren't in the monastery at all." I told her what I'd found in the annals and what Fernando had told me. She nearly spilled her drink when I hit the part about the ivory box which was satisfactory in a way.

"Poor Bernardo sounds like the kind of man psychiatrists write up in textbooks," I continued. "He was a basically nice guy, well-educated and probably with some training in business or government. I'd guess the latter from the look of those files of his. He had to have been religious to start with and something happened to him or his family during the various risings and riots in Barcelona to send him over the edge into mild insanity. Perhaps he had a sister who was a nun. Maybe he wandered around Spain a while, but he finally ended up at San Ildefonso and the monks took him in and patted him on his damaged head and put him to work doing something he was good at.

"When he'd finished organizing and filing and listing all the easy things he started on his inventory. He was well along on that when the Civil War broke. Events accelerated. The war surged up around the monastery, foraging parties came by and carried off anything they could use, and Bernardo, still making his methodical progress, hid the chest with the El Grecos.

"Crazy or not, he must have recognized what he'd found. He knew their value and he was afraid the Reds—dammit—the loyalists would come back and take the pictures for their own use. Instead of telling anyone at the monastery what he'd turned up, he decided to do something about the pictures himself. The prior and Fernando have convinced me Bernardo intended to come back to the monastery, so odds are he packed those pictures on the burro that night to take them somewhere to hide until it might be safe to announce the discovery."

Susan said, "And neither he nor the burro was ever seen again." Most of her elation of yesterday had evaporated, but she wasn't crushed, only wistful. "Do you think they're completely lost?"

"I don't know. It's hard to put yourself in the head of a schizophrenic monk, but for all his mental troubles Bernardo must have been capable of logical thought and action. I'm sure he wasn't going to try a long trip at night with a burro carrying millions of dollars worth of pictures through ground where patrols of two armies were roaming around.

"From taking all his lonesome walks, he knew the terrain around the monastery well. He must have planned to hide them somewhere not too far away because he wouldn't want to stay out very long."

"Planned to?" said Susan. "You think he might not have been able to?"

"Something might have gotten him a hundred yards from the monastery." I finished my drink. "Our last hope, I guess, is to find some indication in the old military files as to where he was headed. What did Don Jaime say about those? And about your finding the chest?"

"I don't know if you do it on purpose but it has a nice effect on me when you say 'your finding the chest.' I'll even fix the drinks this time. Give me your glass." She went to the drinks table. "Don Jaime was fascinated by what we'd turned up and he's willing to look through the Spanish Army archives, but he's not too hopeful there. He says the army archives are better organized than those at Simancas but the archivists are somewhat behind in their work. They've just finished putting the papers for the Second Carlist War in order and are getting ready to tackle the Spanish-American War records. He did say that a great many of the loyalist army files survived."

"That's a help. We'll go talk to Don Jaime tomorrow. Oh, cripes, I almost forgot. Did you see Grey or his two flower children?"

"No, not a sign of them."

"Good. Let that bum stew." My hunch about Luis reporting to Grey instead of Ortega had been buttressed. I figured Grey would have tried to get in touch with Susan if he'd known she were in Toledo.

She gave me my glass and an encouraging smile. "Cheer up, Clancy. How long will we keep looking?"

"A week, maybe. Depends on what Don Jaime may turn up."

"Where do you think Bernardo put them?"

"Damned if I know. I hope to God he didn't bury them or stick them in a cave. That wouldn't do them any good. He might have put them in some old abandoned farmhouse. The prior told me Bernardo was a good stone mason."

"I think he'd have put them someplace they'd be protected. Look how careful he was with those gunstones."

Both of us had come to talk of Bernardo as if he were someone we knew.

I sighed. "If we do tell people about what we've found out so far, I bet you see a search that will go down in the history of the province. They'll probably turn out the Guardia Civil and the army."

"Will you be sorry to lose your big bonus?"

"Hell, yes. Won't you?"

She made a small negative movement of her shoulders. "Yes, but my name will be made in the art business even if we have to give up hunting on our own and go to the authorities."

I wasn't so sure she was as philosophical as she seemed to be about our not finding the pictures all by ourselves.

That was borne out some hours later. I was browsing around her form, my mind on my work, when she sat bolt upright with no warning, nearly catapulting me out of bed onto the floor.

"The inventory!" she said. "He'd have put them in the inventory!"

"What the goddamn hell are you talking about?" I demanded not unreasonably.

"Bernardo! He was putting everything in his inventory. He would have put the pictures in there somewhere. He wanted Fernando's box back so he could measure it and label it for his inventory! Maybe he carried the pictures away, but he'd have listed them first and if he did he'd have said where he was going to take them!"

"Jesus H. McCarty Christ, woman! Are you so female-lib insensitive that—" Of course, Bernardo listed everything in his inventory.

I sat up too. "But the ivory box isn't there. I told you the last items on his inventory for that storeroom are the blasted chest and the gunstones. There's nothing about the ivory box or about the paintings."

"There wouldn't be! They weren't going to be in the storeroom any more. He was giving the box to Fernando and taking the paintings to hide! They're listed somewhere else in the inventory."

"My God! You're right!"

"Yes, I am. Let's go to the monastery tomorrow before we go to see Don Jaime."

"There's only one little problem. That bloody inventory of Bernardo's is like eight big drawers of handwritten Manhattan telephone books. It could take a little time to hunt down any listing of the pictures."

"No, it won't. They'll be the last item in some section. The last things he ever wrote down. Poor Bernardo."

She sighed and lay back down. "Where were you?"

I touched her stomach a short distance north of her belly button. "There. But, you dizzy dame, I'm going to have to start all over. Look at me. You all of a sudden screeching like that."

She purred like a hundred-and-twenty pound kitten and reached for me. "It won't take long."

29

NEXT MORNING, I TOLD LUIS THAT I'D DRIVE MYSELF and he could have the day off. If I really did turn up something in Bernardo's inventory, we might be able to make a quick check and if so, Luis's presence would be a handicap. When he looked hurt, I in turn tried to look embarrassed, which cheered him up. It's hard to keep secrets from valets and maids, so the domestic staff of the palace were probably aware of Susan's and my nighttime activities.

Susan had insisted on coming to wait at San Ildefonso. Out of consideration for Anselmo's feelings and because she said she'd be too nervous to sit inside, she waited in the Landrover.

I wasn't expected but Fernando and Diego were glad to see me anyway. Diego, all ready to spend another fascinating morning diving in and out of cabinets full of pictures, was saddened when I said I only wanted to check through the files again for some information on paintings.

For Fernando's benefit, I went first to the historical records; I didn't want to head straight for Bernardo's inventory, though I felt a twinge of guilt at staging a charade. I did about fifteen minutes of busywork and then had a stroke of luck. Fernando got up, saying it was time for him to do his weekly stint in the cloister garden and if I needed any help Diego knew his way around the archives fairly well.

As soon as Fernando left, I made for the cabinets that held Bernardo's masterwork. I recalled that Fernando had taken the folder with the index plan from the front of the first drawer and had no trouble finding it. I unfolded the three sheets with the small-scale floor plans hoping there'd be some inspiration there. There wasn't. Each held no more information than the designation of every room by a combination of letters and numbers, and nothing was written inside the covers of the folder.

There were literally hundreds of folders in the two four-drawer cabinets. If I had to go through those one by one, we'd have to send lunch and maybe dinner out to Susan.

I put back the index folder and riffled along the tops of the folders behind it. They were in alphabetical order according to the letters in the room designator and then in numerical order within that grouping. Very nice and systematic as I'd come to expect from Bernardo, but no help to me at the moment.

Somewhere in this mass of paper had to be a listing for an ivory box and a bunch of small paintings.

Just on a hope, I looked to see if there was a folder for "Fernando." There wasn't. I found there was a *Farmacia* and a *Forja*, or a Pharmacy and a Forge, but nothing for Fernando. There was no reason there should be. Nothing belonged to a monk. He had only things to use on loan. That rang a tiny bell and I tried looking under *Prestamos*, for Loans. There was a substantial folder there. I took it out and turned to the last sheet. Some of the entries had been neatly lined out. The item had been returned or the monk had died. The last item listed was: "P-721 (AL 1-I) Caja, aparentemente marfil, bien tallada. Hermano Fernando. 10x5x25."

Loan item number 721, from storeroom one on the first floor, was a box, apparently ivory and nicely carved, being held by Brother Fernando. The measurements had been added as an afterthought.

I dredged my mind for all the Spanish words I knew that meant anything like neighborhood, or nearby, or surroundings, or environs, or countryside. I felt a tinge of panic as I unsuccessfully went to where one after another should be found if there were a folder for it. Finally I tried Spanish synonyms for outside. The first one, *afueras*, was one more blank. The second, *exteriores*, was the right one. There was a folder there, a skinny folder.

I took the folder from the drawer, my hand trembling gently. It held a single page, headed "Piedra Cuadrada." There were four entries:

PC-1 Atado de cuadritos sobre madera. EG(?)
PC-2 Idem
PC-3 Idem
PC-4 Idem

PC-1 was a bundle of small paintings on wood, possibly done by EG: PCs 2, 3, and 4 were more of the same. The problem of what he'd found had pushed Bernardo out of his usual routine of counting and measuring. He'd corrected on the ivory box, but he didn't have time nor would it have been wise to open completely the four bundles of paintings. He'd probably only peeked in one and guessed at the others by feel.

I restored the page to its folder and the folder to its drawer. I pushed the drawer shut and sat back in my chair. Susan had been right. Now we had the name of the place where Bernardo had intended to take the paintings. Piedra Cuadrada, the Square Stone. The words in both languages sang in my head. My blood seemed to have turned to soda water.

Diego was working at what looked like overdue cards in the big room. I told him I had to leave but that I'd be back in a day or two and asked him to make my excuses to Fernando. I wished I could get Diego a gold rosary, or maybe a diamond one. Without a doubt he was the best novice I'd ever known in my life.

It was time to talk to Don Jaime. He was a historian and knew the area around Toledo, and he'd have maps.

Susan was walking up and down by the Landrover when I came out. She froze as I walked over. I nodded vigorously. She hugged herself and scrambled into the front seat.

She held control until I'd started up and backed to turn toward Toledo. "Clancy!" she said, sinking nails in my right knee.

"You hit it on the head. Bernardo put them in his inventory. They've got a page and a folder to themselves. There were four separate bundles, each, according to Bernardo, full of small paintings on wood. He thought they were by EG."

"Oh God. Where are they?"

"Some place called Piedra Cuadrada. That means Square Stone. I don't know where it is but—"

"What do you mean you don't know where it is!"

"You grab any harder and I'm going to bleed all over these trousers. Relax and I'll explain."

She let me go and hunched herself against the door. I recounted my clever hunt through the inventory. I concluded, "Don Jaime's our man, now. I was afraid to ask the monks about Piedra Cuadrada."

Susan said, "Clancy, we're going to find them. I know we will."

I didn't say any more about Bernardo maybe never having reached Piedra Cuadrada.

Don Jaime had been worried about our taking valuables from poor monks until I'd come up with the lucky idea that the pictures legally belonged to the non-occupied throne of Spain. I'd still worried about sneaking *El Espolio* or some other picture out of San Ildefonso, but now I didn't have to. By God, if anything we'd be restoring the pictures to the monks, and if I pinched one on the way I sure wasn't stealing from San Ildefonso. I contemplated that fact with pleasure.

Susan spoke abruptly. "Clancy, would you please stop for a bit?"

I glanced around. We were running through flat, open grazing land, with hardly a tree in sight. "We're only about fifteen minutes from Toledo," I said. "Could you wait—"

"It's not that, dammit. I want to talk to you before we see Don Jaime and I can't do it while you're driving. Please pull over." Her voice was serious.

I pulled off on the narrow shoulder and halted. She was getting out a cigarette and making quite a to-do of the process. I waited until she found one the right shape, tapped it and examined it for flaws. I lit it for her and lit one of my own.

"What can't you talk to me about while I'm driving?" I asked.

Her eyes had followed my lighter as I put it in my pocket. With an effort, she raised her gaze to mine. "My bonus," she said.

"Your bonus? That's up to Du Vigny but he'll—"

She shook her head. "I've told you, Clancy, that I liked you but that I stay my own person. It isn't money I want. I want an El Greco."

"An El Greco! That sounds like a half-million dollars or so of money to me!"

She shook her head again. "I don't want it for the money. I wouldn't sell it. I want it to keep—to have the way you say your Du Vigny wants to have the version of *El Espolio*. I want very much to have an El Greco. It doesn't have to be the best or the most famous, but I would like it to be in good condition so I could see it well."

"What in God's name will you do with it?"

"I'll look at it and I'll know I have it."

I took in a deep breath and let it out. I should have realized what would drive this girl more than anything else. "What will you do if I say no?"

"I'll tell the monks and I'll tell Ortega and I'll tell anyone who'll listen to me what we've found out. You have to promise right now that I can have an El Greco or you won't have one single chance of getting *El Espolio* or any other picture." Her tone was high and shaky. She'd had to nerve herself up to this.

I pulled at an ear. "You may be part of the new enlightenment but you are as nutty as the most unliberated female I have ever met."

Her voice became firmer. "I'm not nutty at all. There may be two hundred El Greco's in those four bundles. All I want is one! You're going to get one for Du—"

"That isn't what I mean. You don't really know me very well and if you'll think back a few days, your initial opinion of me was that I was a brute that shouldn't be allowed at large. What makes you think a slip of a girl can blackmail a brute?"

"It's not blackmail, it's only fair. I found the chest and I thought of the inventory last night and—"

I threw up my hands. "You miss the point, but okay! okay! you can have one of these as yet unlocated El Grecos!"

She batted her eyes rapidly. "I can? You promise?"

"I promise on my honor."

"Thank you, Clancy!"

"Don't thank me for something you've extorted. What else can I do but promise you one?"

"You could have been a lot uglier. Are you mad?"

"I ain't pleased. Have you been softening me up for this?"

"Now, that is ugly. I have not."

"Suppose I'd turned you down. Would you have gone to bed with me tonight?"

"Well, no, I probably wouldn't, but—" She fell silent.

"Yeah. Mull that over for a while, Mizz Allgood." I started the motor and we resumed our drive.

She gave the matter her attention until we were crossing the Roman bridge below Toledo. She said, "I might not have gone to bed with you tonight, but I probably would have tomorrow night."

That made me laugh halfway to the cathedral plaza. We were good friends as we started to walk to Don Jaime's house. No Grey nor Dick nor Elaine were in sight.

30

DON JAIME WAS NEARLY AS CONFIDENT AS SUSAN.
Only trouble was, he'd never heard of a place called Piedra
Cuadrada, nor could he find it in an hour's hunt over a couple
of fairly large-scale maps. "In a way, that's a good sign," he
said. "If it were well known that would mean many people
would have passed by or through it. The pictures might well
have been found."

He and I were speaking Spanish for ease of communication. Susan was listening, as bright-eyed as if she understood. I
hadn't told Don Jaime she might be getting a picture and I
didn't intend to until after the event.

"Have you given thought as to how you will take Du
Vigny's picture out of Spain?" he asked.

"Yes. I've seen some El Greco copies in the windows of
the souvenir shops. Would you please buy three or four for
me? On wood if they're available, and please get a receipt to
show any Customs people. I'll substitute Du Vigny's painting
for one of the copies."

He nodded. "That's a fine idea. You shouldn't have any
trouble at Customs either here or anywhere else if you have a
chance to leave before the discovery is announced."

"That's what I'm counting on. But, Don Jaime, we still
haven't found them." I was the only one who seemed to be
thinking about that.

He said, "I'll continue to work on my maps, but I think you would do better to ask a shepherd."

"Ask a shepherd?"

"That's right. You've seen them, certainly. They move their flocks around and they have only their dogs to talk to and nothing to occupy them other than to look at their sheep and the countryside. They know the ground they pass over as no one else does. A great many of the names on the land of Spain have been given by shepherds—not the names of mountains or rivers or towns, but of the small ridges, the brooks and the little folds in the earth. Drive over the tracks near the monastery and ask every shepherd you see."

That made excellent sense. I summarized our conversation for Susan. She wanted to leave immediately.

"Mind your manners," I said. "Finish your wine."

"Oh, no," said Don Jaime. "She is anxious to get on. Frankly, I also am eager. Please call me tonight and we'll exchange any discoveries. You needn't go into detail, but I will be happy to hear anything."

The fever had reached him hard. I borrowed one of his maps that included the area around San Ildefonso. He escorted us to the door and wished us all good luck.

As we walked up the Calle Sal, I saw only local inhabitants. I said to Susan, "We'll get some bread and cheese and wine and go call on shepherds. Okay?"

"For sure," she said, smiling all over her face.

When we came out of the network of narrow streets into the cathedral plaza, I saw Dick leaning against a front fender of our Landrover.

I swore under my breath. I'd thought that without Luis to call in a report Grey wouldn't have picked up our coming into town, but he may have put his pair on observation duty.

"What's that mean?" Susan asked.

"Some more pushing and shoving from Grey. We may have to do something about him."

"Clancy! You said—"

"No, no, I don't mean that. But, damn him, he could get underfoot if we try to move two paintings quietly out of Spain. Well, let's see what this lad has to offer."

Dick was staring idly off into space, but his eyes turned alert when we came into his field of view.

"Hi," he said. "You've been a long time there, Major."

"That so?"

"Yeah, it is. Arthur'd like to see you."

"Sorry. We're in a hurry. Some other time."

Dick grinned through his sparse whiskers. "Arthur thought you might say that, so he gave me a note." He took a folded piece of paper from his shoulder bag and passed it over. On the outside was my name and old rank. I opened it and read:

Dear Major Clancy—

I do believe we should have another talk. There are some factors of which you may not be aware. One of them is the whereabouts of your attractive Paraguayan friend, Miss Nelida González.

I'd like to meet you at the café on the Zocodover where we last talked. Might be less embarrassing if you came alone, but that's up to you.

Yours,
Arthur Grey

I looked back up at Dick. He moved away a pace and said rapidly, "Man, like I just carry the notes. That's all I do."

"Where's Grey."

"He's around. You go to the place in the Zocodover and he'll meet you there, you know."

Nelida was smart as hell about many things but it wouldn't have been hard to convince her that I'd sent for her to come to Spain.

"Tell Grey I'm on the way," I said to Dick. He nodded and strolled off.

"Something's the matter," Susan said.

"Yeah. I have to see Grey. I'm not sure what the hell is going on. Please wait here and—no. Better you go back to Don Jaime's and wait there. You know the way?"

"Yes. Clancy, your expression when you read that note." She bit her lip. "Can I help?"

I dredged up a smile for her. "Just go to Don Jaime's. Stick to the traveled streets. Don't wander. I shouldn't be more than an hour."

She patted my arm and turned. I watched her start across the plaza and headed myself for the Zocodover.

Grey wasn't in sight when I got to the café ten minutes later. I picked a table at the end of a row with no one sitting nearby. For appearance's sake I ordered a beer.

Grey could have bought someone in Asunción. Carlos, the Argentine, wouldn't have come too high. If Carlos had showed up one morning with a telegram supposedly from me and an airline ticket and some tale about Du Vigny paying, Nelida would have packed in five minutes. She'd always wanted to fly in an airplane and a chance to see the Madre Patria would have been a prospect so glittering she wouldn't have examined it at all. If somebody had met her at Barajas, she'd have followed them without question.

Goddammit, I'd thought about Grey making a move to take Susan. I'd never thought of him taking Nelida. Paraguay was so far away.

I looked at my watch. Grey should arrive any minute, and I had to put my head in order. There was one thing I had going for me—he was a cheat and I wasn't. There should be another.

Ten minutes passed and no Grey. I made a move to rise and indecision gripped me like sudden nausea. I forced myself back in my chair. I'd give him five more minutes.

He came inside of three. I saw him walking across the small, irregular plaza. A Polaroid camera case was slung over one shoulder.

He took the chair opposite. "Good morning, Major. Drove yourself today, I see."

"Yeah."

"Could it be that you've twigged your driver who was calling in to us? Or rather not us, but to a Spanish agency I've dealt with before. They think you and Mizz Allgood are a divorce case."

"What's this about Nelida?"

"Let me put your mind at ease on that count, old man. Far as I know, Miss González is well and happy in Asunción. Have to confess we've run a trick on you." He reached into a side pocket and drew out a photograph. "Take a dekko at this."

It was a Polaroid color snapshot showing Susan getting into a Landrover, not ours. Elaine was standing close beside her, her hand inside her shoulder bag. I couldn't make out who was driving. There was enough background to show that it was the cathedral plaza.

"That's right," said Grey. "We don't have Miss González, but we do have Miss Allgood. She'll be quite comfortable, I assure you."

I'd been double-bluffed. The snapshot I held shook. I looked back at Grey.

"Easy there," he said quickly. "We're in a public place." A waiter came up and Grey ordered a beer. We both were silent until it was served.

Grey said, "I really regret this, but you should put yourself in my position. You'll recall that other little trick I played the last time we talked at this café?"

"The bug under the table?"

"Actually what you discovered wasn't a bug, old man. That was just a decoy. The real bug was under my chair. It's a normal technique and I confess not my own invention. One puts a dummy out for the subject to find if he looks and hides the real thing a bit better. Doesn't always work but it's often helpful, and frequently permits you to recover the real bug. If, as you said, you know where you can buy a real bug for a hundred dollars I'd appreciate your telling me. I have to pay the world for these things."

"Get on with it."

"Yes. You were right that I don't know Raspière, but I do have a friend in the Quai d'Orfèvres who got me Xerox copies of your and Du Vigny's dossiers. Had to pay for those, too. Well, it's pretty plain you and Mizz Allgood are on to something rather large. In Du Vigny's dossier there's mention of him and his pal Don Jaime doing some research together. Awfully thorough the French. There's even copies of letters Du Vigny wrote to the present Duke of Rivoli, the descendant of Napoleon's Marshal Masséna. I wouldn't be at all surprised if you weren't scouting around that monastery for an El Greco. The Toledo scene, you know. Care to comment?"

"No."

"Um. Could be mistaken, but I don't think so." He was enjoying himself. "Anyway, yesterday when your driver called in late, I reckoned you were beginning to take precautions. So—and I assure you it was with reluctance—I set up this little scheme this morning. The three of us have been on the main gates into town since seven o'clock." He said this last as if to show me how serious he was.

I kept my face still by setting my teeth until they ached, but something must have showed because his eyes flickered. He might be having fun but he had to use willpower to keep looking at me.

He continued in a reasoning voice, "Now what I propose is this. Let's join forces. Surely in an El Greco—or whatever it is—there should be enough to make nice shares for all. And I can pull my weight you know. I've had experience moving and selling pictures and I'm sure you won't regret my help. May even come to thank your lucky stars."

"And Mizz Allgood?"

"Think she's better where she is for the present. I can bring you photos every day to prove she's in fine health and being nicely cared for. Which I promise you she will be. Up to a point, if you take my meaning."

He had no more than a glimmering of what we were after. That would help.

He sipped at his beer. "Well, what do you say, Major?"

I leaned forward a few inches. "Fuck you, Grey," I said, speaking low but as hard as I could. "You've made a couple of mistakes. Listen closely. First, we're not looking for one El Greco, we're looking for between a hundred and fifty to two hundred El Grecos."

As briefly as I could, I told him the whole thing from Don Jaime's first message to my finding the paintings listed in Bernardo's inventory. I kept back only the name Piedra Cuadrada. While I talked sweat came out all over his face in small, shiny drops.

When I finished the story, I gave him no chance to speak. "Your second mistake was running this stunt today. You've got a copy of my dossier, you say. Then you know my background. You'll bring Susan to the Quintinar palace this afternoon. She can't be far, so you'll deliver her by six this evening. If you don't—from that minute on, you are my enemy. I'll drop looking for the pictures and I'll hunt you and I'll kill you. I won't talk, I won't dicker. I'll come for you and I'll kill you on sight, from ambush or by sniping or any way I can. And I'll do the same to your people—those two hippies and anybody else. You said you have experience in your line. You know I have experience in this line. If you deliver Susan by six, we'll talk about you participating in this operation. You know enough now to block it, so you'll be listened to and your ideas given due weight."

A drop of sweat fell from his chin. He cleared his throat. "You're taking a rather short view, I must—"

"We have nothing more to talk about, Grey." I stood up.

"Really, old man, sit down and drink your beer. Six o'clock is rather soon."

"I don't drink with a man I'm going to kill. Six o'clock." I walked away.

I was taking a risk with Susan and I was doing the best I could for her and I was trying to keep some promises. I cursed myself for not having convoyed her back to Don Jaime's.

A pair of tourists gave me puzzled looks. I rubbed my hand over my face.

I made good time on the drive back to the palace. I told Claudio that Señorita Allgood had stayed in town but would be returning around six, probably with another gentleman. I hoped to Christ I was telling the truth. "Is there a gun room in the palace, Claudio?" I asked.

There was. I said I'd meet him there as soon as I made a phone call. He explained how to find the gun room and went to get the keys. I called the Hotel Gondomar in Madrid. Patricio was pitifully glad to hear my voice. I told him to hire a car and come to the palace with his cousin Ricardo. Patricio wanted to talk more, but after giving him directions, I cut him short.

In the gun room I told Claudio that Patricio and Ricardo would arrive sometime in the evening and asked that quarters and rations be provided. I asked him please to send some sandwiches to me there in the gun room. It was a quarter to one.

Claudio had unlocked all the cabinets and drawers. There were plenty of long weapons for hunting all kinds of game, and some were suitable for what I had in mind. The only pistols were various models of .22's except for one pair of target .32's which I could use though I'd have preferred something heavier. There was a Belgian rifle chambered for .220 Swift and mounting a 4x scope that would come in handy, and a .410 double-barrelled shotgun that could be cut down. The ammunition drawers held plenty of anything I'd need, including slugs for the shotgun and hollowpoints for the rifle. Apparently when the Conde hit a deer he didn't want it to get up and stagger off.

I checked over the pieces and ate a couple of sandwiches without tasting them. When Claudio came to see if I wanted anything else, I asked if there were a place where I could do some practice firing. He had a gardener take me outside to a sort of scratch 100 meter range. The backstop was low but sufficient. I zeroed in the Belgian rifle, adjusting the scope so that the center of impact at 100 meters was about four inches above my point of aim. That should give a hit on a man's body anywhere out to 500 meters. It was a well-made weapon; the groups I got were all less than three inches across.

I had the gardener hunt me out a hacksaw. I went back to the gun room and cleaned the rifle. Then I wedged the .410 between a couple of tables and cut down the barrels and the stock. If I'd not had other things to think about I'd have been ashamed of myself.

I cleaned up the mess and was smoking a cigarette when Claudio came in and my heart almost stopped. He said a gentleman was on the telephone for me but did not care to give his name. I told him to tell the gentleman I was taking no calls from him.

I sat by the window in the gun room and smoked. Pictures of Susan came to me—of her in bed and glad to be there and out of bed and hunting for El Grecos and playing cribbage and chess and hating it when she lost. Pictures of Nelida came, too—also in bed and also out, bustling around the chalet or sitting sewing, which she could do by the hour. Mostly the pictures were of Susan.

The minutes dragged by like hurt bugs. I considered ways to hunt and kill Grey and his people. I'd turn the cops on him if I had to, but if I sent the cops too quick I might have to kill him in jail. On the other hand he might get out of the country. If he killed Susan, he'd probably get Piedra Cuadrada out of her first, and he'd sure make at least one try to get there. If he didn't show by six I'd take Patricio and Ricardo as soon as they arrived and we'd find Piedra Cuadrada and stake it out. Paraguayans are among the best natural scouts in the world and I'd had plenty of training and experience. If I didn't get him at Piedra Cuadrada, I'd turn the police on him in Spain and go to England to hunt.

I still had plenty for expenses and if I needed more Du Vigny would send it.

I wanted Susan back.

The time reached and passed five o'clock.

Claudio came in again. He could be coming to tell me that Patricio and Ricardo had arrived. He said, "Señorita

Allgood and the gentleman you mentioned are here. They're waiting for you in the reception room off the big hall."

I thanked him and said I'd go there directly. After he closed the door, I made a noise. It could have been a sob. It hurt my throat. I had to sit for a minute to let the tension leave me. I stood stiffly, the muscles in my back and stomach sore, and stuck one of the .32's in my belt under my coat.

31

WHEN I WALKED INTO THE RECEPTION ROOM, SUSAN was sitting on a spindly chair. Grey was standing in an opposite corner watching the door. His eyes went to my hands.

Susan rose and walked toward me. I took her by the shoulders. She looked all right except for being pale and her eyes were a darker blue than normal. I shook her gently and said, "Glad to have you back, Susan. You didn't have to wait here with this animal, you know."

"You're right. I hadn't thought of it."

"Did you have a bad time?"

"Not terribly. I was frightened, of course. It was so silly at first. I barely got across the plaza when Elaine called me. I didn't think she was a menace, so I waited for her. She asked me what was going on, saying Dick hadn't told her. We must have talked for a couple of minutes when Dick drove up in a Landrover. Then Elaine showed me a small gun in her bag and told me to get in the car. I probably should have screamed or something but it simply didn't occur to me. I got into the Landrover and they took me away. Once we were outside the town, Elaine blindfolded me. We ended up in some house, where, I have no idea except it's about an hour's drive from Toledo, and they locked me in a room."

She looked over at Grey. That bastard was listening to her

with an expression of concern and sympathy, as if he were hearing the story for the first time.

"Then he came around one o'clock," she said. "I could hear him. There was an argument, I think, but they kept their voices down and I couldn't hear well. Once he telephoned—I think it was here, because although he was speaking Spanish, I could tell he was asking for you. Was it here?"

"Yeah."

"But you didn't come to the phone. Weren't you here?"

"Yeah, I was."

"Oh. Well, a little later Grey let me out and said there'd been a terrible mistake and he'd take me to the palace. So we got back in the Landrover and he brought me here. I had to wear a blindfold again for half an hour or so, but he let me put it on myself. Nobody came with us."

Claudio led in a maid with a tray of drinkables. I hadn't told him not to and there was a guest on the premises.

"Are you hungry?" I asked Susan.

"Very. Dick and Elaine offered me some food but I didn't want to eat."

"Care to have something brought here while I talk to Grey or would you rather have it somewhere else?"

"Somewhere else. In the sitting room."

I gave instructions to Claudio and she followed him out. I turned to Grey.

"Well, well," he said. "Here we are, aren't we. Handsome old place this."

The son of a bitch had kidnapped my girl and stirred me up to going back to war again, and now he was behaving as if we were getting ready to sit down for a jolly chat. I sighed. It was good that Susan was with me and that I wasn't going to have to spend what could have been a short rest of my life

227

finding and killing Grey and a couple of more other people.

"You're right," I said. "We're here."

He sighed too. "Right off, Major, I want to apologize for this business with your young lady. I acted hastily because obviously you were paying scarcely any attention to me and I was frustratingly unsure as to what you were up to. Let me say I think you handled the matter rather well. Quite petrified me when you laid out the full size of the affair, and you were most convincing in your hunting down and killing speech. Most."

I squinted at him. "Grey, you'd do better to let that lie."

"Um. Just in passing, I am expected to show at my place by a certain time or some word will have to be given to the Guardia Civil. Feel sure that comes as no news."

"What do you figure to make out of this?" I asked.

He looked around at the drink tray. "I say, before we get into that, I'd be very grateful for a drink. Would you mind?"

I would mind but I wanted a drink myself. I jerked a thumb at the drink tray and he fixed a whisky and water. I made one of the same.

"Cheers," he said. Ah, the hell with it. I made a motion with my glass. Grey broke into what seemed to be a wide, honest smile which surprised me a moment. He was pleased because I'd told him at the café I wouldn't drink with a man I was going to kill. It gave me a warm feeling to know he was afraid of me. We both sat down.

"Needed that," he said. "To tell you the truth, Major, all along I'd thought I would expect something like, oh, say, a third part in whatever you had in hand. Now I recognize that may sound a little extreme. Still, as I said, I can be a real help. Mean no criticism, but I reckon you could be taking on something you're not familiar with and might need a knowledgeable man about."

"I've got Susan."

"Certainly. Hayden told me about her. No doubt about her extraordinary technical qualifications but I don't believe she's quite the person for this sort of thing."

I raised my eyebrows. "What would you provide other than keeping quiet?"

He became animated. "You may have thought of this, but I most strongly advise that we leave a good many of these paintings right where we find them and arrange for their discovery by others—the monks for example. The stir that it will cause around the art world will be tremendous. It would be a terrible mistake to carry off all the pictures because then the only way we could authenticate them would be by getting some recognized expert in and lads like that who can be trusted are few and expensive. As soon as there's enough of a brouhaha going, we could sell the ones we keep through my contacts. And I have some very good ones, I promise you. That's the sort of thing I can provide."

I nodded. "You're right about not taking them all, but I have a different proposition. Susan and I have our own channels for disposing of the pictures we take. She and I will take our paintings, give you an equal share and we'll all go our separate ways. What you do with yours is up to you. What we do with ours is up to us."

His tongue went over his lips. "You mean I'd get the same number of paintings as you and Mizz Allgood?"

"Yeah."

"The same as both of you together?" The cheat that lived behind his eyes looked out at me.

"Hell, no. The same number that each of us does. A three-way split."

He swallowed. "That's quite fair. How many paintings would that be in all?"

"I can't say until we find them. We know where Bernardo

went to hide them, but we haven't been there yet. You screwed that up. So we don't know what condition they're in. Once Susan examines them we'll be able to say how many we take."

"What about Don Jaime?"

"He'll be our problem."

He took a long swallow of his drink. "Do you have any thoughts as to how we go about finding the paintings and making our division?"

"I do. Come back tomorrow early and we'll go to the place where Bernardo took the paintings. We may have to spend more than a day finding the actual hiding place. Then there'll be the condition of the pictures to be considered. After that we'll talk split. Oh, you'll have to come here alone."

"I'm to go out on this chase alone with you and Mizz Allgood?"

"Not exactly. I have two Paraguayan gunmen coming in tonight. They'll be with us."

"Now, see here, old man. You could scarcely expect me to go off into the countryside alone with just you and Mizz Allgood much less with two hired thugs of yours."

"That's just what I do expect if you want to come along. Grey, you're the one who's been playing the joker, not me. You're in this operation now and I give you my word nothing will happen to you if you play square from here on. There it is. Of course, you don't have to come. You can wait around Toledo and you'll still get your one-third share."

He rubbed his chin. "Major Clancy, you give new meaning to the phrase 'catch a Tartar.'"

"Look, you can do the same as you've done now—leave word with that pretty pair of yours to run for the Guardia if you don't check back within a reasonable time."

"That still leaves me on a very sticky wicket."

I hadn't thought Englishmen really said those things. "Goddamnit, Grey, you are potentially much richer this evening than you were this morning and you got that way by behaving like a half-smart bastard. You've got nothing to complain about. I'll have some rations packed up to take along. Pretend it's a picnic outing mixed up with a treasure hunt."

"I'll try to do that."

"Do your hired help know what we're after?"

"Good God, no!"

"I thought that kind scorned establishment value objects such as money and Old Masters in their search for a more rewarding life style."

"I am not about to test the strength of their convictions. I'm paying them well and they seem quite happy to take it."

"How'd you come to pick them up?"

"They moved some drugs for a fellow I know in London and he recommended them. They've been satisfactory, but they're a bit nerveracking at times."

"Elaine seems to be able to handle firearms."

"Very strange girl. She has one of those pornographic manuals you can buy in Denmark and she and Dick are working through it page by page."

There the two of us were, deploring the decaying standards of the younger generation. In spite of neither trusting the other, a minor rapport was forming between us. Not that it would last when Grey learned his third-part share amounted to one picture.

He looked at his watch. "I'd better be getting on. Here's to success." He finished his drink.

"I'll expect you tomorrow around nine, then."

"Right." He stood. "Apologies all round again. Er—care to shake hands?"

"Okay." We did. I was surely as sincere as he was.

I saw him to the door and watched as he drove away. Not out of courtesy but to keep an eye on him.

I STARTED TO JOIN SUSAN BUT CLAUDIO INTERCEPTED
me. He said Patricio and Ricardo had arrived and were waiting
for me in the servants' wing. I asked him to show the way. He
led me through a door in the back of the main hall.

The Conde's servants were not housed with the seedy
grandeur of his guests, but they sure had a lot of space. There
were rooms and dark corridors all over the place. The heart of
the servants' area was a wide, square kitchen with a tremendous stove. It was filled with activity and people I'd never seen
before. Tables ran all along one side and sitting at one, looking
around out of the corner of their eyes, were Patricio and
Ricardo.

They were certainly completely stunned by their surroundings but being Paraguayan they'd be eternally damned
before they'd show it, especially in front of a bunch of Spanish
strangers.

They were getting a fair amount of attention themselves.
Some housemaids and a couple of other girls dressed for
kitchen work were inspecting them covertly. The two cousins
were different from the Spanish type, being short, square, and
compact, with the swarthy complexion that came from the
Guarani blood.

They were sincerely glad to see me. Patricio gave me a
full *abrazo* and Ricardo who did not share a name-day with

me, gave a half *abrazo*. They both burst into Guarani to tell me about their trip from Asunción to Madrid and what they thought of Madrid and my God they were sick of always staying around the hotel and who owned this place and what did I want them for. I let them rattle on for ten minutes, not understanding it all because Guarani is a tough language, and answering as many questions as I could.

Finally I held up my hands. I wanted to get back to Susan. "*Xamigos*, I can't stay right now. Claudio will give you rooms and food and tomorrow morning we'll have a longer talk. Do you have weapons?"

"*Nahaniri*," said Patricio. "The patrón said we could not carry them on the airplanes. The patrón said you would have guns for us if they were needed."

"I have them and they may be needed. Don't talk about guns with the people here, and be careful about putting hands on the girls. Customs are different in Spain. Get a good night's sleep."

"That's all we have been getting," grumbled Ricardo. "And, my God, the people here stay in bed every day until eight or even nine."

Neither turned a hair at the prospect of gun work. That's what they'd hired out for.

I left them content. They'd found me and I was their patrón in Spain and would take care of them and give them orders.

Before going back to the front of the palace I had a consultation with Claudio. I told him that the next day five of us would be going on a small expedition. I asked him to assemble a hefty picnic lunch, some equipment to include a couple each of shovels, picks, crowbars, flashlights, and a Coleman lantern if he had one, and finally, since one of our party might be camping out, rations and water for one man for five days in a separate basket or bundle. He nodded as if he got such requests every day and said he'd take care of it.

I found Susan in the small sitting room with the French paintings finishing a plate of chicken sandwiches and a bottle of rosé wine. The efficient Claudio had set out another supply of drinks. I was being spoiled by life at the palace.

I went to touch her again, but only to stroke her hair. She smiled at me—not a strong smile, but a smile. "What in the name of heaven happened today?" she asked.

I cleared the pistol I still had in my belt and stuck it back, and sat by her and told her. When I fell silent, she said she was ready for a drink and I fixed us both one.

"You know something, Clancy," she said, taking her glass, "it sounds as if you tossed my life on a scales and waited to see how it balanced."

"Not only your life."

"No, your own and several others. I wondered why you wouldn't talk to Grey when he called from wherever we were. You were just putting more pressure on him. I must say it worked. He's scared of you." She sipped at her drink. "I guess I am too, sometimes."

"There's no reason for you to be."

"I don't mean I'm scared you'll do anything to me. You like me. You must like your Paraguayan girl, too. When you read that note and then looked up at that creature, Dick, there was a time you scared me."

"Susan, I was mad."

"You came with me very quickly for caring as much as you obviously do for that Paraguayan girl."

"See here, Susan. Her name's Nelida and I'm not in love with her, but, yeah, I do like her and I am responsible for her. We are what they call companions in Paraguay. She doesn't think I should stay faithful when I'm away, and I don't believe

235

she thinks she has to either. Those are healthy country girls in Paraguay and when they itch, they scratch. And, if I may point out, I would probably have stayed faithful longer except—"

"Oh, shut up."

A pause ensued. I said, "For what's it's worth, I was madder when I found out Grey had you instead of Nelida."

"Great comfort that." She took a moody pull at her drink. "In New York, I'm careful not to go out alone at night in dangerous areas. If I come to Spain on a crooked mission for a thief and move into the bed of his hired killer assistant, I probably shouldn't be surprised when I'm kidnapped by a suave English something or other and his two dropout helpers."

"You still want your El Greco?" I asked.

"Yes, God help me, I do. Don't you want yours?"

"More now than ever. You'd better know that we can run into trouble. Grey's in now. He doesn't know that come what may, his share of the loot is going to be one El Greco. When he learns that, he's going to be severely disappointed and could well give us new problems. He might not. One El Greco can supply him a good few years' worth of whatever gives him his jollies."

"But you think he will do something."

"He's a hard man to figure. Full of tricks with electronic gadgets and Polaroid cameras, and very quick with a polished lie, but he doesn't have a hell of a lot of iron in him. This may seem a foolish question, but tell me, was Hayden the art dealer who took those fancy pictures of himself and you?"

She reddened. "Yes."

And she let Hayden arrange jobs for her. I found her at least as hard to understand at times as she did me. "I'm pretty sure Grey's telling the truth when he says he and Hayden worked together in the past. There's a flaw in each of them

and they'd get along well together. You can't ever be sure
what that kind will do."

"You think Grey's queer, too?"

"Not the way Hayden is, or maybe not even queer in a sex
way, he's simply cracked inside somehow or other. One thing I
know, he's a cheat, and I'm taking some precautions. Those
two Paraguayans I told you about arrived here this evening. I
called them down to help hunt Grey. I'll use them to copper
our bets."

"How?"

"It'll be easier for you if I don't say. You'll have to be a
part of everything that happens from now on, and if all you
have to worry about is being an art expert, things will be
simpler all round."

"You're not trying to put me in the helpless little woman
role, are you, Clancy?"

"There's a yell." She had her color back. I said, "Please
don't throw your glass at me, but you are a good, tough girl
and I'm glad you're on my side."

"I suppose this is the honeyed tongue of the Irish. So you
and me and Grey will all go out together tomorrow?"

"Yup, and talk to shepherds. Have another drink?"

She would. I made it for her and went to call Don Jaime.
When I told him we'd run into trouble which had blocked our
search for the day, his voice was full of unspoken questions. I
said I'd explain as soon as I could. He himself had found
nothing new about the place we were interested in.

I worried more than a little as to how I was going to break
the news to Don Jaime that as part of this day's work, I'd
promised away not one but two El Grecos.

Just before dinner damned if the Conde didn't call to
accept Du Vigny's offer for the Sisley and the two Morisots.
Thank God, he said there was no hurry in making final

arrangements and he hoped we were enjoying our stay at the palace.

Susan was quiet during the rest of the evening and went to bed early and alone. Said she was tired and I didn't press her.

Sometime after three, I heard my name being softly called. I came out of bed in a rush. There was enough light to see Susan standing inside the door, wearing a nightgown.

"I thought I'd better wake you from a distance," she said.

"What's the matter!" I demanded, keeping my voice as low as hers.

"I woke and I'm too keyed up to go back to sleep, damnit. Since it's mostly your fault, here I am."

I laughed in relief and turned on the bedside lamp. She flipped her nightgown over her head, strode to the bed, stretched out, and lay there half glaring at me.

"Don't you ever wear pajamas?" she said, as if I were a sloppy dresser.

"Nope." I lay down beside her. She was sure neither little nor helpless, but there was no doubt she was definitely a woman, fight it as she might.

We helped each other get back to sleep.

GREY ARRIVED ON THE DOT OF NINE THE NEXT MORNING, all by himself in his Landrover. He was nattily rigged out for a day in the country, wearing tan trousers, a semi-bush jacket, and an African-style straw hat to complete the ensemble. As additional equipment, he was carrying a small attaché case suitable for transporting ten to fifteen small wooden El Grecos.

Susan had completely recovered the bright-eyed, hopeful air she'd worn before her short trip to Grey's place in the country the previous day. Her equipment was her kit bag, a couple of old sheets, and a blanket she'd scrounged from Claudio. She was wearing a blue denim pants suit and looked like a nicely rounded day laborer.

Patricio, Ricardo, and I were the scruffy members of the crew. I'd briefed them that there might be some dirty work and that Ricardo should be prepared to spend time in the field so they were dressed accordingly, and I had hunted out the oldest clothes in my bag. Our equipment was a precise rifle, two pistols, a sawed-off shotgun, and Don Jaime's map. Only the rifle was in sight. I didn't know how I was going to square myself with the Conde over the shotgun.

Luis was glum about being left home again, but he couldn't be taken on this outing. Claudio and one of the manservants loaded the back of our Landrover with the picture-hunting gear, the lunch, and Ricardo's rations. Then the party mounted up, me at the wheel, Susan between me and Grey, and Patricio and Ricardo in the rear seat.

It was another clear day, warm and the sky a million mile blue. We drove for about thirty minutes, Grey chatting with Susan about the south of Spain, the most attractive part according to him. We were on a stretch of the Roman road with no one in sight either front or rear. I pulled over and stopped.

"Sorry, Grey," I said, "but it's search-you time."

When I began to slow he'd gone as abruptly silent as if his throat had been cut, so it should have been a relief to hear we weren't going to do just that to him, but he made a fuss anyway.

He said, "This is embarrassing and useless, since I assure you I'm unarmed. We are now associates. I should think you'd show some confidence. Good God, man, look at the way I'm trusting you!"

"It'll ease my mind, Grey. Don't make me have my people pull you out."

We dismounted and I went over him carefully. I could find nothing dangerous except a big Swiss pocketknife. I had a smaller version in my own pocket. I let him keep his. He started rather huffily to retake his seat but stopped when I opened the rear door and took his attaché case out of the back. He said, "You'll find that empty except for some cloth padding material similar to what Mizz Allgood's carrying."

He was right, but the whole thing felt a few ounces heavier than I thought it should, and the side below the hinges was thicker than it needed to be. I prodded and picked at that and at length did something right, for a small compartment opened and there was a neat little over-and-under, twin barrelled .38 derringer with a dozen extra rounds.

I shook my head reprovingly at Grey. He said pertly, "Well, I wasn't armed. That was not on my person. And look at that rifle your man's carrying. You probably have other weapons, too."

"That's right. Two pistols and a sawed-off shotgun, but there's a difference." I unloaded the derringer and passed it and the ammunition to Patricio.

We resumed our trip. I said, "You'll get it back, Grey, as soon as things are settled."

"I should hope so. Those things are not cheap."

In the back seat Patricio and Ricardo, who had been silent so far, were discussing the derringer in Guarani. They thought it was one of the greatest things they'd ever seen. They asked me a couple of questions about it.

"What on earth are you talking with those fellows?" Grey asked.

I explained about the Paraguayans and Guarani. When I finished, Grey laughed ruefully. "Mizz Allgood," he said, "I hope that you at least may have some sympathy for my position. I did make an error yesterday. I've admitted it and I've groveled for it. As a result here I am now, completely defenseless, traveling through almost uninhabited country in the company of Major Clancy, whose antecedents and tendencies we both know, I believe, and two backwoods cut-throats from the wilds of South America, all three of whom are heavily armed, and all three of whom speak a language I don't understand."

Goddamned if that didn't provoke a little sympathy. Susan said, "I think you have only yourself to blame, Mr. Grey, but you really have nothing to worry about. You are truly safe. You may be even safer now that you don't have that little gun."

"It's nice to hear you say that, Mizz Allgood." Grey put a verbal underline beneath the "you." "I say, must we continue so formal? I'd be happy if you'd call me Arthur."

So we bowled along, Susan and Arthur and me, Clancy.

"Now, as that nonsense is out of the way," said Grey, "may one ask where we are going?"

"We're going to a place called Piedra Cuadrada," I said.

"Where's that?"

"We don't know. It's not on the map. We think within five or six kilometers of the Monastery of San Ildefonso."

"Oh, lord," said Grey. "Clancy, you're bad for my health. Surely we're not going to start quartering over a circle ten kilometers in diameter looking for four bundles of paintings. Please tell me we're not going to do that."

"No we're not." In spite of myself I had to smile. "We're going to ask the shepherds around if they know where Piedra Cuadrada is."

He grunted in comprehension. "Of course. Those chaps should be able to tell us."

I glanced at him. "How the hell would you know that?"

"I grew up in the country. My family had a place down in Wiltshire. I had a splendid time as a boy. Far as I know, my older brother's still there, most likely having a hell of a time keeping it. Taxes are criminal, you know."

Everyone's full of surprises.

He returned to telling Susan about the Costa del Sol.

When I judged we were within ten kilometers of the monastery, I warned all concerned to keep an eye out for flocks of sheep. We could see a good distance over the undulating, almost treeless land.

Ricardo sighted the first flock. I found a track heading in the general direction which took us within a couple of hundred

242

yards. The ground was level so I put the Landrover in four-wheel drive and started across country.

As we drew near, Grey said, "Better stop here. Don't want to frighten the sheep, you know. They're pretty silly beasts."

I halted. Grey appeared to know more than I did about this sort of thing.

He and I got out and walked over to where the shepherd and two dogs were standing in a row watching us approach. All three could be said to be wagging their tails. Behind them around two hundred sheep were in a close bunch, all heads down, all moving slowly to the north.

The shepherd was a man about fifty, spare and brown, with weather lines all over his face. He was dressed in black corduroy trousers and a coarse, brown shirt. A sack was slung on his shoulder and a black corduroy jacket hung from his neck by knotted sleeves. He held a heavy stick with a curved handle. He qualified as a shepherd right to the crook.

He gave Grey and me an enthusiastic greeting which we returned as well as we could. I asked our question and he said he believed he'd heard of Piedra Cuadrada but he wasn't sure. He insisted that Grey and I drink from the wineskin in his sack while he tried to recall. I managed to spill a good bit on my front, never having drunk wine from a skin bag before, and Grey didn't do much better. The shepherd and his two dogs all thought, but at length he had to say he didn't know where Piedra Cuadrada was. He wouldn't lie to us, but he was happy for the company and didn't want us to leave.

Grey asked him where he usually pastured his sheep. That got a voluble reply.

Finally we tore ourselves away. Before we left, I made a move toward my pocket, but Grey said, "Wouldn't do that if I were you. Hurt his feelings. At least we can rule out all the country in this chap's beat. That'll be some help. May I see the map, please?"

I'd have liked it more if Grey hadn't shown any good qualities or good sense.

We went on another few kilometers before hunting another flock. We drew the same blank with the second shepherd, but as a result of Grey's questions we were able to eliminate an additional stretch of terrain to the east and northeast of the monastery.

I said, "Let's go around to the west of the monastery and then down toward the escarpment. Rocks are all over the lot but there are more down there than anywhere else."

"Good idea," said Grey. He still had the map. "A pretty fair track goes off in that direction about half a kilometer on. See?"

He was right. "Where'd you learn to read a map?" I asked.

"Put some time in the army. I really was in Singapore for two years or so."

We found Grey's track and turned off on it. After seven kilometers, we saw sheep on the crest of a near rise. Behind me Patricio and Ricardo were exchanging opinions about sheep. Neither thought much of them, either for keeping or eating.

The shepherd was like the other two. He and his dogs were similarly happy to have us drop in. Grey explained we were looking for Piedra Cuadrada and asked if he knew it.

The shepherd nodded. "Sí, hombre. It's not far from here, over on the edge of the place where the land goes down to La Mancha." He pointed south.

Grey and I looked at each other. He opened the map, and we both asked the shepherd questions as to where Piedra Cuadrada was located with respect to features shown on the map. We got a fair fix on it. It was just about six kilometers from San Ildefonso.

The shepherd peered with interest at our map. "I don't understand those," he said, "but I've seen them."

The map showed a track passing a little over a kilometer from where we thought Piedra Cuadrada would be. I asked if we could take the Landrover all the way there.

"I think nearly so, señor."

"What is there at Piedra Cuadrada?"

"Nothing."

"Nothing at all?"

"Only an old tower from the times of the wars with the Moors, but nobody lives there. There's nothing at all—no water, no forage for animals."

My heart turned over inside me. I said, "Hombre, you have helped us perhaps more than you know." I took out my pocketknife. "Would you please take this gift?"

He took it and smiled at me. "I would to give you pleasure, but only if you will take a little wine." He passed around his wineskin and Grey and I took healthy swallows, getting less on our shirts this time. We all shook hands. The shepherd's was hard as a hoof.

We went to the Landrover and told Susan. "Dear God," she said.

Grey kept the map and navigated. We went south for fifteen minutes along another of the tracks that seemed to run at random over the face of the countryside. Nobody spoke, Patricio and Ricardo because they had exhausted the topic of sheep, the rest of us because we were too full for talk.

The track bent around a low dome in the ground and we saw the tower. It was a kilometer away, silhouetted against the sky. We were close to the escarpment and the soil and vegetation were changing. The land was more rocky and uneven and in and around the rocks there was low scrub and a few twisted bushes.

It required some maneuvering, but eventually I got the Landrover to a small, rock-free space near the edge of the escarpment, about three hundred yards from the tower.

"Looks like we walk from here," I said.

It was easy going but required some detours to avoid large rocks or clumps of bushes. Patricio and Ricardo brought up the rear, carrying the gear and food.

After about fifty meters, I noticed that we seemed to have stumbled over a natural path. It made a fairly clear way through the boulders and tangled vegetation.

The tower was on the point of a narrow tongue of ground nearly a hundred meters long and a few feet higher than the general level to the north. To either side steep bluffs dropped off to deep brush-choked gullies that themselves ran down to join the general rocky fall of land to the plain below.

We walked out the tongue of land and up to the tower. It was like the others I'd seen while traveling between the palace, the monastery, and Toledo. Three stories tall, and about thirty-feet square. The bottom story was completely solid and windowless, the second had slitted embrasures for bowmen, and the last was a battlemented open platform. A few of the battlements were broken and eroded like the teeth of an old fighter, but the tower could probably be held as intended if the pagans came again.

"When was this built?" asked Susan.

I remembered my "Concise History" and said, "Toledo was retaken by the Spanish around 1085. The line of this escarpment was frontier country with the Moors for a long time after. It was probably built before 1100 as part of the general line of watchtowers."

"That's awfully interesting, old man," said Grey, "but how does one get in?"

"An attacking force would probably have to come at it the way we have, so the door should be on the other side. I warn you, it's going to be in the second story and there well may not be any way up."

We started around the tower. "Why ever the second story?" Susan wanted to know.

"These things were only in the alarm system. They weren't defensive works intended to block an enemy advance. If the troops here saw Moors coming, they'd light a signal fire and run off, or if they couldn't run they'd climb a ladder to the second story, pull up the ladder, shut the door, and hold out until someone came and chased the Moors off."

"Or until they ran out of water," observed Grey.

I was both right and wrong. The door was on the far side, close to fifteen feet up, but someone at some time had brought rocks and laboriously piled them against the tower wall to make an irregular narrow stairway up to the door.

I didn't know if that stairway was a good or a bad sign. I moved to examine the rocks that composed it. They were simply unshaped chunks such as littered the land we'd come through and mostly just as weathered, yet on the surfaces which had lain in the earth before they'd been carried here, there were only small spots of the green and brown lichen that forms on exposed rocks. The stairway had been built some years past, but nowhere near as long ago as had the tower.

"Let's go up," said Susan. She sounded as if she had a slight cold in her head.

I told Patricio and Ricardo to wait. They put down their loads and lit cigarettes. I went first, reaching a hand back to Susan and Grey came last ready to catch. She needed no help.

I had to bend nearly double to get through the doorway. There were roomy sockets showing traces of rust where the pins had been seated for the hinges of the long-vanished heavy door. The wall was at least four feet thick. Inside was a single room, dimly lit from the arrow slits that opened into wedge-shaped embrasures and from an open hatch in one of the far corners. A proper set of stairs led up to the hatch and gave access to the fighting top. A single square center column with a bench built around it helped hold up the roof. There was sufficient light to see that outside of a layer of dirt, bits of amorphous natural trash, and bird droppings, the place was empty of anything that looked like four bundles of paintings.

"Let's go up top," said Susan.

That was easy. I was a little leery of the soundness of the stone flagging there. I shouldn't have been. They built to last in the days when the tower had been put up.

The view to the south and to either side along the ragged, broken escarpment ran to infinity. Above, you could see twice as far. There were a few doll villages near the horizon.

"Marvelous OP," said Grey. I agreed.

"There," said Susan, pointing. "Isn't that San Ildefonso?"

Away to the east, the roof of the monastery barely projected over an intervening rise.

"Bernardo came here." Susan was positive. "He came here often."

"I'm sure he did," said Grey. "Question is, where did he leave what he brought?"

"I DON'T THINK HE'D LEAVE ANYTHING UP HERE,"
I said.

We went back down through the hatch to the tower's
single room. "Would there be anything under this?" asked
Grey.

"It's most probably solid masonry, but we'll check it," I
said. I counted the embrasures. There were three in the wall
facing back along the neck of land running up to the tower,
two in each of the others. "The garrison was probably twelve
to fifteen men. Plenty of room for them to bunk in here, and
they'd do most of their living and cooking outside, depending
on the weather and the prevalence of Moors in the area. There
could be some sort of storage space down below, though."

"From what I've read about secret passages and things,"
said Susan, "maybe we should start tapping the walls and the
floor listening for hollow sounds."

The floor was so dirty it was hard to make out how the
flagstones fitted together. I walked to a wall and looked at its
construction. It was made of tightly fitted stone blocks like big
bricks of lengths varying from one to two feet. I didn't think
tapping would help us much.

"The hell with this for a bit," I said. "It's after noon.
We've got plenty of work ahead. We'll have to more or less

sweep this place out to get a look at the floor. Let's have lunch and try a little thinking at the same time."

We scrambled down and joined Patricio and Ricardo in the scrap of shade on the east side. The lunch basket was more than amply filled. Five bottles of wine and bunches of sandwiches made of crusty rolls sliced lengthwise and stuffed with ham or cheese or a kind of omelet. There were pottery mugs for the wine and jars of mustard and sliced peppers and various other condiments and trimmings.

All provided themselves with the necessary and found places to sit. Patricio and Ricardo off to one side, as they were not accustomed to eat with their patrón. Susan and I sat on convenient rocks with our backs against the tower. Grey found himself a rock in front of us. We munched and drank in companionable silence.

For two hundred years or more this had been a border post held by a detachment of soldiers, probably mercenaries because the peasant levies couldn't be put on long service jobs like this. On nice days the men off-duty would often have sat where we were, grousing about the low pay, monotony, lack of women, sour wine, infrequency of passes, and general bastardliness of their superiors from the corporal in charge up to the duke in his castle. At times, battle would have come to the tower. Fast raiding parties might have peeled off from the main body of a Moorish attack force and come to the tower to try to root out the men within. That wouldn't have been easy. Men would have died with arrows or crossbow quarrels in their throats, and if the defenders' water had given out and they'd surrendered, men would have died in harder ways.

Then the frontier had moved south and the garrison had left, likely without a backward glance, and the tower had stood unmanned, for time and weather to pull down a few stones. Shepherds had passed, not many because of the lack of forage, but enough to notice the place and give it a name. Then, around fifty years ago, a monk visited the tower—a monk who liked to walk in lonely places and ease his split mind with solitary prayer. Bernardo must have made the stairway, carrying in a suitable stone or two every time he came by. He was strong enough according to the prior. Then he'd been able to pray on the fighting top, closer to God and farther from whatever had happened to him on the ground of Barcelona. This wasn't the only place he went to, he ranged all around the monastery, but I'd have bet it was one of his favorites.

"He must have been a driven man in some way," said Susan softly.

I almost dropped my sandwich. "You mean Bernardo?"

She nodded. "I've been thinking about him coming here. I wish I knew what happened to him."

"So do I," said Grey with heart-felt sincerity.

"I have a guess," I said. "This place was built for an OP and used as one for a long time. Then war went south and nobody needed it, but when war came back in September of 1936, people needed it again. The Army of Africa was advancing on Toledo from the south and west. If I'd been the Loyalist commander, I'd have put detachments along this escarpment to keep an eye on the plains down there. Bernardo ran into one of those. He got an idea they were after the monastery's paintings and over-reacted. The soldiers who killed him probably neither knew nor cared why he was giving them trouble. A hell of a lot worse than the casual slaughter of a monk took place in those days. The soldiers would have kept his burro—they could always use that—and thrown his body into one of these gullies. It would have gone through the brush to the ground beneath and been mighty hard to find. There's lots of places where it would have been impossible even to smell him from up on the plateau."

Susan made a face. "Poor Bernardo. I hate to think of him ending as a bad smell."

I poured more wine around. "If they got him on his way in, they could have taken the pictures and used them for firewood."

"You have a macabre turn of mind," said Grey. "I refuse to entertain that thought for a moment. I have quite a feeling about that bench around the central pillar. Been thinking there may be space under the stones." He looked around. "Hard to think of anything depressing in a lovely place like this."

"I want to find those pictures," said Susan.

I smiled at her. I did too, but possibly not as much as she did. We'd followed the track that Don Jaime had started in the archives of Simancas as far as anyone could. I had no proof as to what had happened to Bernardo, but I'd satisfied me and I felt easier for that. We could be sitting within a hundred yards of whatever was left of Bernardo. There wouldn't be much, only teeth could have lasted, and if the soldiers hadn't searched his body maybe bits of the ivory box he had taken back from Fernando. I was going to keep looking for the pictures—there was a strong drive in me yet, urged by the prospect of a hundred thousand dollar prize—but I wasn't frantic. Hell, I was sure I qualified for the fifty thousand Du Vigny had offered, and I had a good girl and the wine filled my head and the view was a glory. Grey'd hit it. It was hard to think of depressing things.

Susan rose and, carrying her wine mug, walked to where she could look up at the tower without straining her neck. "It would be so nice if we could pull that apart as if it were a straw basket."

Grey cocked his head. "Expect the Moorish horsemen who rode this way felt much the same."

She shaded her eyes against the brightness of the sky. "Why there's the reason this place is called the Square Stone!"

Grey and I rose and joined her. She pointed. Instead of the regular, almost mortarless, masonry of the inside walls, the outer ones were made of large, rectangular chunks of rock, only roughly dressed and of many different sizes, the irregular joining filled with an iron-hard mortar. High up the wall we were peering at and lying about two feet directly below the middle arrow slit was set a perfectly square stone bigger and of a different color than the rest—almost a light green. Once you saw it, it stood out like a neon sign.

"Susan, I do believe you're right," said Grey. "Very noticing girl, you are."

For a man who'd had her kidnapped at gunpoint the day before, he was being very chummy.

Susan asked, "Do you think the men who built the tower put that there on purpose?"

I stared up at it. For some reason, it bothered me. It was out of place in a way I couldn't define. "I'm not sure," I said slowly. "It was probably just chance that a square stone of a different kind and color from the other rock was hauled out here for the tower building crew, but the foreman may well have put it in the center of the wall because he liked the way it looked there. Could be the name of this place was given to it longer ago than we figured, and not by the shepherds."

"You don't suppose Bernardo could have hid the paintings behind that, do you?" asked Grey.

"From the outside, he couldn't. He'd have needed

scaffolding and a block and tackle. We'll take a look at the flooring in the squad room over where it lies, but it's well below the inside flagstones. Those arrow slits start just about at floor level to make it easier to shoot down at someone out here." That blasted, odd-colored stone had some message I couldn't receive.

I put the last remaining bite of sandwich in my mouth and chewed reflectively.

"That stone is wrong," Susan said positively. I turned my head to look at her. She was frowning up at her discovery. Without shifting her eyes, she reached and grabbed my arm. "Clancy! How many of those arrow slits are there in the walls?"

I raised my eyebrows. "There's three in the north wall and two in each of—" I looked back up. This was the east wall. There should have been only two arrow slits, but three looked back at me. The exterior rim of the slits was made of closely dressed stone, which caused them to stand out even more strongly in contrast to the walls than if they'd been the mere squinting spaces that they were. That was why the square stone was out of place. It was under an embrasure that shouldn't be there.

"Odd," said Grey.

"Come on," I said. They followed me as I walked around. On the south side there was the door above its precarious stair and an arrow slit to either side. On the west, three arrow slits again where there should have been two. On the north side were the expected three.

"They must have closed up the center one on the east and west sides at some time," I said. "The duke might have run into money trouble and decided to reduce his garrisons. Too many arrow slits to be properly manned would have been a weakness."

Grey said, "But they didn't fill them in flush with the outside so that the Moors would think there were more firing posts and more people than there actually were."

"Bernardo wouldn't have known that," said Susan. "He wasn't military. And he counted things, he was always counting things. If he'd seen three on the outside and only two on the inside he'd have had to find out why. He'd have looked."

"Well, let's look, too." Grey bowed to her. "You are a very noticing girl indeed, Susan."

She turned from one to the other of us, her eyes wide. "The walls are very thick. I wonder if they went to the trouble of filling those—those—"

"Embrasures," I said.

"Yes. Of filling those embrasures solidly."

"Not necessarily. They might want to open them up again sometime."

I called to Patricio to bring the basket of search equipment, and we climbed back to the second story guard-room. I took out the Coleman lantern, pumped it up, and lit it. The glaring white light it cast painted black shadows behind the central pillar and behind us as we moved. I gave Grey and Susan each a flash of their own and picked up the crowbar. Patricio watched us with mild interest.

"Okay, Susan," I said, wishing I'd thought to tell her what a noticing girl she was. "Your call. Which wall first? The one over the square stone?"

"Yes, of course."

I carried the lantern over to the east wall and we looked. Now that we knew what to look for it wasn't hard to see. The masonry over where there should have been an embrasure for an arrow slit was the same as the rest of the wall except for one thing. Where the joins of the other stones made an irregular pattern like the broken grid of brickwork, over what would have been the sides of the embrasure were two straight, uninterrupted seams.

I lifted my crowbar and tapped outside the seams, getting an unrewarding clank of iron on stone. I tried between the seams and got the same noise. "So much for tapping," I said. "Let's try prying. Grey, please take the lantern and hold it so my shadow doesn't get in the way."

As he posted himself to the side, minor shadows on the wall changed and moved. Small bumps and notches were easier to pick out. I set the point of the bar under a middle stone at about chest height and pressed down with my right hand. The stone slid out half an inch with only slight resistance. "Jesus," I said.

It took less than a minute to work the stone out to where I could get a good grip on it with my hands. It came free easily. It wasn't as thick as I thought, being only six or seven inches deep. It weighed about forty pounds. There was an empty space behind it. I laid the stone on the floor. "You look," I said to Susan.

She stepped up and shone her flashlight inside. "There's a big space and then another wall where the embrasure narrows. There's something down below but I can't see well. The hole's not big enough."

I bent for the crowbar again. Grey said, "Hold on a sec, old man. It'll be easier now but it's dicky work. Need to go a bit careful or the wall will be down on us and on what's inside. Some of those stones will give no trouble but others are holding up the ones on top of them. Better let me. I used to do stonework once."

"You did stonework?" I said, astonished.

"Yes. Not exactly by my own choice. Didn't like it so I

gave it up as soon as I could. Done quite a few things in my time."

I stepped aside and passed him the crowbar. Working carefully and testing the stones before he pulled or pried, he managed to open a lopsided space about three feet high and two broad at the base. Even before he was half finished, I could see the end of a small, cloth-wrapped bale not quite a foot square. As he went farther down, I could see it was resting on another similar one, their longer axes lying away from us.

Grey put a last stone on the pile he'd formed to one side and backed away from the space. We stood silently staring for maybe a minute, maybe longer. The coarse, brown cloth on the two bundles we could see was dusty but intact. Heavy cords of what could be hemp held the cloth in place.

"Isn't that a lovely sight?" said Grey.

"Okay, Susan." I patted her on the shoulder. "This is your department. Do you have room enough to work?"

"Yes, there's plenty." Her voice was tremulous but with anticipation, not nerves. She pulled a bandanna from her pocket and bound up her hair.

Grey pulled over a couple of stones for her to kneel on but I beat him to getting my jacket off and making a pad so she'd be comfortable. I used a wadded handkerchief to wedge a flashlight between two blocks on one side for general illumination of the cavity.

She knelt and stuck her head and a hand holding another flashlight through the opening. "They're all four here," she said, sounding as if she were inside a drum. They're just stacked one on top of the other. The wrappings are in good shape for the top three but I can't see the bottom one well enough. I hope mold didn't get into it, sitting on a bare stone floor like that."

She ducked back into view and reached for her kit bag. "I'll open one end of the top bundle and see what condition the wood is in."

Grey moistened his lips. "Susan, wouldn't it be easier if Clancy or I simply lifted the whole bundle out here for you to work on?"

She was selecting instruments from her kit, her face as serious as a surgeon's. "Not if the wood's gone to powder. Even if it has, the surface of paint can possibly be saved, but that will mean bringing all sorts of special equipment here."

"But how—how—" He fell silent. To divert his mind from wondering how we could consider bringing special equipment to the tower, I sent Patricio down for Susan's packing material and Grey's attaché case. Old Grey had a bad time coming no matter what the condition of the paintings was.

Grey and I sat on the central bench and watched Susan's shapely stern elevation as she worked at opening the outer wrappings. In the hissing glare of the Coleman lantern I saw that Grey was sweating just as hard as he had been for our talk in the Zocodover the day before. I wiped a hand across my face and found I was sweating myself. Patricio squatted on his heels by the door, smoking and probably storing up questions to ask me later.

It occurred to me that I was pretty stupid. Here we'd found God knew how many El Grecos and everybody was getting one except me and Patricio and Ricardo. Why shouldn't I take an extra one or two or sixteen for me? I had all the weapons and the troops. I could be a millionaire. I wouldn't last very long because every tendency I had toward being a bum would be encouraged to the fullest and there wouldn't be anything else that I would feel like doing. Other millionaires endowed laboratories or they founded colleges, but I didn't think I'd be that kind. I'd simply be a bum millionaire, who never read another book or played another game of chess or screwed a woman who wasn't mentally making a deposit in a bank. So what was wrong with that? A bottle has as many theories in it as an encyclopedia, craps moves faster than chess, skill often prevails over affection. I was already a bum and worse in the books of most who'd ever heard of me.

But I wasn't a bum in my own book yet.

Susan spent more than half an hour opening the outer wrappings. I worked at my inside ones.

Eventually she pulled back into view. "The wood on the end picture seems solid but it's wrapped in linen and I'm afraid the pressure of the cords may have forced the material into the paint. We'll see. Put that blanket of mine on the floor, please."

Keeping her head free this time, Susan reached in and manipulated something. Grey and I were up and standing by her as she slowly drew out a thin square enveloped in fine woven, yellowish cloth. She lay it on the blanket I'd spread on the floor and shifted to sit beside it. She bent over it as if it were a sleeping child and, using two pairs of broad, flat tweezers, started to fold the linen protection to the sides. She stopped almost as soon as she'd begun. "The paint's adhering. This will need complicated treatment."

Grey asked from a tight throat. "Will they all be that way?"

"I don't think so. This is sticking only where the cords crossed it. The idiot who packed it put this one face out. Clancy, please move it over there so I'll have more room."

I thought she was a little hard on the packer whoever he was. The picture had come through a long time. I picked up the first El Greco I'd ever held as I would an unexploded bomb and moved it to where she pointed. I saw that she'd cut a scrap of wrapping from a corner and a gleam of golden yellow showed.

She leaned inside the embrasure again.

It was only ten minutes this time before she emerged. "The second one looks better," she announced. She reached in and slowly withdrew another thin square wrapped the same way as the first. She laid it on the blanket, and manipulating her tweezers so precisely the brittle old cloth stayed intact, she folded back two overlapping layers. There was no problem of them adhering to the paint.

"There," Susan said.

A small pool of jeweled, swirling color lay on the blanket stretched over the floor of the old guardroom and glowed at us.

Grey and I knelt to see it more closely. It was a picture of a man in ornate Spanish armor on a white horse. The horse was halted and the man had a drawn sword in one hand and a green cloak in the other. Standing by his knee was a slender naked man staring up.

"That's *Saint Martin and the Beggar*," Susan said. "The big version is in the National Gallery at Washington."

"You can even make out the tracery of gold inlay on the armor," said Grey in a hushed voice.

I stood. "Grey, we should have a talk." I walked over to the door where Patricio was hunkered down and said to him in Guarani, "Keep an eye on this man. He may either faint or jump at me." I turned to Grey who'd come to stand beside me. His face was pale and his eyes were dreaming.

"Grey," I said, "we stand by our bargain. You get the same number of paintings as Susan and I do, and we'll give you a good-bye drink, and we'll wish you luck and we'll mean it. You've been helpful today and even pleasant company."

"Trying to correct unfortunate first impressions. You

know, I think the way to do this is simply to take the top bundle. There must be forty-odd paintings in there. And though you may have your own channels, we should keep in some sort of touch. Mustn't go after the same prospects and—"

"Grey, I've got bad news for you. Susan and I are each taking one painting. That's all you get, too. One painting. We'll leave the rest right here."

He staggered back as if I'd hit him across the face with no warning—which I guess I had. Patricio and I jumped to catch him.

"No," he said. "No." He shook off the hand Patricio had put under his elbow. "That's so idiotic, it can't be."

I had to agree it was idiotic but that was the way it was going to be.

"Yeah, I'm afraid it can." Yesterday, I'd have laughed heartily at the sight Grey afforded, but I didn't enjoy it today. I didn't exactly grieve for him, but I wasn't gloating.

HE STRAIGHTENED UP WITH AN EFFORT. "CLANCY,
ten is the least we each should have." He was doing his best to
make his voice firm but there was an underlying cracked note
of despair.

"Grey, I've made promises I have to keep. One painting."

"You're insane. Those paintings as they sit there don't
belong to anybody, but you're going to be breaking Spanish
law if you merely take one. What kind of promises have you
made that will allow you to take three and not thirty—or
fifteen?"

"I'm already bending my promises when I give you one.
Jesus Christ, that's not so bad. You should be able to clear a
couple of hundred thousand pounds on it. Yesterday morning
you didn't have anything like that in view."

"For a moment there, I was a millionaire." His voice was
stronger. "It would have been kinder to tell me yesterday
evening."

"I wasn't feeling kind toward you then, and we hadn't
found the paintings." I didn't want to keep arguing with him.
He made too goddamn much sense for one thing. "How about
some wine?"

"Whisky would be better, but if wine's all there is."

I called down for Ricardo to bring up a bottle of wine and

some mugs. I didn't want to send Patricio. Grey seemed to be getting himself under control in the great English tradition of the stiff upper lip, but I thought it was only so he could concentrate on how to get his hands on more pictures, and it would be better to have Patricio close by at all times.

When the wine came, I filled mugs for us. We returned to watch Susan. She'd been working steadily away while we'd had our short chat. I doubted she'd even heard us. As I finished my wine, she brought out another painting. She had no trouble unwrapping it. It was a portrait of a cardinal in his robes of rank. He had the face of a man who burned heretics for the good of their souls. Susan said she'd seen reproductions of the big painting, but she wasn't sure where it was.

She looked at the painting briefly and then went back into the embrasure. Grey and I had another mug of wine. Although his color hadn't returned, his hands seemed steady. I wished the embrasure were closed and we were on our way.

The next painting Susan produced showed the Virgin being crowned by God and Christ with the Dove of the Holy Ghost flying above and an audience of saints below. The golds and reds on the small wooden square seemed to vibrate like soft violin notes. According to Susan, the large version was right in Toledo; she'd gone to see it during our first trip to town.

She lit a cigarette and sat back on my folded jacket, smoking and contemplating the three pictures lying side by side. Grey and I stood by her. *El Espolio* hadn't turned up, but that was nothing to whine about.

Patricio came to see what we were staring at so intently. "Those are very lovely," he said. "The one of the Virgin is the best." He crossed himself and returned to his post by the door.

"Just one more each?" said Grey.

263

"No, goddamnit. Susan, can you put back the picture with the covering stuck to it and close the bundle up so it looks undisturbed?"

"I can try, but it won't fool anyone who knows much."

"Maybe he'll be as eager as we were and won't look too hard." To punish myself, I bent to peer through the hole. The cords on the end of the top bundle hung loose and the outer wrapping had been neatly peeled back. I could see the next painting, anonymous in its linen protection. Grey leaned down beside me, but must have found the sight even more painful than it was to me. He swore in a whisper and went to look through an arrow slit.

I got out of Susan's way. Grey called me over. "Clancy, how do we parcel out that great heap of pictures?"

"Susan gets first pick, you and I toss for the next. Fair enough?"

"Let's toss now. Although I'm sure how it will turn out."

He was right. He lost.

Susan needed longer to close the bundle than to open it, but at last she pulled out of the hole and said, "That's the best I can do." I looked in again. The bundle appeared exactly as it had the first time I'd seen it. I congratulated her. "It even looks full to me."

"I worked some of the other paintings forward to take up the space of the three we have. What's next, Clancy?"

"Let's have share-out." I said. "Which do you want, Susan?"

"I can have my choice?"

"Ladies first," said Grey. "Clancy and I decided." He leered at me sarcastically.

"Then I want the *Saint Martin*. The *Coronation of the Virgin* is from his best period, but I've seen the big *Saint*

264

Martin so many times in Washington." She reached forward and touched her picture with the tip of her finger.

Grey gave her a perplexed frown. He didn't know she was going to keep it. Wouldn't have believed it if we'd told him. He shifted his attention to me. "Well, which do you want, Clancy?" He was resigned.

"Let me make a point. Susan, is that *Coronation* more salable than the *Cardinal*?"

She looked up abstractedly. "Oh, yes, I should think quite a bit more. The portrait of the *Cardinal* is fine, but not anywhere near as well known."

"Okay," I said. "Grey, you can have the *Coronation*. I'll take the *Cardinal*." I wanted the *Cardinal* anyway. If Du Vigny couldn't have *El Espolio*, I thought he'd like the *Cardinal*. There was a touch of the fanatic about Du Vigny that would appreciate the *Cardinal*.

"I suppose I'm expected to exclaim 'Jolly decent of you,' " said Grey, "but I have come to view kindness on your part as a cause for strong concern. What is it this time?"

"Simply want you to leave happy, and I'd appreciate your help putting those stones back. It'll look better if they're neat."

He shook his head, but in exasperation not negation. "You know, I'd decided I wouldn't help on that unless you put a pistol at my head. All right."

"We'd better pack the pictures first," said Susan. She helped Grey stow his. "I'm glad to see you're not too disappointed over getting only one picture, Arthur," she said.

"I fear your attention was on other matters when Clancy broke the news, Susan. I have vast powers of recuperation."

Even with Patricio's help, the two of us had a hell of a time putting the wall back, not that it was hard to slide the stones in place but we'd been too feverish taking them down to pay close attention to the order in which we'd pulled them loose. Since they were all of slightly varying lengths, it was something of a jigsaw puzzle with forty- and fifty-pound pieces. Susan, having done her duty, moved to the bench and smoked a couple of cigarettes and observed. "Bernardo was certainly a better mason than any of you," she commented once without being asked.

She was cuddling the package she'd made of our two paintings to her breast. Every now and then, she rocked it a little.

It was six o'clock when we finished. At my prodding, we policed up cigarette butts and tried to eliminate the traces of our presence in the guardroom. We made a careful passage down to where Ricardo patiently waited. Susan refused to be helped with her package.

Once more on solid ground, I said, "Grey, there's one more formality. Susan and I won't be staying long in Spain. As soon as we're clear, word will go to the proper people about these pictures and where they are. You can guess what will happen then."

"Yes, I can," he said sadly.

"Until that happens, I'm putting a guard on the place. Ricardo, here. I'm going to leave him in ambush. Once more I'm going to tell you a couple of true things. Paraguayans are very good at this kind of work. They can find cover and concealment on a dance floor and they are patient beyond all belief. You can listen to the orders I give Ricardo. I'll speak Spanish."

I motioned to Ricardo and Patricio to join us. I told Patricio to listen and remember, then I spoke to Ricardo. "Hombre, there are valuable things in this tower. You will guard them. Take a position where you can see the ways to come here during the day and hear at night. You can sleep, but no more than an hour at a time. No one should see you. If this man comes ever, alone or with anyone, shoot him on sight and shoot to kill."

Patricio and Ricardo regarded Grey with a degree of surprise. I'd searched him and taken away his small pistol but we'd seemed to be getting along well aside from that.

"Sí, patrón," said Ricardo.

"Now, others may come. A young man or a young girl, both with long hair. Try to drive them off first, but if they keep coming, shoot them, too."

"A young girl, patrón?" asked Ricardo. One normally did not shoot young girls.

"She's a dangerous young girl, Ricardo. I mean this. She'll be armed and she'll kill you if she can."

"All right, patrón."

"Now, sooner or later, other people, probably ten or fifteen or more will come in a group. There'll be monks, and maybe those police with the odd hats, and some civilians. When these come, you leave quietly with no one seeing. Hide the rifle and go. You'll have to walk to a road and then make your way back to Madrid. In Madrid go to the hotel where you and Patricio stayed. Either Patricio will be waiting there or there'll be other orders. You can get the clerk to read them to you. Understand?"

"Sí, patrón."

"Until the group of people come you stay on guard and keep others out of the tower, unless I myself come and order you away. Obey only if I am alone. If there is anyone with me, shoot them without question or talking as soon as you have a sure kill. Understand?"

"Could this young girl be with you?"

"It could be."

"Patrón, you know it is not right to kill women."

"In this case it will be, I promise you."

"Sí, patrón."

"Now, the Señorita Susan here. If she comes, again kill anyone who is with her except Patricio. Do not harm her or expose her to harm. If she tells you to leave your guard, pay no attention to her."

"Sí, patrón."

"You have any questions, Ricardo?"

"How long will I be here, patrón."

"Three days, probably. No more than a week. But stay until the group of people come."

"Sí, patrón."

I met Grey's eyes. "And do you have any questions?" I said in English.

"Will this chap stay out in that boulder field for a week?"

"He will and three days more after his water runs out."

"Something like the Gurkhas, I reckon," he said to himself. "I get your message, Clancy."

"Good. Now I'm going to repeat what I've said in Guarani to be sure he really does understand." I did, and then had Ricardo repeat everything back to me. That may not have been needed. He had the retentive verbal memory of the illiterate. Or better, of the man who's never needed to read.

We started back over the neck of land that connected the point where the tower stood with the plateau. About halfway over, Susan stopped. "You go on ahead," she said. "I'll catch up in a minute."

The rest of us walked on. I looked over my shoulder. She was standing looking back toward the tower. We waited where the neck joined the plateau at the edge of the boulder field. When she rejoined us, I guided her apart from Grey as we resumed walking to the Landrover.

"What did you do?" I asked.

"My business."

We walked another fifty yards. "You said good-bye to Bernardo."

"Damn your eyes, Clancy." But she smiled wryly.

"I didn't think you went in for that."

"I said good-bye and told him we'd only taken three and the monks would get the rest. What were you talking to Grey and your two Paraguayans about?"

"Only one Paraguayan. Look around."

She did. Patricio was following us all by himself. He grinned broadly.

"I'll tell you later," I said. "Let's head for the palace. You want to get knee-walking drunk again? Well-merited reward?"

"Just half-tight, thanks. That will be fine."

At the palace, Grey came in and had a drink, but it wasn't the same as when the three of us had been sitting by the tower eating our picnic before we went in to open the embrasure. I kept him in the reception room off the big hall so he wouldn't strew bugs around the place. He was all the way on the other side again, and trying not to show it. We shook hands when he left, but his eyes were shallow. Don't know what mine were like.

======= *36*

AFTER SEEING GREY SAFELY OFF THE PREMISES, I
telephoned Don Jaime. "We found what we were looking for,
Don Jaime," I told him.

There was a silence. "That is magnificent, my friend. I
congratulate you."

"It's all due to your discovering those papers in Simancas."

"What are your plans now?"

"I'll come see you tomorrow morning, and I'll explain
then. Will that be agreeable?"

"Certainly. Incidentally, I have those things you asked
for."

I thanked him and we complimented each other some
more and hung up. I found Susan in the room with the French
paintings. She was on a sofa, her bundle under one arm and a
martini in her free hand.

"That thing's going to interfere with your eating or taking
a shower," I said, fixing myself a drink.

"No, it won't." She patted it. "Clancy, Grey's a funny
man."

"Most comical bastard I ever met."

"I can't help feeling a little sorry for him."

"Don't. He's somewhere right now, scheming his head
off."

"It must have been terrible for him to have all those paintings within reach and then go away with only one."

"Well, goddamnit, how about a little sympathy closer to home? It wasn't so easy for me."

"I know. I can remember your face when you told me to close up the bundle. Did you think about taking more pictures?"

"Yeah."

"Why didn't you?"

"Too dumb."

"No, I don't know what you are besides tough, but you're not dumb, Clancy. Come give me a kiss."

"You're getting pretty bossy," I complained, but I gave her a kiss together with several pats and pinches. She kept her package under one arm all the time. Bathing and eating weren't the only activities that damn thing was going to impede.

She finally said that was enough until after dinner. "You left Ricardo on guard, didn't you?" she asked.

"Yeah, and with some special orders." I told her about them in detail.

Susan approved. "That should keep Grey away from the tower. It would me."

"There's one weak spot in it. If Grey got you again, I'd be in trouble. I don't have the same leverage as I did yesterday. You are going to stay right here in this palace from now until we all leave with either me or Patricio within arm's reach."

"I suppose that goes for tonight, too."

"Damn right."

"Hmm." She pursed her lips thoughtfully. "Patricio's not bad looking in his way."

She was hazing me lightly and I wasn't minding and it had been a damn fine day.

I told her I'd have to go to Toledo in the morning to give Don Jaime an after action report. As soon as I returned, we'd move out straight for Barajas Airport and get on the first plane heading even remotely in the direction we wanted. As soon as we were clear, Don Jaime would take appropriate steps and Ricardo could come off guard. With any luck, there'd never be a question asked about us.

"Although that means you won't be able to make much of a reputation out of this find," I pointed out.

"I've thought of that," she said with a touch of regret, "but I have *Saint Martin*. What about your friends the monks?"

"I'll write the prior a letter explaining as much as I dare. Which will be everything except that we took one quick peek inside the embrasure." It probably wouldn't fool Father Fermin, but damnit, I was returning the pictures to San Ildefonso.

Susan asked, "Could we unpack the pictures and look at them again?"

"After dinner, sure. We'll have a private show up in my room."

We ate well, both of us being hungry from our day in the open air. Grey and what he could be plotting was a constant minor irritation on my mind, but I kept it from becoming a major one.

We took a bath together afterward, which was bully fun, but as I'd expected complicated by the presence of the bundle. Since she couldn't take it into the tub or even into the bathroom because of humidity Susan let me put it on a chair where she could see it just outside the open door.

Then we had the private show as planned, and it was also pleasant except that Susan had to get up and repack the paintings. The *Cardinal* was simply not the kind of man one made love in front of. I took a spin at it and it didn't work at all. She presented quite a picture in her own right as she wrapped him and *Saint Martin* up again.

We spent the night together with one of the pistols under my pillow and then went down to breakfast side by side. To hell with keeping up appearances. The Conde de Quintinar was going to have a bad impression of me. I went to his palace and shacked up with an art expert, and I brought in two rustic gunmen, and I'd not only ruined one of his better shotguns, I'd also lifted one of his rifles and two of his pistols.

I ate quickly and spent half an hour writing a summary for Don Jaime, a cable for Du Vigny, and letters to the Conde and the prior. That done, Susan and I walked out on the back terrace for a last cup of coffee. The day was like the one before. A few small, round, apologetic clouds to make the blue that held them deeper and a soft wind to spread the sun.

"You're going to take Luis?" she asked. She had the bundle under her arm again.

"You bet. I'm not about to leave a vehicle unattended in Toledo."

"Are you just going to drive right into town?"

"I've thought about trying to sneak in and I don't think it's worth it. Short of climbing one of those damn forty-foot walls, there are only three ways into the place. I've got to see Don Jaime and the least risky way is probably the one that involves the least foot travel. I'll go the same way we always have. I'll have a weapon and I'll be alert."

"You be careful."

"Ricardo's the man Grey wants to get by. There's really not much point in trying anything on me." I didn't add that I would be harder to pull anything on than an unsuspecting Susan.

She came out accompanied by Patricio to say good-bye. I

273

aid, "I should be back by noon. It would be grand if we could eave for Barajas about ten minutes later."

"I'll be ready." She squeezed my arm.

"And don't leave the palace until I show. Not for anything, understand?"

"I won't."

I called Patricio over. "You stay here at the palace with the señorita. Under no circumstances leave before I return. The only time she goes out of your sight is when she goes to the WC, and then you stand by the door. Understand?"

"Sí, patrón."

He had one of the pistols and the sawed-off shotgun. That should be enough.

I flipped her a salute and climbed into the Landrover. Luis was quiet for the first few minutes. I relaxed and admired the countryside.

"Señor," said Luis, "it is not my affair but I think you have some sort of rather delicate business in hand."

I was riding in front with him, mainly so he wouldn't turn around and look at me when he wanted to talk.

"I have, Luis. It's about over."

"Your two Paraguayans are quiet and well-mannered but it is easy to see they are capable of action." He coughed. "I can be active, too, señor, having fought in the war. If you need more assistance, I am at your service."

I looked at him. For a wonder his eyes were on the road. "Thank you, Luis. Thank you very much. I'll take advantage of that offer if I meet any problems. For the moment, there seem to be none."

"I just wanted you to know, señor. You have been a thoughtful employer."

That gave me a glow. Luis, married and with children, was disposed to pick up a weapon on my side. He would obviously love to hear what was going on but was too proud to ask. I was sorry I couldn't tell him.

Inside the walls of Toledo, Luis headed for the cathedral plaza. With the constantly passing locals and tourists it seemed as safe as any place.

"Keep a careful eye on the car," I said to him, "and please forget about a report to that telephone number. I shouldn't be long."

"Trust me, señor."

I made the walk to Don Jaime's house as if it were through unpacified country. I stuck to the middle of the narrow streets and swung wide around corners, my hand near the pistol in my belt under my jacket. I didn't see anyone or anything suspicious. Feeling rather paranoid, I rang Don Jaime's bell and stood with my back to the door until the old maid opened it.

"Ah, señor," she said. "Don Jaime is so anxious to see you." She pulled the door back and I went crabwise through.

Don Jaime was in his library. He came to give me a full *abrazo*. "Hombre!" he said. "Sit, drink, and tell me!"

The wine and nuts were already out and waiting. I took a deep breath and started off by telling him I'd had to promise Susan a picture to keep. That didn't seem to bother him scarcely at all. He liked Susan and if anything was pleased she would have a picture for herself.

It was different when I told him about her being kidnapped by Grey. He turned red with fury and was no more pleased over the way I'd gotten her back.

"You took a great risk, Major Clancy," he said severely.

"I thought I had to."

"Well, I cannot argue with success, and it only cost one more painting. Is there no way you couldn't take care of this rascal, now that he may be off guard?"

275

I didn't think Grey was off guard. "I gave him my word, Don Jaime."

"Oh. That's too bad. But go on."

When I finished, he sat musing and drinking wine. "Some of my colleagues, the historians of art, will go insane when the news of this discovery comes out. It will enable certain doubtful paintings to be authenticated beyond all dispute. Reputations will be made and broken. I am glad I am a mere historian of events." He eyed me. "What are your plans?"

I passed him the report and the letters and cable I'd written. "That top paper explains how we traced the paintings to the Piedra Cuadrada. I hope you don't have to show it to anyone, but the information in it will help you. I'm going back to the palace, pick up Susan, and head for Barajas. As soon as we're outside of Spain, I'll cable or telephone you. You should have word from me by tomorrow noon. Even if you don't, by that time please take whatever steps you think necessary anyway. I'd be very grateful if Father Fermin were the first person you notify, but the important thing is to get the tower under good solid guard as soon as possible. The man I left should be able to protect it until then.

"With luck, no one will notice that we opened the top bundle, but even if they do there's not much that could be proven against us. We've merely made an investigation, left the results with you, and gone to inform our employer, Du Vigny."

He smiled. "In the general excitement, you may not even be remembered. This will be something of a cataclysm."

"I also ask you to send that cable and the letter to the Conde and to see the other letter gets to San Ildefonso. If you go there, please tell the prior, Brother Fernando, and the novice Diego that I'm sorry I could not pass to say good-bye myself. In the letter to the prior, I've said I'd write further about the pictures we bought. Would you mind buying a good rosary for Diego as a gift from me?"

"Of course not. Please allow it to be my gift, too."

I stood. "I must leave, Don Jaime. It has been a great pleasure knowing you."

He went to his desk and brought me a flat package. "Here are the copies you asked for."

I started to ask how much they had cost, but he forestalled me. He said, "No, Major. Let this be as the rosary for the novice Diego. I hope to see you again in Spain someday."

He came down to the door and gave me another full *abrazo*. "This has been a grand adventure," he said. "Adios, hombre."

At the bend of the Calle Sal, I turned. He was standing before his house. I waved and walked on. That was an admirable, slightly lawless, old man.

My return trip to the plaza was the same as when I'd come. There were no signs of Grey or of Dick and Elaine. No one else seemed to take an interest in me either. Nevertheless, I left the maze of narrow streets and went into the busy, sunlit plaza with a feeling of relief.

I halted to make a last full check around. Still no hostiles in sight. But there was one thing. The Landrover was where Luis had parked it, but he wasn't to be seen. The vehicle sat there, empty and unattended.

He could have gone to the latrine. He could be sitting just out of sight on one of the benches in the little park. There were a lot of possible explanations. None of them I liked. I walked slowly over, my head swiveling as if I were back moving through high jungle or across the reed flats in the delta. The vehicle simply sat there innocuously.

I sidled up to it on the driver's side. They couldn't have

booby-trapped the damn thing, but I didn't touch it as I stuck my head through the open window to look inside. There was a small movement. For a fraction of a second I saw, through sun-dazzled eyes, Elaine all curled up in the dim space under the dash. Then the world exploded silently in my face.

I reeled back a couple of steps and dropped like a stone.

I COULDN'T BREATHE OR MOVE BUT I COULD SEE and hear and suffer. Within seconds people were all around me, shouting in several languages about the man fainting. Some kind soul stuck a newspaper under my head and others cried out to give the poor fellow air. I agreed with those last. I needed air. Christ, how I needed air. My lungs seemed to have completely stopped working.

An authoritative voice I knew cut through the babble. "Let me by, please. I'm his doctor." This was repeated in Spanish and English. Grey came into my tortured field of view and bent over me. He gently thumbed back my eyelid. "Yes," he said loudly. "It's one of his attacks. Please help me get him into our car. I have medication at our hotel." Willing hands lifted me. I faded out and was glad of it.

There was nothing and then there was pain again. My lungs had come back on the job but they were half full of a mixture of feathers and pepper. They weren't helped by the sensation of a wide, tight band around my chest. Wherever I was shook and vibrated.

My eyes came open without my willing the act. I was in the rear seat of a Landrover not Luis's. Facing me, her arms folded on the back of the front seat, was Elaine. "Hi there," she said brightly. She was more animated than I'd ever seen her. Dick was driving.

"Feeling better, old man?" That was Grey's voice. I

turned my heavy awkward head and saw him sitting beside me, holding an automatic in his lap.

I made a harsh noise. "Yes," said Grey sympathetically. "That's rather drastic stuff. You've been Maced. You know, that chemical spray your police use on demonstrators and such they want to subdue but public opinion won't let them club. Effects are thoroughly unpleasant but they don't last long. You'll be much improved in a few minutes time and an hour or two will see you fit as a flea."

I made my noise again, trying to let him know that he was a treacherous, sneaking, no-good, son of a whore.

"I'd just rest if I were you."

I took his advice. Elaine regarded me with interest and some pride. I remembered thinking earlier in the day that it would be much harder for this crew to pull anything on me than it had been on Susan. Well, I'd been right. They'd had to go to considerable more trouble and preparation.

The road we were following was nothing I recognized. The tight band around my chest wasn't imaginary; a broad belt of cotton webbing pinned my elbows to my sides, and similar belts secured my knees and ankles. I was also wearing snug handcuffs. Grey had to travel with a trunkful of equipment.

Grey was right; I began to improve. It would have been hard to get worse. After fifteen minutes, I experimented with talking. "Where's Luis?" I asked.

"I threw him downstairs," Elaine volunteered.

"More or less true, I fear," Grey said. "Elaine went and said you wanted him and that you weren't far, so he followed her off. You know those stairs that run from the plaza down to the terrace below?"

"Yeah." Those were steep, long, stone stairs.

Elaine said, "We started down and no one was about so I

gave him a tiny puff of Mace and away he went." She flirted a hand to show how Luis had gone. "I think he broke his neck."

Grey coughed. "Elaine is apt to exaggerate. He was found within a very few minutes and an ambulance came and carried him off. He'll get good care."

They seemed to let Elaine do a disproportionate share of the heavy work. Elaine laughed girlishly. "Dickie and I have been playing Bonnie and Clyde. It's a real high, isn't it, Dickie?"

"A flyer," Dickie agreed.

I should have explained more to poor Luis. "What the hell's the object of this exercise?" I asked Grey.

His eyes slid to the front seat and back. "We'll talk about that when we get where we're going. Not too far now."

It was another half hour, most of it on back roads. Our objective was a small, isolated villa surrounded by poplar trees, the kind of house a city man builds for restful weekends. From Susan's description of where she'd been taken, it had to be the same place.

"Hell of a rent I had to pay for this," said Grey, "but it's got a phone, which isn't too common around here. Came very comfortably furnished I must say."

The strap at my ankles was taken off so that I could hobble in, Grey keeping me carefully covered. I was guided into a long living room and told to sit in a stout wooden armchair. Additional web bands were produced and used to fasten me firmly to the chair. Then the three of them stepped back.

I waited. I could move my feet up and down and that was it.

"Why don't you two take a swim," said Grey. "I want to have a private chat with Major Clancy." He looked at me. "Very nice little pool out back."

"Real fun fucking in it, too," said Elaine. "Last one in is a rotten egg, Dickie."

"You know," he said.

Elaine had her T-shirt and beads off before she was out the door. She wore no brassiere.

"How much have you told those two junior monsters of yours?" I asked Grey.

"I've had to tell them quite a bit. More than I liked frankly. They know that pictures by El Greco are involved." He ran his tongue over his lips. "They both had enough education before they turned into what they are to realize what that means. They'd badly like to have a million dollars."

"As would you."

"I'd like a million pounds. The kids want the money to start a commune of their own. You recall that fellow Manson out in California?"

"Yeah."

"That's the kind of commune they seem to have in mind."

"And what the hell do you have in mind?"

"First, I'm going to call Susan. Would you speak to her and tell her what happened this morning?"

"I would not."

"I simply want her to know that you're all right and being treated just as well as she was."

"I've said it before and I'll say it again—fuck you, Grey."

He sighed. "I've never dealt with a man as difficult as you, Clancy." He opened his coat and took a small tape recorder from his inside pocket. I should have known.

He went to a phone across the room and with some difficulty got through to the palace. From outside came sounds of splashing and a few squeals and once, after comparative silence, a high, rasping whinny.

Grey had to wait while Susan was brought to the phone.

At length, he said, "Susan? Yes, Arthur Grey speaking. I have something I want you to listen to." He activated his tape recorder and held it to the mouthpiece of the phone. The conversation he and I had just finished was played back.

When it ended, he took over again. "You see, I— No, Susan, he's— Please, let me speak a moment. He's all right and odds are he'll remain so. Now— Susan, you must listen. There's nothing you should do, except stay where you are and not inform anyone. That's right, and I'll be in touch tomorrow morning. Yes, tomorrow morning without fail. Until— No, I'm sorry, Susan, but I have to ring off. Good-bye." He hung up.

"Didn't want her to be uncertain," he said to me. "That's always the worst, you know, and she most likely expected you back by now. I have to admit she's upset. Girl's quite fond of you, Clancy."

"You may change some of the details, Grey, but you're not very inventive. What do you expect to get out of grabbing me?"

He shrugged. "Beyond being easier in my mind with you safely tied up, I'm not sure. You see, I'm rather counting on your help here."

"My help!"

"That's right. You know the situation as well as I do, if not better. You know what I want. The top bundle of those pictures. You invent a solution that I'll find satisfactory."

"Why in hell's name should I invent a goddamn thing?" I demanded, although I was afraid I knew the answer.

"Because if you don't, I'll let Dick and Elaine amuse themselves with you. They not only want a million dollars, they know about your part in the Viet Nam war. Disapprove of that war, they do."

I shifted position as much as my bonds would let me. Grey nodded. "Makes you stop and think, doesn't it."

The villa was a long way from the last lived-in place we'd passed. No matter how loud I yelled, no one would hear me except those who'd enjoy it. He had made me stop and think.

"This is nothing I want to do, Clancy, but there it is." Grey's face was that of a dentist who hates to inflict pain but has to in his line of work. "That's a precious pair as you can see. You'll have to come up with some sort of sound scheme rather quickly, old man. We couldn't get to you before you talked to Don Jaime, so I'm sure there's a strict time limit staring at us. But you can tell me about that."

There was movement behind him. The open door there was the one Dick and Elaine had gone through to the pool. I could still hear splashing, but it must have been Dick alone for Elaine came in, naked as a worm, a small revolver in her hand. She grinned impishly at me and held the forefinger of her free hand to her lips. Her feet left damp marks on the tiles.

Grey apparently saw in my face that something was happening behind him. He started to turn, but before he was halfway around, Elaine fired twice. Grey went off balance and his feet frantically tried to catch up with his toppling body. He did a teetering dance past me and there was a crash. Elaine came closer and squinting one eye and sticking a point of pale red tongue from the corner of her mouth took careful aim and fired twice more. The noise of the shots a couple of feet away left my head singing.

I noticed that for some reason, she'd shaved off her pubic hair, just like a showgirl.

Dick came running in, his bare, wet feet almost slipping on the tiled floor. "Did you get him, Elaine!" he cried, skidding to a halt beside her. "Boy, you sure did." He was naked, too. There were needle marks inside his thighs.

"Popped him right, didn't I?" Elaine said proudly. "You know, Dickie, it feels great. It's like coming all over."

Dick stepped past me and returned, dragging Grey by the heels. Grey's right eye was a red ruin, and there was a hole a bit off-center in his forehead.

Dick let Grey's feet drop with a thump. The two of them looked down at him with pleased expressions for a few seconds and then shifted their attention to me. Dread went through me in a flood of icy needles.

"You going to help us, man?" Dick asked me. "Old Arthur wasn't any friend of yours, you know," he added reasonably. "We got pretty tired of him, too, and we don't need him any more. Now we got that one picture and you know we'd like some more. So are you going to help?"

"You better help," Elaine said. She took a pace closer to me and held her pistol about a foot from my face, pointed at the bridge of my nose. Her thumb pulled the hammer to full cock. I could see the dull copper of one unexpended round in a chamber of the cylinder. The other would be under the raised hammer. Elaine's face was avid. "You wouldn't want us to cut off your balls and your prick and poke out your eyes, or for me to pull this trigger."

"What do you want me to do?" I asked. My voice sounded high and unsure in my ringing ears.

"Just, you know, take us to where the pictures are and tell us where they're hidden." Dick continued to be reasonable. "After, we'll leave you tied up but you'll be able to get loose. That's all we want."

Elaine's grip on the pistol never wavered. "You maybe could come on heavy with Arthur, but things are different now. You'll take us right to those pictures or we'll get a knife from the kitchen. I think we'll take your prick first, and save your eyes till last."

Grey hadn't told them where the tower was, or about Ricardo. "All right," I said. "I'll take you to the pictures."

"That's fine," said Dick. "Yeah, man, that's like great. Isn't it, Elaine?"

"Oh, I don't know. We've never tried really hurting someone." She let the pistol droop until it was pointed at the floor. My eyes followed it. I couldn't stop myself. There was the bitter taste of pennies in my mouth. The beating of my heart shook my whole body, tied up as I was. I was as tired as if I'd run five miles. I'd called them junior monsters to Grey. I'd been wrong. They had their full growth and affected me accordingly.

Dick said, "I'll put old Arthur in his room." He picked up Grey's heels again and dragged the body across the tile floor and through an archway. Grey's arms trailed limply behind him and his blazer wadded up beneath his head. Dick came back shortly and used a throw rug to mop up the bloodstains. Dick was the tidy one.

"Okay," said Dick, clean-up finished. "Arthur said the best time to get to wherever the pictures are would be around dusk. Old Arthur was smart in a lot of ways."

"Arthur was a heavy drag," said Elaine, scratching her crotch. "We get to London with those pictures and we can have a time. Nothing but the straight and pure."

Dick agreed but returned, businesslike, to the topic under discussion. "So to get there at dusk when should we leave here?" he asked.

I said wearily, "I don't know where here is. Have you got a map?"

He did and could show me where the villa was. I ran a mental calculation and told him four-thirty should be about right. He smiled and offered me something to eat and drink. I said I didn't care for anything, thanks.

I wasn't sorry for Grey worth a damn but I was sure sorry for myself. They never bothered to get dressed. Once it appeared she wasn't going to begin to whittle on me in the next five minutes, I tried to evaluate Elaine as a woman. The sight of her naked form moved me as much as if she'd been a codfish but there were special reasons for that. She really wasn't much. Rather skinny and untended with breasts not much bigger than teacups and bruises in odd spots. Dick wasn't even that attractive.

By keeping quiet and listening, I learned that Grey had apparently convinced them he'd been left under guard while Susan and I had gone to where the pictures were. That had been half-smart of Grey. They'd held off killing him until they had someone who could take them where they wanted to go.

Dick played the recorder and Elaine sang a couple of songs and they both ate at odd times. I was thirsty and asked for water, which Dick gave me. Elaine started telling me how much she hated what neo-Nazis such as myself had done in Vietnam. She got worked up over the injustice of it all and my blood began to chill, but Dick obviously was stirred in a different way. He took her to the sofa across the room and they copulated there. The high whinny I'd heard ages before belonged to Dick. Didn't fit him very well.

After that they wanted to know what I'd thought of the show. When I said they reminded me of Romeo and Juliet, they thought it a grand joke.

They took turns telling me about some of the diversions Arthur used to favor, a few of which dimly surprised me. I'd known Grey had been flawed but I hadn't known how deeply.

The long afternoon was like spending an equal time staring fixedly into an improperly cared for field latrine in summer. It should be their last afternoon and it well might be mine and there were better ways to have passed it.

AT FOUR DICK AND ELAINE PUT ON THEIR CLOTHES which was a slight improvement. Dick made several trips outside carrying rucksacks and other gear. I saw flashlights and a crowbar in a basket. Grey had gotten equipment of his own together to reopen the embrasure. Hell of a lot of good it would do him.

Elaine's contribution to the preparations was to reload her revolver, stick it in the belt of her blue jeans, and practice quick drawing with me as a target. I hoped she'd shoot herself in the stomach but no luck. She never did clean the poor damn piece. It was hard to imagine her and Dick as small, neat children being sent off to school by doting parents.

Dick came in and announced the Landrover was loaded. He freed me from the chair. I had to urinate and both of them took me to do that, which was what I had feared but I couldn't wait any longer. The humiliating process over, they herded me out to the vehicle. I was put in the front seat and the strap rebuckled around my ankles. Elaine drove and Dick sat in the rear, resting the muzzle of his pistol against my neck. I thought at first I preferred to have him hold a gun on me than Elaine, but after she drove a few miles I wasn't so sure. Not that she was fast, just erratic.

I had tried to time our departure so we'd arrive at the tower around sunset, instead of dusk which Grey had wanted for some reason. As we drove along and progressed into country I knew, it appeared we were going to arrive on schedule. I gave such instructions as were needed.

Dick and Elaine talked about the friends they would meet in London and the drugs they would buy and the fun they'd all have. The swimming pool they'd recently been gamboling in had been a revelation. They decided they'd take a place in the suburbs with a bigger pool where everyone could come and do their thing in and out of the water, all together under nature's sky. The prospects for alternate life-styles had been greatly widened for them. These prospects would narrow soon.

The sun had been below the horizon no more than five minutes when we went around the swell of ground and came in sight of the watchtower of Piedra Cuadrada.

"There it is," I said. "The paintings are walled up inside that tower."

There was plenty of light for Ricardo to get good, clean shots. The scope he had would make it easy. I held in my mind what the pair with me had done to Luis and Grey and were certainly planning to do to me as soon as they got to the pictures.

I guided Elaine to the same place we'd parked the day before.

"Look at that tower," said Dick. "Like wow! I can feel it all the way to here. That's where everything is."

He was close to right.

They dismounted and Dick held his pistol on me while Elaine unfastened the straps around my ankles and knees. Then she covered me while Dick opened the rear of the Landrover and took out the basket of gear.

"Okay, man," said Dick. "Lead the way." He held his pistol in his free hand. "I'll be right behind, and Elaine girl will be behind me, so be like nice. Okay?"

"Okay," I said and started them on their way to meet Ricardo. He'd have taken position at a point from where he could command the neck of land leading to the tower. He'd have heard the Landrover coming a long way off and he'd be ready. I hoped to Christ his gentlemanly reluctance to shoot girls would be overcome by the sight of Elaine and her pistol. I thought his best shot would come when we reached the neck of land and before we turned out on it. That was only a couple of hundred yards away toward the bright, golden flare where the sun had set.

I found the natural path we'd followed before and the going became easier for me. Even though my legs were free it was hard to keep balance with my arms pinned. The shadows between the rocks and scrub in the boulder field were pooling and running together but there was still more than enough light. Elaine began to sing a song she made up as she went along about treasure hunting.

I walked out to the clearer space where the neck started. I felt as if I were a violin, fragile and tightly strung. I tried to keep my pace steady. A small flash, a splat, and a thud came nearly together with a sharp crack right on top. The splat and thud were from behind me, the flash and crack from my right front. I might not have seen the flash if I hadn't been straining for it. I wheeled as Elaine started to scream in high staccato yelps like nothing human.

Dick had been knocked on his back and was staring up at the darkening sky, which had to be black for him. The screaming Elaine was beyond him, her front and face covered with flecks that gleamed yellow red in the sun's dying glow. That was hollowpoint ammunition Ricardo was using and when the bullet had come out, a lot of Dick had erupted over her. Her eyes shone nearly the color of his blood and were no more human than her screams. I wanted Ricardo's next shot as

I'd never wanted anything before. In seconds she'd look for vengeance.

Still screaming, she whipped around and began to fire back toward the Landrover. She got off two rapid shots before Ricardo's second bullet took her and threw her down once and for all, a slender mass, her face in the dirt and her beads and hair flung over her head. I stared at the two bodies. I'd stared at many bodies in my time. Some had just been meat, some I'd killed or helped kill and I'd felt some satisfaction, but these two were more than meat and they gave me no satisfaction.

Elaine must have lost her head and thought Dick had been shot from behind. I turned to look for Ricardo. He was standing not far from where I'd thought he'd be, plain in the fading light. "Are you all right, patrón?" he called, starting toward me.

I wasn't all right, but I might as well lie to him. I drew breath to answer when understanding caught me by the throat. It was absurd for Elaine to have thought Dick had been shot from behind. Even if she hadn't seen the flash or got a fix on the rifle crack, Dick's back had blown up in her face. She should have known whatever killed him came from the front. Unless she had some other very good reason to turn and fire toward the Landrover.

"Get down," I yelled as loud as I could in Guarani. Ricardo stopped, his attitude showing surprise. "Get down," I yelled again, but another rifle shot cracked out and this one did come from behind. Ricardo went down—suddenly and over backwards. I didn't think it was my yell that sent him. I dropped to my knees and snatched up Dick's pistol with my handcuffed hands. I heaved myself to my feet and ran at an angle for the boulder field. I was too anxious and not used to running crouched with my arms strapped to my side, so I over-balanced and fell. As I scrambled to regain my feet something hard hit my back as the rifle by the Landrover cracked again. The impact rolled me once. I pretended to myself that nothing had happened and partly on my feet, partly on my knees, I made it to the shelter of the rocks. No other shot came. I wormed and forced my way blindly into the scanty brush between the boulders.

When I could go no farther, I twisted around to face the way I'd come. I was under a low prickly bush. Through its branches I could see about thirty feet down a lane between the rocks to the open space at the base of the neck of land. The light was going fast. In five minutes, someone would damn near have to touch me to know that I was under my bush, and I'd see him before then against the sky. It wasn't the best place, but it wasn't a bad place. It would do if I could last.

I had the revolver in both hands, gripping it hard enough to bend the butt.

The shot had taken me in the left center of my back when I'd been trying to get up after I fell. I could breathe without coughing, so my lung hadn't been touched. I hurt and I'd hurt worse in a while and I thought I could feel bone grate, so some ribs had gone. My left arm felt wrong also, but I could slide it up and down a little against the strap I wore. The bone there should still be solid. The bullet had come in at an angle, gone off or through a rib or two and then out by way of my strapped arm. It didn't seem to have been hollowpoint that was used on me. I'd already have bled myself unconscious if it had been that. Bleeding worried me, even though the strap in itself made a fair pressure bandage. Too much bleeding was the main thing that might keep me from getting Grey.

Because it was Grey back there. Grey, who'd staged that show at the villa. For a man who liked gadgets and trick devices, it would have been nothing for his equipment box to have held, beside imitation blood and loud blanks, some fake plastic wound marks with quick-stick backing. Christ, I remembered even reading once that we were using such things to train our army medics on maneuvers. Grey'd fallen behind the chair I was strapped to and it probably hadn't taken him more than a few seconds to slap on his make-up. When Dick dragged him back in to sight, I hadn't examined him closely, what with a naked Elaine holding a loaded gun at my face and telling me how they planned to saw off my private parts and blind me.

It wouldn't have been hard for him to con Dick and Elaine into playing along. They'd swallow the pitch that I'd be more malleable if I thought I'd fallen into the hands of a pair of true mad dogs. I told myself they hadn't been far from being that anyway. I don't think they thought for a minute I was going to live long once I showed them where the pictures were.

So just as Grey figured I would, I'd taken them out here, knowing they'd both be dead minutes after they came within range of Ricardo's rifle. He'd killed them as ordered. If it hadn't been for Elaine using the few seconds she'd outlived Dick to fire blindly to the rear, I'd never have had an inkling that Grey had traveled with us in the back of the Landrover. Traveled with a rifle of his own for company. He'd slid out and taken up a position as soon as Dick, Elaine, and I had moved some distance away. He'd watched what happened and had planned to wait until Ricardo came down to cut me loose, when he could probably have hit us both with a single round.

Grey had to come looking for me. Ricardo had gone down as if he'd been well hit, but I'd been scuttling fast the last Grey'd seen of me, and he may have seen me grab Dick's pistol. He might nerve himself to letting Ricardo lie, but he had to find me before he went out to the tower and time was pushing him. He knew about where I'd gone into the boulders although he wouldn't know exactly where nor how far. The moon would rise in about an hour, but that wouldn't give him enough light to follow a blood trace. He'd have to come, sweating and sticking his hat around corners but he'd have to come. All I had to do was be patient and stay conscious.

A half-hour later, I heard him behind me, perhaps fifty yards away. I was sure it was he. The twigs and branches I'd broken or bent in my blind progress to where I was had finished crackling after the disturbance of my passage and the only other sounds in the now full night were those caused by the evening breeze stirring in the brush. Grey threw several rocks around, which made rattling noises exactly like rocks being thrown around. He was likely trying to talk himself into believing I was dead or out stiff. I kept my eyes on my clear lane and the sky above it. If he came at me from behind, I'd hear him. I was getting cold which meant some shock but I didn't feel weaker which meant not much bleeding. Not that I felt strong.

I considered whether anyone would come to investigate the shots, and decided odds favored they wouldn't. We were far away from anywhere inhabited. Only six rounds had been fired, which wouldn't have been abnormal for hunters. I left that and put my entire being into my eyes and my ears. I'd learned how on all-night ambushes.

Grey apparently abandoned the idea of groping down toward me from inside the boulders, for I saw him flash across the end of my lane. He passed too quickly. I wanted him sure. He was desperate to the point of taking chances to draw fire so he could locate me. I waited another half hour.

Part way down my lane the profile of a rock deformed and reformed again. It bulged a second time and stayed so for a long minute. I waited. Grey had to be a good part crazed knowing what was there for the taking in the tower once he killed me. The bulge receded and the rock was the same as before. The moon had risen in the east far enough to deepen the shadow that covered me. I held my aim down the lane I'd memorized.

He came out and started toward me, crouching low. He was good and made the least whisper of noise. When he was ten feet away, I shot him twice without warning, the way Elaine had but with real bullets. I heaved myself up and out of the bush and crawled to him. Carefully, I put the muzzle of the pistol behind his ear and fired again. There was no doubt about Grey now. For the first time since I'd seen him in the bar of the Hotel Guarani in Asunción, I had no doubt about Arthur Grey.

The key to my handcuffs was in his pocket with his fancy Swiss pocketknife. I removed the cuffs but held off freeing myself from the chest strap. It might be the only thing keeping me from bleeding a flood. I had to find Ricardo before I experimented with the strap.

I didn't have to be quiet any more so I nattered away in Guarani as I looked for Ricardo. I had a fair idea where he'd gone down, but a landscape changes under moonlight so it wasn't easy.

He was dead. Grey's bullet had taken him four inches below the throat. I patted his shoulder. He'd been a gunman, not awfully bright, but a good shot and loyal. I couldn't say anything more for me. I picked up the Conde's rifle and left Ricardo there. He probably never had expected a different end if he'd ever thought about it.

I stumbled back to the clear space where Dick and Elaine lay. I smeared the pistol I was still carrying and dropped it by Dick. I had to search Elaine to get the keys to the Landrover and I didn't like that. I told myself again that she and Dick had been true mad dogs and not a pair of kids playing nasty parts just for the kicks. They'd meant it. The keys were in Elaine's shoulder bag with assorted pill boxes and other trash.

For all that my left side was a white flame it seemed colder when I reached the Landrover. I opened the right front door, stuck in the rifle and sat panting in the seat. A big decision was coming up. Did I cut off the strap or did I sit where I was? I couldn't drive the Landrover with my elbows pinned. It was one of those decisions that require a lot of thought. I was sawing inefficiently away at the strap when I heard a motor. To the north the glow of headlights shone over the swell of the land. Maybe someone had heard and decided there was too much firing going on too late for a normal hunting party. I hoped the Guardia Civil would be broad-minded when they found me shot through the side in close proximity to four dead bodies.

The headlights to the north swept around into view and advanced. They left the track as they drew close and bumped erratically straight toward me. I was armed but not inclined to do anything. I sat and watched them come.

The vehicle stopped about ten yards away, pinning me in the glare of its lights and blinding me to whatever happened beyond them. Doors opened and slammed. Susan walked into the white flood spilling around. I couldn't make out her face. She stopped a few feet away.

"Oh, Clancy," she said. "Look at you!" Her voice broke.

"What are you doing here?" I demanded.

"What happened? What is happening?"

"Where the hell's Patricio?"

She gestured. "He came with me. Where's Grey?"

"Grey's dead." I called as strongly as I could for Patricio. He answered from well outside the lights. He knew better than stand in a lighted area when there was trouble around. I snarled weakly for him to get his ass over where I could talk to him.

"Don't blame Patricio, I made him come with me," Susan said. "And whether he obeyed or disobeyed isn't important. You've been shot, haven't you?"

"Yeah. Not too bad, I hope. I told that goddamn Patricio just as plain—"

"Shut up, Clancy." She reached to touch my face. "You're all scratched, too. Aren't you glad to see me? I'm glad to see you."

I paused. "Okay, I admit it. I've never been gladder to see anyone in my life." I looked over to where Patricio stood hangdog at the edge of the light. "Patricio, because the señorita asks—and because I need you, too—I'll let you off this time. Don't ever disobey orders again. I have bad news. Ricardo is dead."

"Ai!" he said softly. "He was a good man, patrón. Who killed him?"

"That man named Grey. I killed Grey a short time after but not before he shot me once. Please come bind me up."

"Sí, patrón." Patricio had some knowledge of wounds and could do country-style first aid.

Susan said, "Stop talking that gibberish. We've got to get you to a doctor."

"No. Listen, Susan. There are four dead bodies out there. I don't know about doctors."

"Four dead!"

About twenty minutes later, I knew Susan's story and she knew mine and Patricio had bandaged my arm and rigged a pad compress on my side, using one of the extra straps that had been around my legs to hold it in place. Repair work had been easier than I'd expected since he and Susan had brought our baggage with them so there were shirts and the like to use.

After Grey's call, Susan had made Patricio and the servants load all our belongings in the car Patricio had rented for his and Ricardo's trip from Madrid to the palace. Then she'd set out to convince Patricio he should come with her to the tower.

"How the hell did you talk to him?" I asked.

"I didn't talk. I drew pictures, and once I tried to sneak away. He got the message," she said.

She'd been sure that no matter what Grey would go to the tower again. She'd come to make some sort of deal with him. Any sort of deal. She'd brought our two pictures to give him. They were in the car with our suitcases.

Patricio fixed a sling for my bad arm and asked if he could go to Ricardo's body. "He was a cousin, patrón, and he wore a cross he would like me to give to his companion."

I told him how to find Ricardo and he went off, carrying a flashlight. Susan lit me a cigarette. She was bearing up well for someone with small experience.

I said, "Give me a kiss, Susan. You are a damn fine girl."

She kissed me lovingly on the lips. "What do we do now, Clancy?"

"The only person I've killed was Grey but Ricardo killed two at my orders. All of those might be called self-defense in a way, but it could be pure hell to explain to the police, not to mention answer some hard questions they might ask about pictures we have in hand. So we'll run. We'll have to leave the paintings."

She nodded, and looked over toward where Dick, Elaine, Ricardo, and Grey each lay where they'd died. "Who are you going to leave the pictures with? Don Jaime?"

298

"No. We're going by the Monastery of San Ildefonso. We'll leave them there."

She lit a cigarette of her own. "Do you think Grey could have brought his painting? He mustn't have planned on going back for anything."

"Let's look." I could walk without much extra pain.

In the back of the Landrover, under the rucksacks where Grey also must have traveled to Piedra Cuadrada, was his attaché case. The *Coronation of the Virgin* was inside. Susan put the package of our two with it.

Patricio returned. He wanted to talk about the terrible pictures the señorita had drawn, even had a few he'd saved to show me.

I passed him the rifle I'd brought back from Ricardo's body, and told him to stop worrying and drive to San Ildefonso.

I LEARNED ON THE RIDE TO THE MONASTERY THAT I could travel but that I didn't like it. It wasn't as bad once we got on the Roman road. We pulled up before San Ildefonso at a quarter to midnight.

"Wait with Patricio," I said to Susan. "I'm not sure how long I'll be." As if I were going through thick mud, I trudged over to the door, carrying the attaché case. I put it down and worked the bell pull. The monastery took in distressed travelers. I was eligible.

There was a wait and then shuffling footsteps the other side of the door and a yellow line appeared at the sill. The door opened and Brother Anselmo peered out. "Who is it and what is it?" he demanded in a tone to send most travelers on their way. He was carrying a candle in a light tin lantern. They wouldn't want to waste electricity at San Ildefonso.

"Señor Clancy. I am hurt and I need a priest. Please take me to Father Fermin."

That got the door swung wide. He raised the feeble lantern to see better. "You're hurt," he agreed, "but the Father's gone to his bed."

"Would you let a man die unconfessed?"

He couldn't stand against that. "Come in," he said. "Can you walk?"

"Enough." I picked up Grey's attaché case and followed Anselmo.

He led the way to the prior's office, muttering under his breath. He opened the door and flicked on the electric light. "Sit. I'll tell Father Fermin," he said. Anselmo didn't believe I was dying, but he couldn't take the risk of my doing so unshriven because of him.

I didn't have to wait long. The prior came in the side door. His eyes widened as he saw me. "You are hurt, my son. We'll call a doctor."

"Please no, Father. Hear me first."

Father Fermin's eyes narrowed again. "Do you want to confess?"

I shook my head. "I don't have the right. I haven't been a communicant for many years. I must tell you something, though."

"Not under the seal?" His long, intelligent face showed surprise.

"No, Father." I raised the attaché case. "Please look in here and unwrap the parcels inside."

He carried the case to his table and turned on the lamp. In five minutes the three El Grecos were lined up before him. He knew what he had as soon as he'd uncovered the first. I saw his eyes go from the painting—it was Susan's *Saint Martin*—to my face and then to my crippled arm and padded side. He unwrapped the *Coronation of the Virgin* last and like Patricio crossed himself at the sight.

He came to sit beside me. "Tell me what you will."

I did. All of it. I had to swallow when I told him of leading Dick and Elaine forward for Ricardo to kill.

When I finished, he said, "I recall hearing what I thought were hunters over to the west. It was four lives being taken."

301

He regarded me sorrowfully. "If you're not confessing why are you telling me this?"

"Because of what happened I want to leave these pictures with you and tell you the story so you can do what you think you should."

"What do you plan to do?"

"I have clean clothes in a car outside. I ask that you let me change. Then, I'll run. Run like a rabbit. I hope to get clear of Spain before the police put controls on airports and frontiers."

He pointed wordlessly at the telephone on his table. I shrugged my working shoulder.

He rose and walked up and down across the room. Finally, he stopped. There was a sad smile on his face. "Greed is a terrible thing, but it seems to be one of the sins you aren't charged with, and I believe there is honor and truth in you. Technically, I think you are not even a criminal. I can't see how either the justice of the law or you would be helped by the police arresting you. I am willing to call the Guardia tomorrow after morning prayers to tell the commander I have reason to believe there has been trouble at that watchtower."

"That's more than I hoped for, Father."

"I said, 'I am willing.' There's a price."

My mouth worked a moment. "A price, Father?"

He gave a short bark of laughter. "Yes, a price. Repeat what you've told me under the seal. Make a confession, my son. It'll be easier for me for one thing—here the law never questions the inviolability of the confessional—and also, I am by vocation and command a fisher of souls."

Tears blurred my eyes. I started to drop to my knees, but the prior stopped me. "We can dispense with that," he said.

I crossed myself and began, "Bless me, Father, for I have sinned."

He sat by me and listened to the whole story over again. When I said that was all, he raised a finger. "It is not. You have more on your conscience than the past few days' work. I said make a confession. The rest, too—the sins accumulated over the years since last you did this."

That set an appalling vista for me to contemplate. By giving round estimates as to the number of times I'd broken various commandments, the telling took less time than the first part but it was as hard on me. Father Fermin handed me a penance that would keep me busy for days and went through the Latin that absolved me.

He said, "You're in a State of Grace, at least temporarily, my son. Fernando tells me you were a soldier. Spanish priests have been confessing Spanish soldiers for centuries, so we are realistic. We don't hope too high, but we never give up hope." He smiled. "Let's send for our brother who cares for our minor aches and pains and for your clothes." He rang the bell on his table.

Anselmo led in a wide-eyed Patricio carrying my suitcase, and another monk came a few minutes later with proper bandages and tape. My arm and side were rebound—hurt worse than when Patricio did it but the results were neater—and I was helped to dress in another outfit. That done, I resembled a halfway respectable survivor of a middling bad automobile accident.

I left a check for two thousand dollars with Father Fermin for Luis's care and said that more would be coming.

He nodded and said, "Go with God, my son."

I followed Anselmo blindly away. I wasn't converted or anything like that, but Dick and Elaine lying dead on the escarpment weren't as much a sore place in my head.

When we reached the car, it was one-thirty. Susan was fit

to lose her mind. "What were you doing in there!" she nearly barked.

If I'd told her, it would have upset her worse. "Talking to Father Fermin and getting repaired," I said. "If we can get clear of the country by eight o'clock this morning we'll be all right, I guess."

40

WE REACHED BARAJAS AT FIVE-FIFTEEN. I TOLD
Patricio to leave the car in the parking lot. He protested that
he'd had to post a bond of twenty thousand pesetas and why
didn't we turn it in at the airport office. When he'd rented it
the people had told him he could. There was no point in trying
to explain to him we were on the run. In Paraguay, what had
happened earlier in the night would have needed maybe a
morning's conversation with the proper people to square away.
I snapped at him as strongly as I could and ordered him to
leave all the weapons under the seat. He knew he couldn't
take those on the airplanes so he didn't complain about that.

The sleepy porter who took our bags asked on what
airline we were traveling. I gave him a couple of hundred
pesetas and told him simply to follow us. We went to the
departure board.

The first flight out left at six for Orly, Paris. The next was
a Polish plane to Warsaw via Prague. I'd rather have gone to
Warsaw than Paris but didn't like that either.

There was a flight to Caracas at seven. I said to Susan,
"That's for us and we'll see about a connecting flight to
Mexico City."

"Why Mexico City?"

"Because Mexico has no diplomatic relations with Spain
and good hospitals. Also fair plane connections to Asunción."

"Can you make that long a trip, Clancy?"

"I'd better be able to."

She bought the tickets on my credit card. There was space and there was a connection to Mexico. We even had time to get me a drink in the bar before boarding. We went through passport control, climbed a gangway, found our seats, and left, just that easy. Nobody came out in vehicles with flashing lights to stop the plane. With the help of several unhealthy double whiskys I managed to sleep an hour or so.

I worried about being held at Maiquitía Airport in Venezuela, but the only tough part there was an endless two-hour wait in damp heat because the air-conditioning was on the fritz. I was running a good fever when we boarded the plane for Mexico.

Patricio was having a great time. He was seeing the world and there was free beer in first class.

An hour out of Mexico City I called a stewardess and said I was really much worse than I looked and would she please have an ambulance meet the plane. That caused a stir and would cost Du Vigny more money but damned if I was going to look for a cab.

Since we were traveling west it was only late afternoon when we landed at Mexico City. I was assisted down the gangway and by that time I needed the help. A stretcher was at the foot with two bearers standing by.

As I tottered onto the asphalt, a man from the airline stepped forward and announced he would take Susan and Patricio through Customs and send them on to the hospital I was bound for.

I turned to her and said, "Susan, we've made it. We'll stay here a week anyway. I think we're going to find out we're in love."

She burst into tears and solicitous people led her away. I

306

was disposed on the stretcher and carried to the nearby ambulance. Everyone couldn't have been kinder until the receiving surgeon at the hospital unwrapped me and took a look at what ailed me. Then a certain steely note entered the atmosphere. I was efficiently X rayed and injected and cleaned up and bandaged all right, but there were few smiles.

I still had enough travelers' checks and cash of several currencies to be wheeled into a private room, but right behind came a gray-haired man in a white coat followed by an unmistakably tough cop.

The man in the white coat informed me he was Doctor Maldonado. He took my pulse and looked at the clipboard hanging on the foot of my bed.

He said. "Señor Clancy, you are in satisfactory condition. You have some infection and will almost certainly develop a light case of pneumonia, but in my opinion you can answer questions. This gentleman is Inspector Rivera of the Federal District Police."

"How do you do, inspector," I said. "I'll be happy to answer pertinent questions. First, let me say that I was shot in Spain."

"Oh!" the doctor and the inspector said in unison, breaking into smiles of relief. "Spain!"

There would be a minimum of brouhaha over me whatever I'd done, as there was no Spanish ambassador to holler and make démarches and complicate life for everyone.

I went on to say that my shooting although possibly a violation of some sort under Spanish law had been a private affair among foreigners in that country and that I doubted the Spanish police would even have held me for long. This made my hearers practically cordial, although the inspector had reservations, which grew when I said the most I expected the Mexican authorities to receive would be a routine Interpol inquiry as to my whereabouts. Gunshot wounded travelers don't stagger off airplanes and know about Interpol inquiries if they are completely blameless.

The inspector had numerous questions then. Most I refused to answer, on the grounds nobody'd accused me of anything and I was fairly sure I hadn't broken any Mexican laws. Eventually, he gave up and said he'd be back the next day. Doctor Maldonado went off with him. The doctor smiled as he wished me good night and said he hoped I'd be comfortable.

Susan and Patricio came by about an hour later and were allowed in to see me. Susan had recovered from her tears and Patricio thought Mexico City was even better than Madrid and much better than Buenos Aires. Susan wrote down a cable for Du Vigny at my dictation. A small, determined nurse chased them out after a few minutes and fed me a pill that planked me for twelve hours.

Over the next few days I had the light case of pneumonia Doctor Maldonado had promised me and didn't find it fun, but by the end of the week I was sitting in a chair, and was whining about not getting enough to eat and wanting to know when I'd be released. I wrote a report for Du Vigny and more letters to the Conde, Don Jaime, the prior and to Luis. The last I sent to Don Jaime for delivery. I hoped Luis was in condition to read it.

I spent a lot of time getting my penance out of the way, and I also got in some worrying as to what I would do about Nelida.

I had visitors. A sleek lawyer ordered long distance by Du Vigny showed up and let me know he was mine to command, and Susan and Patricio came daily, Inspector Rivera not quite so often. He was annoyed over my getting a lawyer but accepted my apology and excuse that my employer had taken the action without my knowledge and consent. He admitted the only communication he'd received about me had been the routine Interpol inquiry I'd predicted.

On Monday, Doctor Maldonado said I could go on out-patient status the next day. He allowed as how I could indulge in limited physical activity. Susan said it was damn well about time. We were playing cribbage that afternoon when Rivera came in, filled with suppressed glee.

He wanted to verify that I would still be in the hospital the following morning. I told him only until eleven o'clock and he said that would be fine. Rivera beamed at me fondly as if I were a favorite nephew who'd won an esteemed scholastic prize. He patted me on my good shoulder, shook my hand, and said he'd be by around ten.

Susan was in my room at ten the next day when Rivera arrived. I was fully dressed for the first time in over a week. Rivera asked in a rather loud voice if I would mind receiving a caller as a personal favor to him. I replied of course not, and he went to the door and beckoned.

In strode Señor Ortega Crespo of the Spanish Department of National Security, looking like a viceroy of Imperial Spain who had been betrayed into the hands of savages.

Rivera effusively made introductions. It would have been cruel to stop him. Ortega thanked him in a polite manner calculated to go through Rivera and stick a foot out behind his shoulderblades. Rivera paid no attention and withdrew, all coy smiles, so that his valued colleague could talk privately with me.

I invited Ortega to sit down. He suggested that Miss Allgood might find this boring. Susan said she wouldn't. He switched to Spanish but I answered in English deprecatingly motioning at Susan.

Ortega sighed and fell back to English. "Señor Clancy, we

had to beg them—beg them!—through every neutral channel for permission for me to talk to you."

"I'm at your disposition, Señor Ortega."

"What in the name of the angels of God happened at that watchtower? Our forensic experts are going mad. Who shot who? And how is it that three of—three of those paintings are at the Monastery of San Ildefonso and one hundred and sixty-nine are walled up in the tower? Do you know the Vatican has written a letter expressing interest?"

"I didn't know about the Vatican but I'll tell you all I do know. Incidentally, I haven't seen anything in the papers about the—should I just call them the paintings?"

"That would be better, yes. Please tell me what you do know."

I did. I'd told or written the tale so many times it flowed smoothly. When I reached the events around the tower, he made careful notes in a small, leather book. Once I'd finished, he leaned back in his chair, and stared at his notes and me alternately.

"You can't extradite us from here, can you?" asked Susan hesitantly.

He eyed her. The viceroy was being tormented by the natives but standing it as best he could. "No, Miss Allgood, we can't."

She was emboldened. "Why hasn't there been any announcement about the paintings?"

The viceroy had been tied to a stake and they were beginning to pile brush around his feet. "The affair is delicate. It may distress you as a citizen of a country dedicated to freedom of the press, but it has been judged expedient to suppress all information as to what was found in and outside that tower. Even so there have been rumors and agitation in influential circles. Then the letter from the Vatican." His eyes rolled heavenward. "The *Caudillo* has been informed and he has directed that regular reports be sent to him."

"What happens if we go to another country?" I asked. "Would you try extradition proceedings then?"

Now someone was advancing on the viceroy with a lighted torch. His fate was one to endure as a grandee of Spain. "I am ordered by my masters to say that if you keep quiet, you can count on not being hunted by us. It will take the government some time, months at least, to decide what to do. If you cause no further complications, we will have no reason to pursue you vengefully."

Susan sat straighter. "Could we go back to Spain and visit?"

"We'd love it if you did." Ortega grinned the wolf's grin that I'd seen on his face once before. A corner of his mouth quirked up, the grin widened into mirth, and he laughed heartily and long. He wiped his eyes and said, "We Spaniards are frequently accused of having no sense of humor and perhaps we don't in the Anglo-Saxon sense. We often laugh at deadly things. But we do have a sense of the ridiculous. No, Miss Allgood, I would not return to Spain for quite a while if I were you or Señor Clancy."

I asked, "How is the man who drove for us, Luis Morillo?"

Ortega was again the grandee. "He had a fractured skull, a broken arm, and several broken ribs. He's being cared for and will recover."

I heaved a sigh of relief. "Good. I left money with the prior. I'll send more as soon as possible, but if there's an emergency I'd be grateful if you'd let me know."

Ortega raised his eyebrows. "The prior claimed the seal of the confessional. You left that money?"

"Yes."

Ortega threw his notes in the air. "Come to dinner with me tonight. I'll include my Aztec colleague Rivera and have him recommend one of the better places for the incredible food of this land."